DYING TO FIT IN

DYING TO FIT IN
By J. E. Henricks

iUniverse, Inc.

New York   Bloomington

Dying to Fit In

This is a work of fiction. All of the characters, names, incidents, organizations, and dialogue in this novel are either the products of the author's imagination or are used fictitiously.

iUniverse books may be ordered through booksellers or by contacting:

iUniverse
1663 Liberty Drive
Bloomington, IN 47403
www.iuniverse.com
1-800-Authors (1-800-288-4677)

Because of the dynamic nature of the Internet, any Web addresses or links contained in this book may have changed since publication and may no longer be valid. The views expressed in this work are solely those of the author and do not necessarily reflect the views of the publisher, and the publisher hereby disclaims any responsibility for them.

ISBN: 978-1-4401-4317-5 (pbk)
ISBN: 978-1-4401-4318-2 (ebk)

Printed in the United States of America

iUniverse rev. date: 5/12/2009

There are too many people who gave me their support and friendship throughout the years to personally thank, but special appreciation goes to those who took the time to review this book in its many earlier forms. In particular, thanks to Guy Newland, Larry T. Reynolds, Mary Senter, and Jill Taft-Kaufman—all of whom made helpful suggestions; and to Dennis Thavenet, in appreciation of his excellent proof-reading abilities. If there are any mistakes left, they are solely my responsibility.

Chapter 1

Dear Sam,

What am I doing here? Why didn't you stop me? I've never been so lonely, and I miss you even more than I thought I would!

People are friendly enough, but it's not the same as being in a big city. There's nothing to do here, except for a few movie theaters. You know how I don't like to eat alone in restaurants—though I haven't found many of those around. And you can watch just so much TV before losing a few IQ points.

Perhaps when classes start up I'll feel better—at least I'll be busier. But, I'm here for the year—can't break a contract, you know. Unless things change significantly, though, it'll only be a year! And I can't imagine anything exciting, no less significant, happening here. After all, I'm at a state university in the middle of nowhere!

I have, though, found a nice coffee shop, Isis, where I can sit with a cup of coffee and read or write. It's quiet, and there are comfortable chairs in little cozy alcoves where you can have a private discussion without worry of being overheard. In fact, I met an interesting woman there today—a swimming instructor at the university. We're going to get together once I'm more settled in.

I guess the first time I'll be able to see you will be the Christmas break. Keeping that in mind will help get me through until then. I know you don't like phones, so these emails will do have to do—except for those times when I need to hear your voice.

I love you and miss you.
Maggie.

....

Maggie had finally settled into her new apartment. It was small, smaller than she was used to, with a large room that served as a combined living, dining and bedroom, a kitchen, and a bathroom. It was certainly adequate; its main drawback was the lack of storage space for clothing, furniture, and books. The daybed she had found at the local thrift store served quite well as both bed and couch. She had also found a desk and chairs at the auction put on by Claxton State University every fall–leftover items from offices being refurnished–which served as her desk, and, with vividly colored placemats, as the dining table.

The white walls had become gray with time; the landlord had refused Maggie permission to repaint them, which led to an investment in some interestingly patterned fabric which she hung on the walls. She could tell, without needing to ask, that it was permissible to hang things on the walls by the nail holes that were already there.

When she looked out the window of her new apartment at the street below, she could see young people, mostly students, laughing as they walked by, exuding excitement about the start of the new semester and the meeting of old friends. It was evening, the setting sun turning the sky pink, with streaks of blue and mauve. The end of summer was near and the leaves were just starting to turn. Classes were not yet in session and she was at loose ends. She had just arrived and had met only one person–the swimming instructor. She had spent her time buying some furnishings for her small apartment and walking around the town, trying to get her bearings. But she was lonely. What was she doing here–so far away from home?

Margaret Bell–Maggie to her friends–had lived all her life on the East Coast, Boston and New York, in particular, so, while accepting a job in Michigan was exciting, she was apprehensive. Would she "fit" into a small college town? Would she miss a big city? Her friends and family, none of whom had been further west than New Jersey, thought she was heading for the wilderness and questioned her sanity. "If you're going to leave New York, at least go to California!" they had said.

But the position at Claxton State offered her a chance to teach at a state university, and to teach what she loved, rather than continuing in her position at Bennett College, a small, private women's college where she spent most of her time dealing with young women who thought they were entitled to good grades because they paid a high tuition. Social philosophy was not high on their list of "things to know when one leaves college," and talking to them about feminism had proved to be a waste of her time.

So she is now in Michigan–in the middle of Michigan. If you were speaking to a Michigander, he would hold up his hand, and point to the middle of his palm–a gesture Maggie found strange when she first arrived from New York, but now found herself using.

She still can't get used to the politeness that greets her wherever she goes. She can't shake her New York skepticism that makes her wonder what they are *really* thinking. Even the local TV news announcers seem overly polite, actually upbeat, when they announce some disaster. How can you smile and laugh with your fellow announcer after reporting about a man who murdered and then dismembered his girlfriend in the woods north of town?

Perhaps it's the small town atmosphere that she's reacting to. While the total population is 50,000, about half are students, making it a fairly typical college town. However, it doesn't have the feel of a college town–or what she's imagined a college town feels like. It doesn't have the coffee shops or meeting places where students and faculty get together to discuss great ideas; it doesn't even have a book store where she could browse among *New York Times* best sellers as well as textbooks; and it doesn't have trendy restaurants specializing in the last fusion fad. What it has is lots of bars, where students seem to spend most of their evenings, and hamburger and pizza places. She was surprised when told not to schedule any of her classes on Fridays because Thursday night is Happy Hour at all the bars in town and students would be too hung over to attend classes on Friday. She wonders if she's formed her picture of a small college town from romantic novels about college life. This may be exactly what small college towns are like!

. . . .

"Well, here you are. It's not much, but at least it has a window and you don't have to share with anyone." With those words, Louise, the department secretary, opened the door to Maggie's new office. Louise was right–it wasn't much. A desk and chair, with an extra chair for students or visitors, a small bookcase, a file cabinet, and a phone.

Maggie scanned the small office. She was a small woman in her late 30s, with long dark brown hair that she typically wore in a ponytail, only occasionally letting it loose. She dressed casually in jeans or black slacks, but avoided the somber look by wearing brightly colored shirts. She had worn high heels when she first started teaching, to enhance her 5'3" frame, but switched to "sensible" shoes as her confidence grew, thinking that if she couldn't garner respect from students without adding 4" to her height, she probably shouldn't be a teacher.

"Will I have access to a computer?" Maggie asked.

"Oh, of course. I forgot to tell you. We requisitioned one for you, but it won't be available until classes begin next week. It's not a new one–we go by seniority–but it's in pretty good condition. We don't have a printer available, though, so you'll have to send your printing through to the main department office, which is just down the hall."

Louise Carroll was a woman in her sixties and had been secretary to the department for more than fifteen years. She looked apologetic, as though she wished she could have done better for a new member of the faculty. But facts were facts and there was not much money available for new computers. As she said to Maggie, "There doesn't seem to be much money for anything these days! I know where every penny goes, and in my opinion, *some* people get more than they deserve. But it's not up to me, so no use complaining."

"Is it possible to get another bookcase? My apartment's real small and I don't have enough room for the books I'll need for my classes. And what about personal stuff, you know, like a lamp, a rug, things like that?" Maggie looked around the room, already thinking of ways to make the stark office into a place where she wouldn't mind spending time.

"Sure, whatever will make it more pleasant for you," replied Louise. "Now let me show you the workroom and where your classes will be held."

As they walked down the hallway to the classroom wing, Louise reminded Maggie of the meetings scheduled for the next few days. There were new faculty orientations, the college meeting, the department meeting, the dinner at Dean Sweeney's house, and then the President's address welcoming everyone to a new academic year and undoubtedly reminding everyone of the budget problems faced by the university. In other words, a new year, an old problem.

....

4

The rest of the week went by so fast that when Maggie returned home Friday evening, she was exhausted. She had spent the morning carrying boxes of books to her office, along with a lamp and an old faded rug she had found at the thrift store downtown. While unpacking the books and sorting them into the bookcases–yes, now there were two–she thought of the posters she would put up on the walls, and the picture of Sam that she would put on her desk. She was determined to make this into a pleasant place to work.

But it wasn't so much the physical exertion that exhausted her. She was lonely. She missed having someone to greet her with a smile when she returned from classes. She missed having someone patiently listen to her describe the silly frustrations of her day. She missed having someone to share her thoughts with. She missed Sam.

She put the Lean Cuisine dinner in the microwave and, as she waited, poured herself a glass of scotch and put on a KD Lang CD. That had been a part of the evening ritual: a glass of scotch for her, a glass of red wine for Sam, and music. Fortunately, she and Sam had similar tastes in music–everything from classical to blues. Sam was the cook, though–Maggie stuck to frozen dinners and take-out. But they always took time to relax with each other, to catch up on each other's day. They used this time to connect with each other–to forget that there was a world beyond them, a world that, if they allowed it, would demand too much of their time. Sam was the one who insisted on the dinner hour, knowing how Maggie could get caught up in her work and forget everything else. Who would keep her balanced now that she was alone?

As she refilled her glass, she thought back over the day. It had been one of those days when you feel you've accomplished nothing, but have been busy every minute. She had taken her lunch to the office as she hadn't yet met many people and hated to eat alone in a restaurant. Besides she had been so busy unpacking that she had only a few minutes to gulp down her sandwich and coke before the college meeting began. That had taken about two hours, during which time she and the other new faculty members were introduced. It wasn't unpleasant, but neither was it interesting. The best part was the reception on the lawn outside the building, where she got to meet some of the other faculty. In particular, she was pleased to meet Jessie Hamilton, the Director of the Women's Studies Department at Claxton, who invited her to attend their next meeting.

The day ended with dinner for the new faculty at Dean Sweeney's house. Again, not unpleasant, as she did get to talk to some of the new people there, but most of them were in the English Department and talked about post-modernism as if they had invented it. Everyone seems to forget that most of these new ideas come from philosophers, and then are rejected by philosophers as untenable and picked up by other fields as the new "ism" of the day. This was true of faculty in the English Department where she had been, especially if the new "ism" came from France! She didn't think very highly of post-modernism. But the people at the dinner were pleasant, and interesting–in a post-modern way.

They were talking about someone in the English Department who had had his manuscript stolen–or at least that was what he thought. Others thought he had simply misplaced it, as he was known to be absent-minded, and that it would turn up in an unlikely place one of these days. A lost manuscript was a constant worry for academics, although with computers and backups it wasn't as much a concern as when the only copies you had were the ones you typed on carbon paper. She was pretty careful about backing up everything she did on disks and placing the disks in a secure place. Her book, *Aristotle, Friendship, and Women,* had just come out the previous year and she was working on a series of articles on friendship and the different views of what friendship required. All of this was neatly stored both on her own computer, on disks in her locked file cabinet at the office, and on a flash drive she kept with her at all times. With her career dependent on a steady flow of publications, she was taking no chances.

....

Dear Sam,

Well, I'm all settled in–and really missing you. I hope I haven't made a mistake in coming here. I know we've been apart before, but it was always for a short time. This time it feels like it's forever. This place is so different from what I'm used to. It's not a big city and it's not a small town.

It's a pretty town, though. The streets are lined with old maple trees that are already starting to turn red, gold, and orange, and the houses in the center of town, the old part of town, are fine examples of the turn-of-the century Victorian style. Many of these old houses are now owned by fraternities and sororities and, except for the occasional garbage tossed out after a party and the beer bottles strewn on the lawns like odd-shaped flowers every Saturday and Sunday mornings, are fairly well maintained.

Now brace yourself for a little history I've learned this week: The town had once been the oil capital of the Midwest. When oil was struck in the 1920s, it became a boom town, with people coming from all over the country to make their money in oil. It grew rapidly in a short time. But when the oil production slowed, major businesses moved out and the town was left with Claxton State University, the state mental institution, and large Victorian houses. Claxton itself has undergone major changes since its inception in the early part of the 20th century. It started as Claxton Community College; it is now a state university with an active graduate program in applied areas. Like many similar universities, it suffers from trying to prove that it is more than it is.

You know I've always been committed to providing a quality undergraduate education, thinking that an important officemate of my work is to educate the next generation to be productive, aware, and successful citizens, who are prepared to contribute to the community. But like many universities, it seems that Claxton wants to present itself as a first-rate research institution, developing graduate programs rather than focusing on a quality academic experience for undergraduate students.

I can tell already that teaching philosophy to undergraduates is not going to be considered a top priority by the administration. I've been told that my classes will be capped at 50 students per class, what the room can accommodate. It's a good thing that the rooms aren't larger—generating good discussions with 50 students will be challenging enough.

But I feel out of place, even though everyone has been quite nice to me. I'm exhausted—that's probably why I'm so down. I'll close and write more tomorrow. I miss you terribly.

Love, Maggie

Chapter 2

Finally, Maggie got to meet the members of her department. She had met three of them when she interviewed for the job, but the other five were new to her. She was pleased to see that she was not the only woman. Not that it mattered much; she had been the only female in her previous position and that had worked out just fine. But it would be nice to have another woman with whom to share similar interests.

Most of the meeting was spent making committee assignments for the year. Maggie, to her delight, was not expected to do any committee work her first year, but, true to form, she found herself volunteering for the library committee, which, she was told, met only once a year and was largely perfunctory: you asked what books and journals the department members wanted to order, submitted the request to the library, and were told by the librarian that there was no money in their budget.

All in all, it was an interesting department, with some fine teachers and some very accomplished scholars. Maggie was looking forward to working with them and getting to know them better. At least there were colleagues with whom she could discuss her own work–which was not true at Bennett, where she had been one of two philosophers, the other one not at all interested in social ethics or feminism.

She spent the rest of the day preparing for her classes and, in the evening, had dinner at the swimming coach's house. Doris Redden was a red-headed woman in her forties who taught swimming at the university. She had the physique of an athlete, although one who is past her prime. She didn't cook, but she was quite adept at ordering out. They dined on some quite good Thai food and listened to music.

They were interrupted during dinner by a phone call that seemed to upset Doris. When Maggie asked her about it, she said, "Oh, I don't know. I keep getting these calls and there's no one there."

Maggie tried to convince her that it was probably one of those solicitation calls but Doris seemed unusually concerned. "It just sounds different from those calls. It's like there's somebody on the line, but not saying anything."

Maggie didn't pursue the issue, thinking that Doris was clearly overreacting. At 10:00, she returned home, having spent a pleasant evening with an interesting woman.

....

Dear Sam,

You'll be glad to hear that I'm better today. I guess I was feeling down last night–missing you and the gang. But things were better today. Yesterday was a day of meetings, mostly boring, but I did get a touch of the gossip going around. It seems that one of the Vice Presidents was found by the campus police in the gym hot tub with a woman–not his wife. He accidentally set off the alarm (at 2:00 a.m.) and police came to investigate. Embarrassment all around–she's also married–and since many people don't like him, it's been a major source of entertainment around campus.

I also learned that a faculty member donated a kidney to the daughter of the Provost–no relation–and has now been "promoted" to a dean. That didn't elicit laughter, but a shrug–"Oh, well, that's how one gets ahead around here."

I met the director of Women's Studies yesterday, and I'm anxious to see what that group is like. I'm not the only woman in my department, but it doesn't look as if she is around very much, so it would be nice to meet some women with similar interests.

Speaking of the department, we had the first department meeting today. The chair, Charles Richards, seems like a decent guy. He runs an open meeting, doesn't require Robert's Rules, anybody can speak and raise issues. He's in his mid forties, and is starting to show his age. He's still a good-looking man, but I hear he's constantly being nagged by his overly ambitious wife to watch what he eats and to dress more professionally–he tends toward casual clothes–as she has higher administrative positions in mind for him. They have no children because, as Leo says, Mrs. Richards is fond of saying that taking care of Charles is a full-time job.

And speaking of Leo, remember him? He was the one at the interview that I told you about. He's a renowned scholar of 18th century philosophy, in particular the work of David Hume, but he doesn't flaunt it. He's a small man, in his 60s, with an impish look about him—I've already heard some female students call him "adorable." He says he's getting ready to retire, but I think that even in retirement, or perhaps especially in retirement, he'll continue his writing. He's married to Susan, a school teacher, and has two sons, one a biologist and the other a commercial airline pilot. Leo was complaining today that it was just his luck to have a pilot for a son when he didn't like to travel.

Write soon. I need to hear from you. Better yet, call!

Love, Maggie

P. S. I've already learned about a mystery here. I heard some people talking at the Dean's dinner party the other night about a guy in the English Department who claims his manuscript has been stolen. It's on Aemilia Lanyer—no, I don't know who that is—and the joke is why would anybody want to steal that? Anyway, he's looking at everyone in his department with suspicion and threatening to go to the police if it isn't returned by the time classes begin next Monday. Maybe I was wrong about the Midwest—it's not all that dull!

Chapter 3

Maggie met Doris for lunch at *Isis*. Doris was sipping an herbal tea and eating her vegetable wrap, while Maggie was mainlining plain black coffee–no latte or cappuccino for her–and devouring her turkey salad sandwich.

Maggie, in between bites, recounted her week. It had been hectic, with campus police interviewing everyone in the building where she had her office. It seems that not only was Prof. Grimsky's manuscript missing, but he had been getting hate mail. And, to make matters worse, someone broke into his office and slashed a painting he had on his wall. It wasn't valuable but it had sentimental attachments for him as he had bought it on his first trip to Paris when he was a young man. Of course, the police were more concerned with the vandalism–and perhaps with the possibility of this escalating and endangering university property– than they were with the missing manuscript.

In any event, Maggie continued, when she wasn't being interviewed by the police, she was caught up in conversations speculating on whom and why. The only thing that was settled was that Grimsky's officemate was at a conference in Ohio during the time the manuscript disappeared so he was no longer a suspect–at least in the eyes of the police. Grimsky wasn't so easily convinced.

"I hope your week hasn't been as hectic as mine," Maggie said.

With a sigh, running her hand through her short hair, twisting it so that she ended up looking like a porcupine, Doris replied, "Not hectic, but horrible. I'm really worried. I'm running out of patience. I'm not the only woman in the Athletics Department, but no matter what I do I don't seem to fit in. I seem to be the only one who doesn't go along with the good old boys. And they don't like that, so they get back at me by giving me a terrible schedule and not supporting the programs that I'm involved in. I'm sure they'd love it if I found a job somewhere else."

"Who does this? The chair? The whole department?"

"It's ultimately the chair who makes these decisions, but he has the support of the rest of the department. You see, there are only seven other regular faculty members–all men. The other three are adjuncts and you know what that means".

"Yeah, they don't have the security of tenure and the university can pay them less than the regular faculty and dismiss them at the end of their contract. And since they're on short-term contracts they're always worried about being reappointed."

"Exactly. Well, the three other women in the department are adjuncts, which means that even if they wanted to support me there's no way they can since they can't participate in department matters."

At this point, Doris put down her cup and drew up closer to the table. Bright red spots appeared on her cheeks as she pounded on the table with clenched fists.

"If they had their way, I'd be out of here. In fact, two of the men went to the Provost to protest my reappointment saying that I was unprofessional and a hindrance to the harmony of the department. They also made some comments about inappropriate behavior with students–you know, inappropriate sexual touching, things like that. Hell,

when you're teaching people to swim who have never been in the water before, you do have to touch them–hold them up, show them how to move their arms and legs. But there's nothing sexual about it–there's no other way to teach swimming.

"I come up for tenure next year and I'm convinced this is all a way to make it easy for them to make a negative decision–you know, get the Provost on their side before the issue even arises. It's bad enough to lose your job, but if you're denied tenure, it makes it hard to get other jobs. People always ask, 'Why did you leave your last job?' and you have to admit that you were fired."

Maggie looked at her, clearly concerned. The few years she had spent studying law before going to graduate school prepared her to detect sexual harassment when she saw it. "When they make these charges of 'inappropriate' behavior, are they talking about male or female students? What I'm getting at is: are they insinuating that you're a lesbian?"

"Insinuating, hell. They've all but come out and shouted it. Of course, they know they can't discriminate against me on that ground, so they just make jokes about it."

"What kind of jokes?"

"Oh, you know, when I walk into a department meeting, someone tells a joke about lesbians at the beginning of the meeting before things start. The chair then says, 'Okay that's enough, let's get down to business,' but there's no reprimand for the joke telling. And someone once slipped a picture under my office door from a magazine showing two women having sex. When I complained the chair said, 'Oh, lighten up! Can't you take a joke?' I didn't want to bring any more attention to myself so I didn't do anything about it."

"You know you don't have to put up with that. That's sexual harassment and you can file a grievance. But I think there are two issues here. One is the scheduling issue and the other is sexual harassment. I've dealt with sexual harassment issues at my former college, so if you decide to do something let me know. Maybe I can be of help. Think about it and get back to me, okay?"

"Thanks, I will." At this point Doris looked at her watch, finished her lunch, and got up, saying, "I have an appointment in ten minutes. I'll get back to you, okay?"

"Sure, just let me know what you want to do—no pressure."

....

Dear Sam,

I met with Doris Redden today—you know, the woman I told you about. I think she should file a grievance against her department, but she seems hesitant. Her department, or at least her chair, seems either very cruel or oblivious to what anybody else would see as sexual harassment. I just hope that she doesn't back away from filing a complaint because she's afraid of alienating people. From what she's said, she's already alienated them, although I don't know what the particulars are. She seems pretty normal, in fact, quite nice. We've had some good discussions—mostly about music.

I had dinner at her place the other night and it was quite pleasant. I discovered that she shared my interest in classical music. It seems she had been a music major before getting involved in coaching; she actually plays the violin. We spent the evening comparing our favorite performances of *various symphonies and concertos, with Doris playing CDs of the different performances of Beethoven's 9th to prove that her favorite was clearly superior. Fortunately, she was a good sport and didn't mind my defense of my preferences. If we can stop the harassment, she might be able to focus on other things in her life. I'm looking forward to attending some of the concerts coming up with her. None of my friends here seem to appreciate Beethoven—or maybe they're too busy to go to concerts. Hmm, maybe they're more like you than I realized!*

Love you, Maggie

Chapter 4

The weeks went by so quickly that Maggie didn't have time to realize how lonely she still was. It was only in the evenings when she had finished dinner and was relaxing that she questioned her decision to leave New York. But tonight she had work to do before calling it a day. One of her students was doing poorly in her class, even after many visits to her office for help. She was afraid that he needed more help than she was capable of giving. Clearly, she needed to get advice from someone. She made a mental note to speak to Charles the next day. She wasn't sure he was the best person to consult but, since the situation might call for some special tutoring for the student, a chair was more likely to be aware of the bureaucratic hoops to be jumped through.

She liked Charles, found him pleasant, and realized that he had gone out of his way to make her feel comfortable in the department. But he always seemed to be hurrying off someplace. Mostly to meetings, she thought; but it also seemed he ran quite a few errands for his wife. Maggie hadn't met her yet, but she had heard about her and her ambitions for Charles. She felt sorry for Charles; he seemed perfectly happy doing what he was doing. It was hard to picture him in the administrative position his wife was planning for him.

She was thinking all this the next morning when she knocked on the door to his office. "Hi, I hope I'm not interrupting anything important. But I have a problem in one of my classes and wanted to talk to you about it. Do you have time now?"

Maggie stood in the doorway, waiting for Charles's response.

"Sure. Come on in. sit down. What's the problem?" Charles was seated behind his desk, which was covered with papers organized into neat piles. He was wearing his usual outfit of jeans and a tweed jacket over an opened-collar shirt. A green and blue striped tie, which he had probably worn that morning at the insistence of his wife, was now hanging over the back of his chair. His office was adorned with vibrant tapestries depicting medieval battles, one of his non-academic interests.

"Well, I have an African American young man in my introductory philosophy class who is going to fail. He seems quite bright, but he's totally unprepared for university work. He tells me that he's a participant in something called 'Project Twenty' and that he didn't have to deal with any of the admission requirements. Is that true? Do you know anything about that program? "

"Yeah, he's right. Those kids were recruited to diversify the university. As you've probably noticed, we have a predominantly white student body, not to mention faculty and administration. That program was put into effect a few years ago and from what I hear it's been quite successful. Most of the kids who don't drop out are doing quite well–an average grade of 'B'."

"But this young man has trouble with the readings and his writing is terrible. Are there tutorials to bring him up to speed? Or group sessions, or something? Should I be doing something special?"

Maggie's face clearly showed the frustration she was experiencing. She prided herself on her teaching and was distraught when she couldn't reach students and turn them on to philosophy. After all, she herself had turned to philosophy because everything was fair game in that discipline. You could–and must–question everything, even the so-called "self-evident" tenets you had been taught. Surely, she could find something that could grab a student's attention. And yet, in the case of this student, she *had* grabbed his attention; he was interested; he asked good questions; he saw the significance of the important distinctions. But he could barely read or write! How could he have been admitted?

Seeing the expression on Maggie's face, Charles sought to ease her mind. "No, there's nothing special you should be doing for him. But remember, since these students don't have the academic background the other students have, perhaps you should grade them accordingly. I mean a 'B' for these students would probably be a 'C' for the other students. After all, they are working at a disadvantage, not having the adequate background."

Maggie didn't respond. What could she say? That it would be unfair to other students, not to mention the young man himself? That it was a form of racism? She prided herself on her grading. Realizing that grading essays was never a purely objective exercise, she tried to counter that built-in problem with grading each paper without knowing the name of the student, and using a form of a "rubric" (that recent buzz word of the composition faculty) to help maintain the same criteria for each paper, whether it was read first or last. To use a different standard for some students was abhorrent to her. If Claxton was going to admit students who weren't prepared for university work, they should provide some help for them. She was an advocate of an "open admissions, fairly closed exit" principle. Everyone should be able to get a university education, but they had to attain certain levels of competence in order to graduate. And if that required some tutorials and special workshops, well, then that should be provided. Deciding that some students, because of a poor academic background, or membership in some group, weren't capable of meeting those standards and therefore should be judged more leniently was unacceptable to her.

However, she didn't say anything to Charles. After all, she had just recently met him and didn't know if he agreed with Claxton's practice or not—and besides, she felt too insecure in her position to do the right thing!

She left the office feeling compromised. It was times like this that she missed having Sam to talk with. While she had met many people here, she had yet to meet anyone with whom she felt comfortable enough to have this kind of discussion.

....

A few days later she ran into Jessie Hamilton, the Director of the Women's Studies Department, and was invited to join her for coffee. Jessie was a woman in her sixties, with graying hair pulled back into a French twist. She was what used to be called "pleasingly plump" and tried to minimize the effect by wearing loose-fitting shirts or jackets over skirts. Her one vanity seemed to be shoes—she wore the latest styles, with the highest heels she could walk in. Her friends chided her on this: "Wear sensible shoes," they said. But, as she pointed out, her legs were her only asset and she was going to show them off to advantage.

They were just finishing up their coffee in Jessie's office when Sarah Lowell came in to join them. Sarah was an anthropologist, specializing in Native American studies. She was five foot two with blonde hair worn in a Dutch Boy style which made her look younger than her 50 years. Her trim figure–achieved without "working out"–added to her youthful look. She wore no make-up of any kind, claiming she didn't have time in the morning to fuss. Maggie felt like giving her a few tips on how to do the job in five minutes each morning, but not knowing Sarah, restrained herself. She had learned many years ago that not everyone was appreciative of her well-intentioned advice.

Feeling comfortable with both Jessie and Sarah, Maggie raised the issue of differential standards for minority students, wondering if it was as accepted a practice as Charles had indicated. To her relief, neither woman approved of the practice and neither practiced it themselves nor thought that many of their colleagues did. Quite to the contrary, Sarah seemed to think that many of the faculty were insensitive to the needs of these students. Once she got started, she went on to recount examples of faculty and administrative insensitivity.

"I was on a committee my first year here to study adding a foreign language requirement for all first-year students. At first Greek and Latin were the two languages proposed, but that was discarded when someone pointed out that Claxton didn't offer courses on Greek or Latin! Then they proposed German and French. Which was fine–the university has those courses. But when I suggested adding Spanish, since it is probably the language that more students would be likely to use than French or German, the committee members balked. 'What research worthy of reading was in Spanish?' they asked. When I told them that their fucking prejudices were showing they backed down and added Spanish to the list. But it all came to naught as the committee's recommendations were filed away and the curriculum wasn't changed."

Once started, Sarah seemed on a mission to bring Maggie up to date on campus culture. "They don't know how to accommodate international students here, either. Since most of them live in the dormitories, or as they call them today, 'residence halls,' they have to move out of their rooms for the Thanksgiving and Christmas breaks as the university is closed during those times. Where are they supposed to go? Well, it's up to the students to make their own arrangements!

Fortunately, some of the local churches find people to take them in for the holidays. That's at least something good that churches do."

"Enough already," interrupted Jessie. It was clear that Sarah was on a roll and would continue listing problems at Claxton if given half a chance. "We don't want to tell Maggie all the negative things about the university in her first few weeks here. She'll find out about them soon enough. And, to bring you up to date, international students are now housed in Mason Hall, which is set aside for them during the vacation periods."

"Big deal," said Sarah. "They still have to move out of one dorm and go to another –that's certainly inconvenient for them."

Jessie agreed and suggested they move on. The rest of the hour was spent explaining the plans for Women's Studies that were in place for the coming year and the agenda for the next meeting. Maggie left the room feeling strangely comforted by the conversation with Jessie and Sarah.

The next evening when talking to Sam, she related the conversation she had had with Jessie and Sarah. Sam, always attuned to her subtle changes of mood, pointed out that perhaps she had found some compatible souls. Maggie had to agree.

....

When Maggie entered her office the next morning, she found a voicemail message from Professor Grimsky. For some reason, he wanted to meet with her. At first she was reluctant to return his call; what could they talk about? But then, feeling sorry for him, she picked up the phone and made an appointment to meet with him the next day.

The rest of the day was spent grading papers so that she could have a free evening to watch TV. She was a closet TV watcher–something that her friends, and even Sam, didn't understand. "How can you watch that crap?" was a constant question asked of her when she settled down to watch a cop show. Her only reply was that she enjoyed it! She would remind them that Wittgenstein, the famous philosopher, enjoyed Western movies; but the typical response was, "Well, he had no taste, either."

Now she could watch what she wanted without having to defend her choices. That was one good thing about living alone.

....

Dear Sam,

Thanks for the call last night. It was just what I needed. You seem to understand me better than I do myself. You're right about my sounding better—I'm feeling better. I think of you only ten times a day now instead of every hour; in fact, sometimes I can go a whole day without realizing that I miss you!

I'm getting the feel of the place. My classes are going fine—even my "unprepared" student is doing better. I've met with him a few times and we've set up a schedule for some informal tutorials that I think will help. Those workshops on how to teach reading that I attended back in New York have come in handy. He asks the right questions, which convinces me that he not only understands what's being said, but wants to know why the author said it. Now if only the other students would get to that point!

The mystery about the missing manuscript has gotten more serious. The police have been called in and talked to other members in the English Department and the rest of us in the building. There are no "official" suspects at this point, although the prof has his own suspicions. He thinks that his officemate, a man who hates post-modernism, has taken the manuscript out of jealousy.

But enough about me; I'm concerned about you. I know how difficult it is for you, how hard it is to get a showing. But you're a great photographer— and you know it! You're just tired. After all, it's only a year since you left Erickson Advertising. You have to give yourself time to get noticed. And you will. Remember, you hated Erickson! The work you're doing now is so much more creative, more you.

So no more talk about getting a job—you have a job. I've put a check in the mail to help pay for groceries—you need to eat. They pay me quite well and, since there's nothing to spend it on here, I'm actually saving money.

Get some rest, watch a good movie, drink a glass of wine—and start tomorrow with the knowledge that you are *going to get a showing.*

(I wish I were there to comfort you, but emails and phone calls will have to do for now.)

Love, Maggie

Chapter 5

Maggie had agreed to meet with Professor Grimsky, although she was still unsure why he had invited her. Maybe he just wanted to talk to someone who hadn't taken sides yet in the big debate: was it stolen or did he misplace it?

"He seems a nice enough old guy, a little on the fuddy duddy side, but then one would have to be in order to spend years on the work of some obscure, 17th century author who wasn't even famous in her own lifetime. It's a marvel that any of Lanyer's works have survived, especially when one realizes that the works of many others have been lost to the future." Maggie's audience was Jessie, who listened quietly as they were sharing some homemade coffee cake in Jessie's office.

Jessie's office was in the Women's Studies Center, which included a conference room, a small lounge which served as the library, and her office. The furniture was clearly hand-me-down, but Jessie had managed to claim the old furnishings from the Dean's office when it was being remodeled—a cut above what the average department had. With the few objects she brought in from home, the rooms had a comfortable, warm atmosphere. There was a coffee pot, a microwave, a small refrigerator used for food served at meetings, and bookshelves filled with issues of journals and books dealing with women's studies. A few colorful posters and a vase with fresh flowers from Jessie's prolific green house completed the cozy effect.

"What will we talk about? I certainly don't know if his manuscript was stolen, and if so who stole it. What if we get on to his favorite topic—the marvelous contributions of post-modern analysis to all things intellectual? I'll have to restrain myself in order to be polite. Perhaps I should simply claim to be ignorant of the whole post-modern fad and brace myself for a lecture on it. I can always start the meeting with an announcement that I have an important appointment, and so can only spare a few minutes talking with him."

Maggie quickly learned that Jessie, although not an advocate of post-modern critical analysis, was not as negative toward it as Maggie. Politely pointing out that Maggie's adamant rejection of post-modern analysis might be the result of the philosophical tradition that Maggie worked in, Jessie pointed out that not everything can, or should, be subjected to rational analysis.

"Maggie, you're right about one thing at least. Professor Grimsky is a nice man. He's feeling particularly isolated right now. People are quick to assume he misplaced his manuscript and that he's getting too old to be productive. He's only 64, and he's no more senile now than he was at 30! He never learned to use a computer–he types everything on an old Remington and then has the secretary do the final version. He thinks people are laughing at him, and that even the police don't take the loss of his manuscript seriously.

"You weren't here last year when he applied for a leave to work on the book. His department turned him down and some of the comments his colleagues made regarding the worth of his project really hurt him. You see, you're not the only one who dislikes post-modern analysis. And even the colleagues who *are* post-modernists think that his work on Aemilia Lanyer isn't worth publishing; in fact, they think that she isn't worth studying at all. So, you see, he feels that in you he can at least have a neutral listener. Just don't offer to help him solve the mystery of the missing manuscript!"

With that, Jessie got up to clear the table, and Maggie thanked her, promised to be polite, and left for her appointment with Grimsky.

....

Grimsky opened his door and welcomed Maggie with a hearty handshake. He was a small man, with a shock of thick, wavy graying hair. He was wearing what appeared to be bedroom slippers and a shawl of shades of brown wool woven into geometric patterns. His side of the office was filled with books, papers, posters, and music tapes–on the desk, the floor, the bookshelves, and even the window ledge. If anything had been stolen from his office, it would be hard to know. Chaos was the dominant impression one received upon entering the room. And yet, contrary to the taunts of his colleagues on the state of his office, he seemed to know where everything was.

He gestured to Maggie to sit down–although she had to remove a pile of books in order to do so—and launched into a lively discussion of his life's work: the writings of Aemilia Lanyer. His thesis was that she was a 17th century feminist whose works—*Hail God, King of the Jews* and *Eve's Apology in Defense of Women,* in which she argues for women's equality, or even superiority, to men in spiritual and moral matters—were worthy of study because women rarely published at that time and because her works were influential expressions of women's perspective on religious issues.

Maggie, true to her promise to Jessie, politely listened to him, as he described the significance of Lanyer's work and its influence on Shakespeare. After twenty minutes, Maggie, looking at her watch, apologetically pointed out that she had a meeting with a student in ten minutes. Grimsky took that as the sign to get to the point of the meeting.

"As you probably know, the manuscript of my book has been stolen. I know who did it, but nobody will believe me. Andrews, my officemate, has been jealous of my work for years now and the thought of the fame the book would bring me was just too much for him. People laugh at my interest in Lanyer and the conclusions I've reached about her literary significance. They think she was just another mistress to famous men in her time, but I know she was more than that. They reject the possibility that any woman at that time could have had any literary influence on writers like Shakespeare and Donne. That's because they're all sexist! Oh, I know, some of them teach courses on women writers and participate in the Women's Studies Program here, but you should see how they treat their wives. Underneath all their PC rhetoric, they expect their wives to cook and clean for them, raise the children, and entertain when necessary—even when their wives have their own professional careers! Feminists, indeed!"

At this point, Maggie interrupted him. "I'm sure you'd know if the manuscript was missing—you seem to know where things are in this room. But how can you be so sure that Professor Andrews stole it? I thought he was in Ohio at a conference when the manuscript was taken."

"Oh, that's how clever he is. He was in Ohio when I *discovered* the manuscript missing. But he knew that I wouldn't be in my office for most of that week as I was working in the library those days. He could have stolen the manuscript days before he left for his conference, trusting that I wouldn't notice its loss until he was safely in Ohio."

"But what about the hate mail you've been receiving? Do you think he's responsible for that, too?"

"Either he is or he's more likely manipulated some student to do it. I don't understand modern technology, but it seems possible for someone to send an email that can't be traced–or at least the police aren't interested in tracing it. Some of our majors are also very knowledgeable about computers; he could have paid one of them to send the emails."

Maggie nodded, hoping that by doing so she appeared sympathetic. She rose, extended her hand to Grimsky and said the polite things about how sorry she was for his loss and how she hoped that the manuscript would eventually turn up. She couldn't help but ask, though, why he didn't have any backup or copies of the manuscript.

"Well, I never thought I'd need it. After all, I trusted my colleagues." With that reply, Maggie nodded again and took her leave.

....

Dear Sam,

I told you that things would look better in the morning. Which series did you show the gallery? I thought the ones on the playgrounds were fine, but so were the ones on the windows. You know how I like pictures of windows, but I'll defer to your better judgment about which ones to show.

I met the professor whose manuscript was stolen, or so he thinks. He's an interesting guy, a stereotypical English professor. He's really into his work– 17th century literature–and his general thesis is certainly plausible: women are hidden from history. But he does tend to jump to conclusions. He's convinced his officemate, a Professor Andrews, whom he hates, has stolen or destroyed it out of jealousy. Everyone thinks he's gone too far, but I feel sorry for him. He does get ridiculed a lot and most of the time it's for nothing but his enthusiasm about his subject.

Other than that, things are pretty much the same here. Well, I have to get back to grading. Keep me posted on the interview.

Love, Maggie

P.S. Stop being so sensitive about money. When you become rich and famous you can take care of me and I can retire and spend my life reading, writing, and eating bonbons.

Chapter 6

"Well, I guess we should begin–maybe others will be along shortly." It was the start of the monthly department meeting, and Charles had distributed the agenda and the minutes of the last month's meeting.

"Any additions to the agenda?" he asked. "If not, let's have a motion to approve the minutes."

"We don't have to approve minutes, according to Robert's Rules." This was the main contribution Henry seemed to make at these meetings, and it was promptly ignored by everyone at the meeting.

"I'll move approval," said Ben. "And I'll second it," said Doug.

"There's a misspelling in section IV–it should be 'judgment' not 'judgement,' and there's a misplaced comma in section V." This, too, was contributed by Henry.

"I believe that both spellings are appropriate–the OED accepts the British as well as the American spellings," replied Leo.

"But we're not British. These minutes go to the Dean; they should be correctly spelled–in American English," declared Henry, whose face was now a startling shade of red. "If we don't maintain proper standards what can we expect of our students?"

"Okay, Henry, we'll make the changes," groaned Charles, in an obvious attempt to prevent the escalation of Henry's lecture on the department's responsibility to single-handedly defend academic standards and fight the encroaching influence of those who maintained that a student's attendance in class was deserving of at least a "B" whether or not they had mastered the material of the class–assuming that there was some content to master. Everyone in the department agreed with Henry, but no one was willing to spend half of every department meeting hearing him wax, ineloquently, on the topic.

In a somewhat clumsy attempt to take charge of the meeting and move things along, Charles relayed the usual messages from the Dean: enrollments in the university were steady (bad); enrollments in the department were up (good); the state was decreasing its funding to the university (bad); the department had the least number of grants in the university (bad); and applications for promotion and tenure decisions were due next Friday.

At the announcement of the lack of grants in the department, everyone started talking at once. "Doesn't he realize that grants in philosophy are not as easy to get as they are in the natural and social sciences?" asked Leo.

"I'm tired of hearing about the importance of grants," chimed in Doug. We have an outstanding research record. I think we topped everyone in the college last year in publications, all without external funding. What more do they want?"

"Money!" exploded Charles. "With external grants, they can use that money to fund assistants, and even your salary; so it saves them money when our work is funded by outside agencies."

"But we don't have research or teaching assistants," replied Leo, who was winding up to continue the argument. Even though he had received a grant to complete his book on Hume, he was supportive of his colleagues who didn't have the same resources.

"Okay," said Charles, "We all agree it's unfair to compare our grant activity with other departments but there's not much we can do about it. We've presented our position every year and it's gotten us nowhere. We never get any more funding and we hadn't had any new hires in the last few years until Maggie. We've made these arguments before, but they've never impressed the Dean. Let's move on."

The discussion went on with the same points being made repeatedly. Maggie realized that it was cathartic for everyone to weigh in on the issues, so she sat through the discussions, saying nothing, not feeling comfortable pointing out that forty-five minutes had passed and the main points of the agenda had not even been mentioned. There was the discussion of the proposed changes to the requirements for the philosophy major, and the vote on whether the department should buy a new copier for the main office or new computers for two of the faculty. She was opting for new computers, hoping that would ensure she got a slightly better hand-me-down than the one she presently was using.

The discussion gradually got around to the main agenda topics, which ended up being postponed because the report on the proposed changes to the major requirements had not been submitted–Barbara Bradshaw, the chair of the committee, wasn't at the meeting and hadn't finished writing up the committee recommendations; and there was no agreement on copier or computers–Henry wanted to know about the specifications on the copier and the computers before he would vote.

At the end of the meeting, Toby approached Maggie and invited her for coffee in the lounge. They had been trying to meet for coffee all week, but their schedules hadn't matched. Toby was known throughout the university as eccentric. He was often seen walking in the hall, with what would be a pretentious air in other people, but seemed truly genuine in him. Hands behind his back, or hand stroking an imaginary beard–a typical gesture of male philosophers–as he paced up and down, deep in thought. He usually didn't notice her when their paths crossed, so absorbed was he in whatever he was pondering. But when he did notice her, he had always smiled and asked how she was doing. Maggie had not met anyone quite like him before, but she found him fascinating–and sweet. She looked forward to their coffee sessions.

As they were walking to the faculty lounge, a small room painted purple, with tables, chairs, a refrigerator, and a coffee pot, Maggie noticed that Toby had a tear in the back seam of his jacket. When she politely called his attention to it, he looked at his jacket as if seeing it for the first time and said, "Oh, my; so it does." and then proceeded to take a seat at the small table set aside for casual conversations such as theirs.

"Well, how are you adjusting to the strange ways of Claxton or should I say our department?" he asked.

"Well, things are different here, but I'm getting used to them. This was the first real department meeting I've been at–the first one was just getting to meet people before classes started. Was this a typical meeting?"

"Actually, it was more productive than most. At least Henry didn't go on too long, and Charles did try to move the agenda along."

"I noticed that some people weren't there, is that typical?"

Toby laughed. "Oh, you'll rarely see our Barbara at a meeting. She's quite the *prima donna* and seldom has time to do much for the department. But she's a splendid teacher and that counts for a lot here.

Ben has been ill, otherwise he'd be there, and Yamato—Felipe—randomly comes to meetings, but that's okay. When he's there the meetings go on forever because he has to comment on every bloody thing that's said. Have you met Felipe yet?"

Maggie smiled. "No, I haven't had the pleasure. He's the one who's interested in cognitive science, right?"

"Yes, he's trying to introduce a master's degree in it. He's not getting much support from the department or from the Dean, so he's been bloody frustrated. I'm surprised he hasn't approached you yet to get your support."

"I don't know what kind of support I could give at this stage. I'm still trying to learn about the courses and programs we do offer. And the degree structure here is different from what I'm used to. It seems that most of our philosophy majors get a Bachelor of Science degree rather than a Bachelor of Arts. I always thought that you had to have a science major in order to get a B.S. degree."

"Well, you see, in order to get a B.A. degree you have to take two years of a foreign language. And since most of our students don't want to learn another language, the system has adjusted to the demand and allowed any major on the B.S. It's most unfortunate, but what can you do—we're all 'market-driven' these days."

At that moment, the door opened and a tall, thin young Asian man entered. "We were just talking about you, Felipe," said Toby. "I was explaining to Maggie—have you two met yet?—about your attempt to get a cognitive science master's here."

Felipe came over to the table where Maggie and Toby were seated and extended his hand to Maggie. "Hi," he said. "Yeah, I've been trying for two years now to get this place into the 21st century, but they're all Luddites. We have a chance to be on the cutting edge of where philosophy can go and this administration can't see beyond its nose."

Felipe would have continued in this vein except Toby got up to leave, claiming that he had to show Maggie where the department kept its journals. This was clearly a ruse as Maggie had already used the journals, but she rose to join him, making the usual polite comments about meeting Felipe.

When they were in the hallway, Maggie looked at Toby with raised eyebrows. "Oh, if you encourage him, he'll go on forever. The problem is that not all the department is behind him on this. Some would like to see a general philosophy graduate program, and others want us to concentrate on the undergraduate students and are afraid that, without significant additions to faculty, a graduate program would take away resources from the undergraduate one. I'm sure he'll get around to you before the department takes up the bloody proposal again."

"I'm not sure which side I'd support. I don't feel I know enough about the programs here yet to take a stand. I'm still trying to get used to the students in my classes. They seem bright enough, but not very motivated. I don't think they are doing the readings, although they do come to class; I guess that's something. Speaking of students, I have an office hour in ten minutes, so I'd better get there. You never know if a student will show up! Thanks for the coffee and the update."

....

Dear Sam

Just a quick note to say I miss you. I'm starting to feel comfortable here. I'd love for you to come for a visit–maybe a long weekend soon? I'm anxious to show you that the Midwest in the fall is beautiful. The trees should reach their peak in about two weeks and you don't have to drive two hours to see them, as we did back in New York. I'll call you this weekend. Think about a visit!

I just had coffee with Toby Fletcher. He's the metaphysician in the department and he's probably the most eccentric person I've ever met. But he's also an extremely nice guy. At first I thought his "absent-minded professor" behavior was an act, but I've come to realize that it's quite genuine. He truly lives in his own world, only occasionally making contact with what the rest of us call reality. He's in his late 50s and was educated at Oxford. He speaks with a slight British accent, although he was born and raised in Nebraska. He's a really kind person and seems to volunteer for jobs that others run away from. He's single, but seems to have developed deep and long-standing friendships with former girlfriends. I have the feeling that he would love to have a "relationship" that lasted, but his eccentricities, while charming enough for continued friendships, are obviously not charming enough to keep a relationship going. But he's a sweetie. You'd never know he was born and raised in Nebraska; he peppers his talk with "bloody" and "jolly well"–must be the influence of his years spent at Oxford. We have coffee at least once a week and he keeps me up with the local gossip. People complain that he grades too easily–he gives mostly 'A's and 'B's–but his response is that the students are surprisingly good. As he says, they ask questions he had never thought of!

You would enjoy talking to him. He's quite knowledgeable about music and film, and he loves to ski. They're predicting a lot of snow this winter and he's invited me to go skiing with him. I haven't skied since I was thirteen years old, so I think I'll decline the invitation.

The other guy I met today is Felipe Yamato, a young Japanese man, who I learned was born in Chile but speaks English as if he had been born here. His specialty is philosophy of science and he seems on a mission to introduce a master's program in cognitive science. He's a type I've dealt with before. Seems bright, but rather arrogant. He followed me to my office after we met and tried to get my support for his cognitive science program. When I said I didn't know enough about the programs here, he didn't see why I couldn't support it anyway. He couldn't understand why anyone would disagree with him. I've heard that he applied for an internal grant–his project was on "Robotics and Evolution", which ties in with his interest in cognitive science. When he heard that someone in the Psychology Department received the grant and that her project was something on studying autism in young children, he couldn't understand why anyone would consider that project more important than his. Some think that the resistance his program is receiving from the administration is partly due to his abrasive personality.

Now that I'm talking about department members, I might as well tell you about some of the others. There's Henry Bellows, the department's aesthetician. He's small and trim, with a Hercule Poirot mustache. He walks with short mincing steps and has a thin reedy voice. He seems to be only concerned with rules and regulations, and doesn't seem to hesitate to remind them when they are in violation of such. He lives alone with his long-time companion, Minette–not Minnie!–a short-haired, tortoiseshell Abyssinian cat whose activities and health are known to all of us as Henry emails a "bulletin" each Monday about the amazing things his Minette did during the weekend. Needless to say, no one looks forward to these announcements and most of us hit the "delete" button without reading the message. He seems a real fuddy-duddy–not much fun to talk to.

The youngest department member is Douglas Wilson, a tall, lanky young man with curly blond hair that he wears in a long pony tail. The *female undergraduates think he's "hot" and he responds by trying to date them. He's a logician and seems to use the large logic course for easy access to potential dates. Toby tells me that he's been warned many times by Charles that it was unprofessional—as well as perhaps unethical—to date students, but Doug ignores that advice. Some members are waiting for some student to file a sexual harassment charge against him; some seem to be eagerly anticipating it.*

Then there's Barbara Bradshaw. She's a strikingly attractive young woman. She has jet black hair and very white skin, and wears clothes which, while professional, reveal considerable cleavage. She's called "Gothic Barbie" by her students, both because her specialty is ancient Greek philosophy and because she dresses in all black, including black lipstick. Her courses seem to be quite popular, especially with the young men.

So, now you know some of the people that I work with. Some good, some not-so-good, but all-in-all a pretty good department.

Well, this didn't turn out to be a short note, did it? I'll close now. Call me this weekend. I'll be home grading papers—again.

Love, Maggie

Chapter 7

"Maggie? It's Doris. I need to talk with you–weird things are happening. Please call me when you get in."

Maggie didn't listen to the message until late that evening, as she had been busy grading exams at *Isis*–a place where she could sit quietly with a cup of coffee and not be interrupted. She typically spent time there when she had no classes. It was quieter than her office, and there was no refrigerator calling to her with yesterday's leftovers.

When she returned the call, Doris answered immediately, anxiety apparent in her first word.

"What's happened?" asked Maggie.

"I don't know who's doing this, but I keep getting these strange phone calls. No one says anything but I know someone's there. And then someone's been putting up pictures on my office door–like pin-up pictures, you know? Sexy women, scantily clad."

"Do you have caller ID on your phone? You know sometimes when solicitors call there's a delay in their spiel–they dial multiple numbers and keep you on hold until they're finished with the previous call. Maybe that's what's happening with the calls."

"No, I don't have caller ID. But I don't think it's a solicitor. I can hear breathing on the line. It sounds different from the solicitor calls. And what about the pictures?"

"Yeah, that's serious. That sounds as if it's someone in the building, maybe even in the department. Have you complained to anyone about this? Your chair? The dean?"

"No, it wouldn't do any good."

"Look, it's late and you're upset. Let's meet tomorrow morning. I don't have class until 11:00. Can we meet at 9:00 at *Isis*? This is getting serious; we need to be clear about our next step."

"I'll be there. Thanks."

....

The next morning saw the first snowfall of the season. It was only November, but clearly winter was approaching. Maggie was grateful for the many heavy sweaters her family had given her when she left New York. Their reason for thinking that Michigan would be much colder than New York was based on the typical New Yorker view that discounted everything between New York and California, the only two states worth thinking about—except for Florida when one was considering retirement. In their eyes, Michigan's weather was the same as Minnesota's, and they knew it was cold there.

The bare trees looked as if in full bloom with fluffy white flowers on every branch and the air had a crispness that matched the crunching sound of her footsteps on the frozen ground. She dressed warmly, slipped on her trusty UGG boots and walked to *Isis* where she sat down with a cup of coffee to wait for Doris.

She didn't have long to wait. At first she didn't recognize Doris, all bundled up in a furry-type coat which made her look twice her already large size. But it was her face that startled her. Doris looked as if she had aged ten years in the two weeks since Maggie had last seen her. There were dark circles under her eyes; her hair, which was sticking out of a black woolen cap, looked more gray than red; and she had lines in her face that were not there before. It was clear she hadn't been sleeping and that she was not well. Given last night's phone call, Maggie would describe her as scared.

"Are you all right?" asked Maggie.

"No, I can't take much more of this. This morning when I went to my office, I ran into Danny—he's the track coach, a nice guy—who said he was sorry I was leaving. Leaving! I asked him where he heard that and he said he had been talking to Jack, the chair, who said I wouldn't be here next year. Danny was embarrassed when I told him I wasn't leaving and said maybe he had misunderstood Jack. But you can see what's happening. They've already decided that I'm not going to be reappointed for next year, no less tenured."

"Whoa, slow down. I've read your department's rules and procedures. You have to be given at least a year's notice—so no matter what happens you're here for next year. But, more importantly, let's focus on what's happening. I think that you really ought to file a grievance against your chair. And the first step is to get the dean involved. Deans are supposed to see that departments are run properly, and that includes the chair's behavior. If the dean supports the chair, or does nothing, then we file the grievance against the dean, who didn't do his job–or is it a her?"

"It's a her, Dean Morris," replied Doris.

"So, let's prepare what you're going to present to her."

"What do I have to do?"

"The phone calls are iffy. You can mention them, but there's no evidence that they are harassment calls. They could be pranks, or solicitors– yes, I know they sound different, but I'm not sure that'll count as evidence. You can mention them, but I wouldn't stress them too much–you don't want to come across as paranoid. You want to present yourself as reasonable but concerned, maybe even scared. The pictures, though, are another thing. Have you kept any of them? Was anything written on them?"

"I kept them, but nothing was written on them. When I complained to Jack about them, he just laughed and said I had no sense of humor, that it was probably just a joke and I shouldn't take it so seriously."

"What a jerk. But we need to tie them into the larger picture of your treatment in the department. Last time you mentioned some ways you're treated differently than the men in your department. Lesbian-baiting, if I remember correctly, was one issue. Can you remember specific incidents? It would be good if there was someone else present who was willing to support your claim. But, wait, didn't you say something about the Provost?"

"Yes, two members of the department went to the Provost and accused me of inappropriately touching students."

"Great, that's what we need. That way you can show that you're not being overly sensitive to a few old boy jokes. How did you find out about that?"

"One of the adjuncts, Marge, overheard Jack talking about it to the secretary."

"Jeez, talk about unprofessional! Okay; you also mentioned that your schedule was unfair. Can you support that with hard evidence? You know, compare your schedule the last few years with that of others?"

"Sure. I'm the only one who teaches an extra class without it counting and without getting paid for it. It's called 'advanced life-saving', but since it's an elective and only has about ten students each time, they don't think it should count. But lots of other courses are electives and have small enrollments–and they count."

"Okay, get the data on that: courses, dates taught, enrollments, and who taught them. Include whether they counted as part of their load and then compare it to yours. Try to do this by the end of the week, if you can, so we can make an appointment with the Dean early next week. There's a time limit to start the grievance process, but we're okay on that. But there's another issue. You look–what can I say–frazzled? Maybe scared? Are you worried about your safety? Has something happened to scare you?"

"I don't know. Sometimes I get the feeling that someone is watching me, but there's no one there. I think I'm just on edge about this whole thing. Like, the other evening after my last swimming class. I was tidying up the pool areas–there are always things left behind by the students: water bottles, towels, you know that sort of stuff–and I had the weirdest feeling–like someone was watching me, but there was no one there."

"Well, it's hard to believe that someone would actually physically attack you, but I'd keep to well-lit, public places with people around– just to be sure. Okay, if you get that material to me this week, we'll make the appointment with the Dean. And if anything else happens, call me right away."

"You'll be the first to hear. I can get the info on schedules today and get them to you by tomorrow. Thanks so much for your help."

"Doris, this is an important issue. It obviously affects you in a very immediate way, but it also affects other women on campus. What you're experiencing is sexual harassment, and there are laws against that. Granted, laws don't always change attitudes, but they're sure helpful in changing behavior when they're enforced. Get the info to me tomorrow, and get some sleep."

Doris left and Maggie got another coffee. "Shit," she muttered to herself. She had fought–and won–the battle of sexual harassment at Bennett and thought that by now everyone was aware that lesbian-baiting was taboo. Obviously not. She wondered what the guys in the Athletics Department were like. Could they be so insulated that they weren't aware that what they were doing could get them in trouble? Or did they feel so protected by the administration that they didn't care? After all, athletics was big even at a place like Claxton. Maggie had read in a recent campus paper that many college coaches made more money than their presidents! And that even though football brought in money from the gate receipts, the athletic program at Claxton still received $14 million from the general fund in order to operate. Was this going to be an uphill battle because of the importance of athletics on campus?

She finished her coffee, gathered her briefcase with the exams she had finished grading, and left *Isis* to trudge through the snow to her office.

....

Dear Sam,

Well, I met with Doris again. If what she says is true, she is being sexually harassed. I think jocks are probably the most sexist men. I know you disagree and I'll grant you that I don't know much about athletics and can't stand football, but you have to agree that it's particularly difficult for women in athletics. They're always having to fight being labeled lesbians, as if that were the worst thing in the world. Some of the female athletes that I've met seem to go out of their way to appear feminine, i.e., heterosexual, even if they're not. And the others are just dismissed as "butch." Remember the trouble that Janet and Lily had at Bennett? They had to hide their relationship for years—until sexual orientation was added as a legal no-no.

Okay, enough about athletics. How are you? You haven't written lately so I assume you've been busy. How is the work going? Have you heard from any of the galleries yet? Do you see the gang often? Give my love to them and tell them I'm looking forward to seeing them at Christmas.

Love, Maggie

Chapter 8

Maggie received the scheduling information from Doris the next day, clearly supporting the claim that she was treated differently from others in her department. Maggie spent a few hours reviewing the provisions for processing a grievance. Never having handled one at Claxton, she sought the advice of Ben, who had been involved in many grievances throughout his years at Claxton. She had not met Benjamin Hopkins before arriving at Claxton, but in the short time she had been there she had heard a lot about him. He was a soft-spoken man in his late 50s who specialized in social ethics. He was of medium height, with thick brown hair turning gray at the temples. Most importantly, he was well-known on campus as the person to go to if one needed help.

He and his wife Julia had adopted three African-American children. They had decided not to have children when they married, partly because of his age and partly because of the racial difference—Benjamin was white, Julia was African American. But Julia's sister had died unexpectedly and they had adopted her three children. It turned out that Ben's age and the racial difference had not interfered with their turning out to be wonderful, loving parents of delightful, thriving children.

When Maggie presented the facts about Doris's situation, she found him to be helpful, giving bits of advice on how to approach certain issues, what to stress, what to downplay. But, he warned, the main weakness of the procedure was its lack of time limits for the administration's reply. He suggested that applying pressure on the dean was perhaps the best way to get a response, even if it meant being a nuisance.

Maggie left, feeling a bit more confident in what she was about to be involved in. It also helped to know that Ben would be available for more advice, should she need it.

....

The following weekend, Maggie had her first taste of culture at Claxton. She was impressed with the number of events sponsored by the university, but had been so busy with classes and her writing that she hadn't been able to take advantage of any of them. Tonight, though, she was at the theater.

"This was a great idea. I haven't been to a play–or anything–since I came here. I miss the big city's music and theater, not to mention restaurants," said Maggie as she and Nina Nichols were settling into their seats in the campus theater, waiting for the play to begin.

Nina was a tall woman with wispy long blond hair, who seemed to prefer wearing black tights, accentuating her thin legs. She was a member of the Theater Department whom Maggie had met at a Women's Studies meeting. They had hit it off when Nina found out that Maggie had played Beth in a college production of *Little Women*. Maggie had always wondered why the director had Beth die unusually early; he seemed to have changed the script so that she wouldn't have too large a part! Tonight they were attending the opening night of *Death of a Salesman*, which Nina was critiquing for a department evaluation of a colleague.

"Oh, yes, restaurants. That's the biggest problem with this town. There's only one good restaurant and it's at best mediocre. They do a good salmon, but they have a very inferior selection of bottled water and their wine list is limited. I once tried to get a San Telmo cabernet, a lovely Argentinean wine with a hint of anise along with the fruits, and they only had a 2007. Clearly not aged enough." Nina spoke with a deep breathy voice, pausing at just the right moments for the appropriate impression.

She was a foodie. She imported as much of her food as was possible. Cheeses and bread from New York, fruit from *David and Harry*, wine from California, and special condiments from other on-line companies. She would always remind friends about the bottle of Gevrey-Chambertin she was once given as a gift by a long-gone boyfriend. She seemed to be still searching for that perfection in her wine and food. But she did not consider herself a "yuppie." A friend had once told a joke at dinner about yuppies: "A yuppie was someone who was in search of the perfect mustard." Everyone at the table had laughed, except Nina, who was offended. "The quality of food is very important," she had said. "It's not something to joke about."

Maggie had heard about this encounter and wisely decided not to mention that she drank tap water. Food was important to her, too, but not in the same way as it was to Nina. Maggie just liked to eat and was always balancing her love of food with her love of fitting into her jeans.

At the intermission, Nina turned to Maggie and asked what she thought of the play. Maggie, who had enjoyed it immensely, who was impressed by the acting of the student performers, gushed that it was great. She had seen the play on Broadway and thought that this production stacked up pretty well, allowing for the limitations of student actors. Nina looked at her with raised eyebrows. "Really?"

"Why? Aren't you enjoying it?"

"No. You see the blocking is all wrong; they're not using all of the stage to its fullest potential. And the casting is all wrong. Willy Loman is supposed to be a tired, world-weary middle-aged man, not an old man as he's being portrayed. No, the director didn't do a good job on this one."

Maggie just nodded, saying, "I never thought of the blocking I guess I have a lot to learn about theater. I actually thought I was enjoying it!"

....

The following Monday, Maggie met with two of her students after class to help them prepare for the presentations they would be giving in class the next day. On her way out of the building, she dropped in to say hello to Ben, whose office was down the hall. He was sprawled in his chair, with the keyboard to his Mac on his lap. He was wearing faded jeans, a gray sweatshirt with letters that had once read "Virginia" but now read "Virgin," and green hightops. His thick head of graying dark hair was disheveled, a result of his habit of massaging his scalp when working on a problem. After the usual pleasantries were exchanged, Ben said, "I'm on my way to a workshop on diversity. If you're not busy right now, why don't you come along. I think you'll enjoy meeting the diversity director." Not having any plans for the rest of the afternoon, Maggie accepted the invitation.

The workshop was being put on by Olympia Anapopolous, the Director of Diversity at the university. The invited speaker provided no new information for Maggie, but the discussion over coffee proved interesting. There was a group of faculty who were trying to get a course on diversity required for all students. Some people argued that there was a need for courses on African-American history for the African-American students; others argued that it was the white students who would benefit most. Maggie thought both groups were right and didn't see why they were spending so much time on the issue. It was finally decided that Olympia, working with Ben, would work up a proposal and present it to the group at a later date.

Olympia, originally from Greece, was an attractive, older woman, given to wearing colorful long skirts and shawls. Her thick dark hair, which she wore pulled back from her face in a tight bun, did nothing to enhance her appearance—but Maggie wisely refrained from pointing that out. After all, she didn't even know the woman!

While Olympia was not a native speaker of English, the only indications were the lack of contractions in her speech, and the precise pronunciation of every consonant so that the cadence of her speech gave the impression of a very formal person. She was what Maggie's mother would have called a "lady." Even the position she took at the table was ladylike. No spreading out as the men—and Maggie—were doing; no taking more space than necessary. When she had applauded the speaker, her manner of applauding was restrained: hands held close to her chest, moving quickly and daintily. But the modest impression she presented was coupled with what appeared to Maggie to be a fierce determination when it came to supporting and advocating diversity.

After the meeting, Olympia invited Maggie to her office, which was connected to the Diversity Center. The office contained a small library filled with publications and DVDs that were loaned out to be used for classes, and a large desk, which occupied most of the room. The desk was covered with colorful folders—all neatly labeled and arranged in alphabetical order. The overall impression was a profusion of chaotic order.

Olympia started the conversation by saying, "I heard from Leroy, the young African American man in your class, about how you had gone out of your way to help him. He really appreciated that." Looking at

Maggie, she smiled and asked, "Would you be willing to work with Ben and me on this new proposal? I think we could use a new perspective on what we are trying to achieve here."

At first, Maggie demurred, claiming that she had had no experience in developing curricula, but, with Olympia's prodding and promises that it wouldn't take much of her time, she agreed.

....

Dear Sam,

Well, I've done it again. No matter how much I try to say "no," I end up accepting more committee assignments. This one, though, might be more productive than most. They're trying to implement a diversity requirement for students—not that the students have to be diverse, though that wouldn't be a bad idea, considering that the student population here is predominantly white—but that they have to take a course on diversity. The committee has been asked to work up the outline for the course. I'll be working with Ben – the guy in the department who always raises the ethical and social implication of everything we're doing—and Olympia, the Director of Diversity Studies. I just met her today and she seems quite nice. Quiet, but clearly committed to the program.

And Ben is a kindred soul. He is always the first one at a department meeting to see the social and political implications of the decisions we make. And he insists on bringing campus issues to the table. Right now he's concerned that the Military Science Department is changing its name to the Leadership Department, and that they will be changing the name of their "Small Tactics" course to "Leadership Ethics." He convinced the department to challenge the course name change as being deceptive – it's the same course as before, with a new name –but he couldn't get enough votes to protest the departmental name change. People wanted to think about it!

Of course, that takes up time at the meetings, and that annoys Barbara, who seems to want to leave as soon as she arrives. I had hoped that having another woman in the department would be a nice experience for a change, but she's busy with her own projects and doesn't come around very often. She's really quite attractive and intelligent—and a good teacher. She's married to a very wealthy older man. I've met him a few times at various functions and he's really quite a windbag. Thinks he knows everything, even everyone else's fields. She runs the program committee for the department and as such can extend invitations for speakers to come to campus. She seems to invite a lot of cronies of her husband, who made his money in the electronics industry. She seldom attends department meetings or other activities on campus, including Women's Studies activities; she's primarily involved with those she sponsors through her program committee.

So, how are you feeling? The last time we spoke you were coming down with a cold. Is it getting any better? Perhaps I should send you a "care package" of my chicken soup. That would have the benefit of helping you and getting me to do some cooking. I find that I have no desire to cook dinner for myself, so I end up eating salads, and omelettes a lot–along with frozen dinners (Ugh!) Fortunately, I go out to dinner at least once a week and always bring back leftovers for the next day (or days).

But seriously, are you getting enough rest? Enough fluids? And remember, Vitamin C and zinc do work, even though they can't prove it.

Tomorrow is another Women's Studies meeting–I actually enjoy those meetings. I think I'll raise the issue of sexual harassment, see if anyone has any advice. I don't have a feel for what the climate is around here. Do they just ignore these complaints, or do they actually condone them? Some of the women I've met in the Women's Studies program seem to be solid feminists, so I'm hoping they can give me some advice.

Well, it's time to finish my preps for tomorrow. I miss you and wish I could be there to cook for you and soothe your brow, and other things.

Love Maggie

Chapter 9

"It looks like we have a quorum so let's get started." Jessie looked around the conference table at the women and men who were busy passing around the cookies that were an essential ingredient at any Women's Studies meeting. Jessie always said that she learned early in her career that the best way to get people to meetings was to feed them. She had earlier gained the reputation of being the only chair in the university who could get a quorum at department meetings. Of course, at that time she was the only female chair of a department and somehow that was considered the reason why she had such good attendance at meetings. But being female was irrelevant; anyone could do it–all you needed was food! As she told people, she had learned that lesson as a mother and carried it over to her administrative roles. And it worked.

The agenda for the day was largely bureaucratic, assigning people to work on the yearly assessment plan, a chore that most departments hated but the administration insisted was the key to improving the quality of programs. Since there was no general format, departments simply used whatever data was available to show that their students were really learning what they were supposed to learn. And in cases where they couldn't find such data, they just changed the goals.

It was a joke in Maggie's department that the first time they tried to assess the effectiveness of the elementary logic course they found that students' reasoning ability at the end of the course was no better than at the beginning. Clearly, the instrument used to assess this was defective! So they came up with another one that worked better. The fact that this new instrument used technical terms that a student would know only after taking the course was ignored by those in charge of assessment and the department was praised for its success. To the department's credit, though, they did change the course content so that it was more challenging for students, but the administration never knew that.

After all the assignments were made, Jessie looked around the table. "Okay, that was productive. Anything else we should be dealing with?"

Maggie had learned that Jessie had started the Women's Studies program more than thirty years ago at the height of the women's movement. It had floundered when it was attacked by faculty members who accused it of being "soft," "propagandistic," "lacking academic rigor," and just "silly." Jessie, along with others, had fought those charges, providing evidence of serious, nationally recognized scholarship being conducted by Women's Studies faculty; she had provided evidence of the rigor and relevance of the courses they offered. But, in the end, what helped to establish the program and stifle the criticism was the high student enrollment in the classes. Numbers matter!

It was clear to Maggie that Jessie was fond of the people around the table. Most of them were young—at least younger than Jessie—and while they were more interested in academic feminism than in activism, they were committed to the program and its goals. Jessie was near retirement and would soon be joining her early collaborators in retirement, but not just yet. She had told Maggie that she still had a few projects to finish before she took off to warmer climates and evenings with her husband, a retired professor of literature.

Maggie was unsure whether to raise the issue of Doris's situation at the meeting, but ended up saying, "Well, yes, I have an issue I'd like advice on. I can't mention specifics, but it's a case of sexual harassment—in particular, lesbian-baiting. What's the 'climate' here about that? Have there been other instances? What's the official university position? I know it's illegal, but are they supportive, do they enforce the rules?"

Sarah, a long-time member of the Women's Studies faculty, and an avowed Marxist, responded. "It's all talk around here. There are policies regarding discriminating on the basis of sexual orientation, but no one ever acts on them. It's interesting that the Affirmative Action Officer has never found a case of gender or racial discrimination worthy of acting on! And the university does everything it can to keep any complaints under wraps; after all, they wouldn't want the public to know what goes on here. It's all a matter of marketing—you have to make the public believe that the 'product' they're receiving is worth the money they're paying. And who wants to send their kids to a place that's getting negative publicity; that's also why the university reports six cases of sexual assaults on campus, but the student hotline has handled more than 200 calls for help."

"I think that's too harsh," claimed Brandy, a young woman who taught family studies. She spoke softly, with just a hint of a Georgia accent. "I know that the Provost is very supportive of women's issues and would certainly not approve of any form of sexual harassment. He's told me many times that he's very supportive of his gay son's new partner." Brandy Alexander—yes, that was her name—was considered naive by many of the people sitting around the table. She formed friendships with high-level administrators because of the programs she produced on campus—very good ones, in fact. But many people thought that she lost her objectivity about people once she became friendly with them, carrying loyalty to friends too far.

Sarah obviously couldn't let that comment go without response. "I'm sure he loves his gay son, and I'm pretty sure that he's supportive of gay rights. But does he have the guts to be public about it? I think not! Not if it means going against the rest of the administration, especially the President, who doesn't care a fig about gay rights, or any one's rights, except those of his and his cronies. Remember how he handled that conflict of interest issue when he asked the Board of Trustees to rescind the policy requiring freshmen to live on campus? Everyone on the Board knew that he was a partner in the new housing complex being built near campus, and that he and his cronies would profit from rescinding the policy, but they did it anyway. And the Provost, who privately admitted that he saw it as a conflict of interest, didn't say anything publicly! Why should we expect anything different now?"

Brandy shook her head and was about to say something when Jessie interrupted. "Okay, can we give Maggie any advice on how to handle her case? Are there people who could be useful? Are there any precedents that would be helpful?"

Names were suggested, some rejected after discussion, but there was general consensus that there hadn't been any cases of lesbian-baiting that had become public. Everyone could relate instances, but there had never been a charge filed and the university never had to take a stand.

Maggie left the meeting feeling strangely empowered. While she wasn't as "left" as Sarah, she admired her fire. She didn't mince words and she had a pretty persuasive analysis of what typically happened at universities, at least as far as Maggie had experienced. While she hadn't gotten any real help from the group, she did get the feeling that they were as concerned as she was about sexual harassment.

Now why would that surprise her, she asked herself? That brought back painful memories of trying to convince her women friends back in New York that Anita Hill had benefited the women's movement by introducing the issue of sexual harassment into the public's vocabulary. They had been so focused on whose version of the events was true–Hill's or Clarence Thomas's–that they failed to see the larger picture of sexual harassment and the eventual acceptance of the illegality of it.

Gail Robbins came in as the meeting was coming to a close, apologizing for having been delayed at a department meeting. Maggie had met Gail when she first arrived and had found her pleasant and quite helpful. They shared an interest in mystery novels and were movie addicts and so had made the usual invitations of "let's get together sometime," without being specific. Maggie was hoping they would get together soon.

From what Maggie later learned from Jessie, if Gail had attended the meeting, it would have been hard to predict which side of the argument she would have supported. She and Sarah were famous for clashing many times in the past over their conflicting analyses of just what was going on at the university, and why. Gail, having been an associate dean for five years before going back to the faculty, tended to think that her administrative experience had allowed her to "see the big picture," which regular faculty, such as Sarah, could not. And, of course, Sarah saw her as a "sellout" to the administration.

On the other hand, Gail and Brandy also had a history of clashing. Gail, along with many others, considered Brandy ignorant about political matters, including university politics. Even Maggie could see that Gail made no attempt to cover up her disdain when talking to or about Brandy. It didn't help that their disciplinary backgrounds were so different, either. Gail was an economist who was enamored of hard data, whereas Brandy was a devout disciple of Jungian psychology and had recently been convinced that all human violence was a direct effect of our fear of death. Ergo, once we understood and confronted death, and no longer feared it, violence would disappear. Clearly, this was nonsense to Gail, who thought it was as silly as claiming that violence was caused by eating meat—and she didn't hesitate to tell Brandy what she thought.

After the meeting, Gail caught up with Maggie at the mailboxes and they actually made plans to see the latest movie in town. The really good movies seldom came to town, and, if they did, they stayed for only a week, as opposed to the slasher films or the ones targeted at an adolescent audience that seemed to last forever. The theaters probably knew their college-age audience, but when a decent movie came to town, Maggie was anxious to see it before it left.

....

Dear Sam,

I'm glad to hear you're feeling better—see Vitamin C does work. I got a strange call from Gwen last night. I think she had been drinking. She didn't make much sense, just went on about how Tim isn't the same man she married, blah, blah, blah. Are they having problems or is she just in one of her moods? I hope she's not drinking too much again.

Things here are pretty much the same. I'm anxiously waiting for the Christmas Break. I've already made my plane reservations and can spend the whole two weeks with you. I feel lost without you. The days are fine, they're usually busy, but the evenings are lonely. I miss our evenings, even the ones where we're each doing our own thing, me reading or grading papers, and you in the dark room. Just your presence surrounds me with a feeling of belonging. And I miss our nights, holding you after we've made love. Maybe I need to get a cat—not to have sex with, just to cuddle!

Well, Christmas will come soon enough and then we'll have time for each other. Don't make too many plans with others, I want you to myself.

Love, Maggie

Chapter 10

"Come on in, Maggie. Have a seat. What's up?" Jessie motioned to the only comfortable chair in her office.

Maggie sat down, letting out a loud sigh of relief. "It's been a really hectic day. I had ceiling problems in my classroom–but I won't bore you with the details–and I've got a stack of papers to read before tomorrow's classes. How do you manage to get any of your own work done? By the time I get home at night I'm exhausted."

"It's not easy. Now that the university has decided to try to compete with the big guys, they've increased the requirements for publications, but haven't reduced the teaching load. The only departments that are seeing any relief are those that have doctoral programs. They get reduced teaching loads. So, what else is bothering you?"

"I don't know. I just wonder if I'm the best person to be helping Doris. I think the situation is serious–at least it's seriously affecting her. I was at her place yesterday evening when she got this phone call. All of a sudden, she turned pale. I asked her what happened, and she told me that it was an obscene phone call. I tried to make light of it, saying that it's probably a drunk student who thinks it's fun to shock older woman. But she didn't buy that. She looks terrible; in fact, she looks scared. I don't think she's sleeping well and if that affects her teaching they'll use that against her in her reappointment. I don't know much about athletics–they seem to be more, what should I say, 'traditional' in their gender stereotypes. And as I read their rules, the department has a major say in personnel decisions. I don't know how to avoid her losing her job if it's up to the department, except to claim sexual harassment, or even sex discrimination. And I don't know what the general climate here is about such things, and how the administration would respond."

"I'm not sure about the general climate, but I do know that the administration will try to avoid any bad publicity. So, if you and Doris can present a good case–one that could at least plausibly get to court–I think the administration would do something to prevent it going that far. How is her case? Is there enough evidence?"

"She gave me the information about things like scheduling and overloads, and I think she can easily handle the 'inappropriate touching' charge–what a joke. So, we'll see what else she can come up with. We filed the grievance but haven't heard anything. It's more than three weeks and whenever I try to schedule a meeting with Dean Morris I get the run-around. What really bothers me, though, is that there are other women in the Athletics Department, but they're adjuncts and don't want to jeopardize their jobs by supporting her."

"Well, unfortunately, that's not so unusual. Academic jobs are scarce these days, and people are afraid of losing what they have. But I'm sure you're doing all anyone could do. It's not unusual for cases like this to drag on–the time limits are really too generous. Say, I heard you talked with Grimsky again. He seems to like you. He told me he feels you understand him."

"Well, I don't know about that. He's a nice enough guy but he sure seems to dislike his officemate–I think his name is Andrews. He does go on about his suspicions, and all I really do is listen. He talks about what he's working on–some unknown, at least to me, 17th century woman. But that's not my area so I don't know if she was important or not."

"Well, it's not so much a matter of how important she was. There were many other writers at the time who weren't really important, in terms of influence at the time or later, but most of them were men and we have heard of them. I think Grimsky's point is a valid one, although I'm not sure he knows how to make it salient. Many women's writings and ideas have never come to light either because they weren't able to get their work published, or they worked through the men in their lives–or worse, the men in their lives stole their work! The famous case is Rosalind Franklin, you know, the chemist–or was she a physicist? Anyway, she's the woman whose work on crystals gave Watson and Crick the idea for the double helix model of DNA. They received the Nobel Prize; she wasn't even mentioned. And they did steal her work–snuck into her laboratory after hours, found her notes on crystal formation, and used them as a model for the structure of DNA. And then there's the case of Einstein's first wife–see, I forget her name! There's not much documentation in that case, but there is the rumor that she deserved at least some credit for Einstein's early theories. But then there's my favorite example of the opposite–John Stuart Mill and Harriet Taylor. Are you familiar with them?"

Maggie nodded. "Of course, I know about Mill; and I more recently learned about Harriet Taylor. She wasn't taught in any of my graduate courses, but feminists know about her, although I don't think they do much reading of her stuff. They just know that she was his wife and probably had an influence on his views about women."

"Well, we'll have to have a long conversation about Mill and Taylor when we have more time. But, no, she wasn't just his wife; in fact, she wasn't his wife for much of their collaboration: she was Mr. Taylor's wife! You might be interested in that story. But, getting back to Grimsky. The police have decided that there's no evidence that the manuscript was stolen; they probably think he's an absent-minded professor and just   misplaced it. He's furious and the department is thinking about moving Andrews out of the office as the two of them just can't get along. Andrews claims that every time he enters the room, Grimsky starts a harangue about how Andrews can't get away with it, he'll be found out, and so forth.

"It's really sad, they're both decent men, but they should never have been put in the same office. It's not just that their interests and methods are different; each one has absolutely no respect for the work of the other, and they let it show. It was bound to cause problems. It's surprising that they've lasted this long without something happening."

Maggie shook her head. "You know, I thought I left the competitive life behind me when I became an academic. But it's just as bad here as it is in the corporate world, only the issues at times seem even more petty."

"Yes, well no matter where one is ego and self-interest do pop up," Jessie responded. "But it's possible to keep your nose out of these issues, so just focus on your teaching and your own work and you'll do fine."

"Thanks, well I'd better get going or my own work won't get done. See you later."

....

Dear Sam,

Sorry I haven't written lately, but I seem to be like Alice in Wonderland, running faster and faster to stay in the same place. The holidays are coming *up soon and I look forward to getting some rest, getting caught up, and, most importantly, seeing you! Let me know what the plans are so I'll know what clothes to bring with me.*

I was glad to hear that Wayne and Kristi have finally decided to make it legal. You'd think that they wouldn't have needed seven years together and two kids to know if they were compatible or not. I was sorry to hear that Gwen and Tim are divorcing. I guess I'm not surprised, but I hope it's a "friendly" divorce since they have to continue to work together.

I had a strange experience the other day—yes, I know, another strange experience. When I got to my classroom I found two janitors there, poking holes in the ceiling tiles with a long aluminum pole with a sharp instrument duct-taped at the end. When I asked them what they were doing, they replied that with all the snow we've been having, they were poking holes in the ceiling because the roof leaks (the classroom is on the top floor of the building) and they didn't want the water to build up and collapse the ceiling. When I looked up, I could see that there were some bulges in the ceiling tiles. No water came down, but I guess this is a precautionary measure they take. Anyway, now that I was aware of the possibility of the ceiling tiles falling down, or water coming in, I was concerned about the students. I certainly didn't want them to sit in places where they could have water, or worse, ceiling tiles, fall on them. But when I told them to sit where there weren't any holes poked in the ceiling, we found that there weren't enough "safe" seats! When questioned, the janitor said, "This is nothing new, we've always done it this way."

I didn't know what to do. I couldn't cancel class—I'd have to cancel it for the rest of the semester. So we had class, but I could tell the students were as nervous as I was. I mentioned it to Charles and he was more helpful this time. He's going to try to get me a room on a lower floor. But that doesn't really solve the problem, does it? Someone will be using that room. It would seem that the sensible thing to do would be to repair the roof before it collapses.

Well, enough complaining. In general, things are going well. My manuscript is coming along, and I'm looking forward to the Thanksgiving break to get some more work done. The grievance against Doris's department has gone to the Dean, but she hasn't responded. I wish the waiting were over; Doris is getting more and more worried—even scared! I was there when she got an obscene phone call and it really unsettled her. I made light of it, not wanting to increase her anxiety, but I'm hoping that all of this isn't going to affect her teaching.

Well, give my love to the gang; tell them I'm looking forward to some evenings of good food, good wine, and lots of good arguments when I visit at Christmas.

Love, Maggie

Chapter 11

The town was blanketed with fresh snow and the air was crisp. As Maggie and Sarah walked the few blocks to *Willows*–the only real restaurant in town, excluding the many burger and pizza chains that seem to populate college towns–their footsteps could be heard as they broke the thin layer of ice on the snow. Even the short walk in the cold air was enough to redden their faces and freeze their glove-clad fingers.

Sarah was explaining to Maggie how the restaurant had started. It was run by two former graduate students in the History Department, Glenda and Sybyl. They had been catering parties for their professors while they were students, and word had quickly got out about the excellent quality of their food. Soon they were in great demand for other university functions. They might have limited their catering and concentrated on receiving their doctorates if they had not felt unfairly treated by the department. But when they were both overlooked for more prestigious teaching assignments, losing out to two of their junior male classmates, they started to consider other career options. This was perhaps made easier by the fact that history Ph.D.s are not in great demand.

When the opportunity arose to invest in an already established restaurant in the downtown area of the town, they scraped together the necessary down payment and took a leap of faith. And it required quite a bit of faith. Sarah was quick to point out that most of the restaurants in town at the time were owned by a prominent person who had an undue influence on the Planning Commission, one of whose functions was to decide the conditions for new businesses in the city. Many people had started up restaurants only to find that they weren't able to get a liquor license, or that they had restricted parking rights –two conditions which made it difficult to succeed. Fortunately,

Glenda and Sybyl inherited the liquor license from the previous owners and a parking lot across the street was easily accessible.

"Shit, it's friggin' cold, and it's not even Thanksgiving," complained Sarah, as she rubbed her hands together. Maggie found it amusing that Sarah, who had lived in Michigan all her life, had never adjusted to winter and was always complaining of the cold. Maggie had heard other people laugh at the on-going contest of who could get to the thermostat in their office first. If Sarah turned it up, her officemate would open the window; if he turned it down, Sarah would turn on the space heater. People agreed that if they hadn't been such good friends, they could have asked to change offices, but neither wanted to be the one to do that, and so the battle continued throughout the cold months.

Not until they were seated and had ordered their drinks did Sarah remove her parka and relax. The restaurant was quite empty, people choosing to eat at home rather than face the cold, and it seemed even more cozy than usual. The flames from the corner fireplace gave a warm glow to the room, enhancing its rich maroon and mahogany décor.

"What are you having?" asked Maggie.

"I think I'll have the whitefish, but without the sauce. Who needs sauce?"

Maggie, for one, needed sauce, but chose not to point that out. She ordered the teriyaki chicken, where the sauce was an integral part of the dish. After all, she didn't have a cholesterol or blood pressure problem; what she had was a slight weight problem, which she solved by wearing her looser jeans and resolving to eat less the next day.

They spent the time before their food was delivered complaining about the latest student behavior. Maggie noticed that there was a sort of rhythm to all conversations among academics. First you complained about the latest egregious behavior that had occurred in your class that day, then you generalized your complaints to students in general, then to all young people. Next, you complained about the amount of grading you had to do that weekend. After that, if there was an administrative decision you disapproved of that week–and there usually was–you spent a good ten minutes ridiculing it. Once you got all of that off your chest, you could go on to other issues. Depending on the individuals involved, some of those other issues could be state or national politics, your own research interests, the latest films seen or books read, or just plain gossip about people you knew.

By the time their food arrived, Sarah and Maggie had reached the gossip stage. Maggie asked, "What's with that guy who has the office next to mine? Every time my door is open he comes over, stands in the doorway, and talks. I usually leave my door open except if I'm busy with something–that way students can see that I'm available–but he is quite a nuisance, especially when he goes on about his trips to Russia and his Russian wife."

"Wives, you mean. He's had two. The first one came over, learned English, got her green card and divorced him. The second one, his present wife, has a high school-aged son. I think she'll stay with him until the kid finishes college. We get tuition waivers for dependents, you know. But she's really his third wife. He was married with two kids when he first went to Russia. Came back with the Russian woman, divorced his wife, and married the Russian. The sad thing is that his first wife still does all his typing and manuscript editing. She comes in at night and works in his office when no one else is around. We all know what's going on, but what the hell–she's not hurting anything."

"What is it with some women? They put up with shit. And he's not even good-looking!"

"Oh, it's worse than that. Many years ago, I worked on a project with him. I was at his house one afternoon and we were so engrossed in our work I didn't notice the time. Anyway, his wife came in and asked if I wanted to stay for dinner. I said no thanks, I would be leaving in a few minutes. She then proceeded to put a platter with a large steak and a bowl of baked beans on the table. I assumed they were going to have steak and beans. But, no, he was having steak, she was having beans. I asked her if she was a vegetarian, and she told me that, no, but they couldn't afford two steaks! I couldn't believe it. Neither of them seemed embarrassed.

"Another time when we were working together, he complained that his morning bath was too cool. It seems she used to 'draw' his bath for him, and she didn't time it right so it wasn't the proper temperature. So you see, it's a well-established pattern for her to be a doormat. I don't know enough about her background, but I suspect she was brought up that way and ended up marrying someone who encouraged it."

"That's sad. It's so damn hard to work with women like that. I was on the Board of Directors of a battered women's shelter back home. Now I'm not saying that his wife was physically battered, although she's certainly had her self-esteem battered. But it's so hard to get these women to change their behavior. It usually takes three or more times in the shelter to convince them to leave the guy. And in a case like this, especially if there's been no physical abuse, you end up criticizing a way of life and you come across as imposing your own views on them. 'After all,' they say, 'this is the way we do things and our women, as well as our men, like it that way. Who are you to tell us we're wrong?' It's damn frustrating. I think if we could get these women to see other alternatives, we might have more success; but that involves breaking with their family and friends and that's very difficult for most of us.

"But on a larger scale, this is an issue I've been interested in for some time. I have an article on it–it's about tolerating intolerance–taking so-called "relativism" too far. Most of my social science friends disagree with me, claiming that one can't judge other cultures or cultural practices. But I think more distinctions need to be made, and that once these distinctions are clear, they would agree with me. But that's a discussion for another time."

"I'd like to read your article. But, yeah, patriarchy is alive and well in the USA. The issue you raised at the last Women's Studies meeting– the one about sexual harassment –that's another example. These guys think there's nothing wrong with what they do–after all, boys will be boys. And, we all know, feminists have no sense of humor!"

"You know, I'm really worried about her. She's under a lot of stress– phone calls, lewd pictures left on her door. I'm wondering if there's not more going on than the typical sexual harassment. You know, some other agenda working. Well, we filed a grievance, so we'll see if that does anything. The Dean hasn't responded yet. You'd think they wouldn't want this kind of complaint hanging out there, with the legal ramifications and all. But I'm told to be patient; administrators must be slower readers than the rest of us!"

The conversation eventually switched to a discussion of their plans for the holiday break, which was coming up in a few weeks. Maggie would be going to New York for two weeks and Sarah would be in Washington, DC working on her latest project. As an anthropologist whose area was Native Americans, she was often hired to work with native groups who were trying to get federal recognition of their tribal status. Sarah explained that thousands of pages were submitted documenting that the group had a common language, common religion, and common ceremonies, and that they had been a group for a certain number of years. Much of this had to be based on oral testimony from the elderly members of the group, who could remember the past. Sarah would sometimes spend years getting this information, putting it into context, and then documenting it for the federal government. She was now at the stage where it was necessary to meet with members of the Bureau of Indian Affairs and so she was off to DC.

It was after ten when they left, each one with head down trudging through the soft snow. Maggie waved to Sarah as she got into her car. She was looking forward to a nice long bath and a phone call from Sam. They were at the stage of finalizing plans for the holidays and Maggie knew that Sam was too involved in trying to get up an exhibit to be any good at plans. It would be up to her to contact friends and make all the arrangements for get-togethers.

Sam's call came through while Maggie was still soaking in the tub. Fortunately, the water was warm enough for her to remain immersed while they talked about the high points of their respective days.

Chapter 12

Isis was relatively empty. Maggie sat at her usual table, reading the campus paper before heading off to class. Nothing caught her interest so she was quite willing to join Nina when she arrived with Carl Ericson, a retired professor of history. When Maggie mentioned that she was new in town, Carl was delighted to give her advice on restaurants and events in the local area.

After recommending various restaurants in the surrounding area, the conversation turned to the theater and Carl told Maggie about the Shakespeare Festival in Stratford and the Shaw Festival in Niagara-on-the-Lake, both in Canada. He was a devotee of the theater and he and Nina often compared notes on recent productions.

"I've just returned from London. Saw four plays–three at the National, a marvelous theater and one at the Hampstead in Swiss Cottage, a small but lovely theater. That's where new plays are often produced. I've sat next to famous actors who are looking to see if they want to perform in the play when it gets to the National, or some other larger theater. In fact, once I sat next to two men who were obviously producers, discussing whether they wanted to produce the play as a film. And you can get wonderful deals on plays; the price is quite reasonable."

Nina agreed. "Yes, that's true. The same was true when I was in New York a few years ago. And you can get tickets at the last minute for very good prices if you line up in the morning. There are always some empty seats. The other thing I remember is 'rush' tickets. You go about a half hour before the performance and you can usually get a rush seat for very little money."

"Yes, but those rush seats are usually the very small ones at the side of the theater. Very uncomfortable," replied Carl.

"Not necessarily, I've gotten very good seats that way."

"No, what you want to do is ask for a seat in the upper balcony–the cheapest seats. After the first act you can usually be transferred to a better vacant seat. I've always had success doing that. Why, once I was transferred to a seat in the third row of the orchestra. I could see the sweat on the face of Albert Finney. Of course, I'll pay the regular price for something with Maggie Smith or Judi Dench–their plays are always sold-out." Turning to Maggie, he said, "If you're interested, I can give you the listing of the plays that are worth seeing this season."

"That would be lovely," replied Maggie, "but I'll be going home to New York for Christmas."

Turning to Nina, Carl said, "I don't know why you don't go to London or New York to see what they're doing on stage nowadays. It's truly innovative."

Nina looked offended, saying that she had neither the time nor the money for London and while she did get to New York occasionally she found the plays derivative. What Maggie knew was that Nina was afraid to fly, which greatly limited her visits to theaters outside of the Midwest.

The conversation then turned to places to eat in New York. Nina turned to Maggie, and in her breathy voice said, "But when you're in New York you must eat at Le Bernardin on the upper west side. Their shrimp ravioli with truffle sauce is to die for. You'll need reservations, of course, and it's not cheap, but it's worth it."

Maggie politely thanked them for the various recommendations and took her leave.

....

I'm sorry to call so late, but I didn't know what to do." The fear in Doris's voice was noticeable from the first word she uttered. Even though Maggie had been awakened from a deep sleep, she quickly gathered her senses enough to know that Doris was frightened.

"What happened?" she asked.

"Someone just called and said horrible things. Like if I didn't withdraw my application for reappointment I'd be sorry. Called me names–'lesbian bitch,' and other things. I'm scared."

"Did you record the message?"

"No, the call woke me up and I wasn't thinking clearly. That's bad, right? Now, I can't prove anything." Doris started to cry, deep sobs echoing through the phone.

"No, it's not bad, but you need to report it to the police right now. They can sometimes at least trace where the call came from."

Maggie considered what else she could do. It was clear that Doris was not okay, and that she would not get any sleep tonight. "Do you want to spend the night here? I've got room and then in the morning we could both go to the police and find out what else we can do."

"Thanks, but I'm okay here. I guess I just needed to talk to someone. I'll see you tomorrow morning. Thanks for listening."

....

It was now five in the morning and Maggie knew that there was no point in trying to get back to sleep. She made herself some tea and tried to focus on what the next step should be. They had filed the internal grievance against the department and were waiting for the Dean's response. Doris had documented the inconsistencies in her scheduling. She was correct—there was a clear pattern that she had been assigned more classes, with more students in each, than other tenure-track people in the department. It would be interesting to see how the department could justify that. And the pictures on her door? While it wasn't clear who had put them up, it was clear that the department—in particular, the chair—had done nothing to investigate the incident. In fact, if she remembered correctly, he had brushed off the incident, claiming that Doris couldn't take a joke. The success of arguing that point would depend on the administration's attitude toward sexual harassment. But keeping in mind the administration's aversion to bad publicity, the threat of going public was a card she was willing to use.

Tomorrow she and Doris would go to the police to see if they could trace the call. While it wasn't a clear death threat, it certainly was a threat and the police usually took that seriously.

....

The next morning, bundled in their heavy coats and scarves, bracing against the wind whipping loose snow in their faces, they entered the police station. When they told the woman behind the desk what they were there for, they were told to take a seat and that an officer would be with them shortly. Doris's eyes were red, whether from lack of sleep or crying wasn't clear. And she was clearly nervous. She held her scarf in her hands and was systematically parting the fibers, making a small hole in the lacy fabric much larger. Maggie tried to calm her, but succeeded only in getting Doris to leave the scarf alone.

Within ten minutes, an officer approached them and invited them into a private office.

"I hear you want to report a crime." He was a young man, with the physique of an out-of-condition linebacker. His red hair was clipped short and his face had the mottled look that some red-heads have to contend with. It was more apparent on men than women, as women could use make-up to even out their skin tones.

Maggie responded by relating the phone call incident and how it was a clear threat to Doris.

"Did you record the conversation?"

"No, it was the middle of the night and I wasn't thinking clearly—I had been sleeping." Doris's voice was so low the officer had to lean forward to hear her.

"Well, there's not much we can do if there's no evidence. You should have an automatic recorder on your phone so that every phone call is recorded. Then you could delete the ones you don't need, but you'd have the evidence that you need to start an investigation."

Maggie was not satisfied with that response. "Can't you trace where that call came from? She knows the exact time it came in and you have her number. Surely, you have access to that information."

"Ma'am, you've been watching too many cop shows on TV. There's nothing we can do without more evidence. You could contact the telephone company yourself and ask them to monitor future calls, but I don't think they'll trace a call that's already been made without authorization—and we don't have enough information to authorize that."

Doris got up from her chair, ready to leave. But Maggie was not ready to drop the issue. "So, you're saying that she has to wait until she gets another threatening call, or maybe until someone actually attacks her, in order for you to do anything? Is that your position?"

"I'm afraid it is, ma'am."

She turned to Doris, who was already at the door. "Let's go; these guys aren't going to help you at all."

Once outside, Maggie tried to comfort Doris by reminding her that they had filed the grievance and should be receiving word on Dean Morris's decision any day now. Doris seemed to cheer up slightly at the mention of the grievance and agreed to keep in touch.

....

Dear Sam,

I'm counting the days until Thanksgiving break so I can get some rest. So much has happened here I don't know where to start. Perhaps the most important is Doris's grievance. It's going through the university procedure and it's taking forever. We handed in our list of complaints, and the process requires that the dean have an opportunity to resolve the issue. If not, we then include her in the complaint. But she hasn't responded to the complaints yet, so we're in limbo! There are no time limits so we just have to wait. The police weren't very helpful, either, but the telephone company was. They've put some kind of monitoring device on the phone so the next time Doris gets a threatening call they can trace it. However, they only do that for a limited time—a month, I think. And the harassment in her department continues. I need to pick your brain on other things we can do. You have such a good devious mind!

I met a most interesting man today at coffee. He's a retired history professor and he is truly charming, but rather opinionated. But not more so than Nina who told me not to see any of the plays on Broadway because they were "derivative." I'm not sure what that means, but it's clear it's not good! I've gone to a few plays here at the university and I have to admit I've learned a lot from Nina about what to look for in a play. Things I never noticed before now are so apparent that I can't believe I hadn't noticed them before. We've developed a routine: at each intermission I ask her if I'm enjoying the play, and she laughs and says "no." We'll have to go to the theater when I get home so I can show off my new expertise.

She also raved about a restaurant and I'm almost tempted to go there, just to see what she regards as good food; clearly not much here meets her standards. Food is obviously very important to her. Now, don't say it; I know it's important to me, too—but I like to eat it, not talk about it.

Love, Maggie

Chapter 13

It was the Wednesday before Thanksgiving and Maggie was looking forward to four days without teaching or committee meetings. She could hear the persistent ring of the phone over the noise of the shower. It was 8:00 a.m., too early for a casual call, but she was in no state to get to the phone in time. Finishing her shower, she wrapped herself in a towel and went to the phone.

The message indicator light was on; there was a message from Jessie. Maggie knew that it had to be important for Jessie to call this early in the morning. Pushing the button, she heard Jessie's voice saying, "Maggie, call me as soon as you can. I'm at the office."

There was an urgency in Jessie's voice. Maggie quickly dialed her office.

"Jessie, Maggie here. I just got your message. What's up?"

"I don't know how to tell you this, except to be blunt. Doris is dead. They found her in the pool. Apparently she fell, hit her head, and drowned. There's an investigation, but everyone seems to be convinced that it was an accident. I know you'd gotten to know her pretty well so I thought you ought to hear the news from me rather than read it in the paper tomorrow."

"Oh, my god. I can't believe it. When did this happen? Are they sure it was an accident? Could she have been pushed, or something? You know she was afraid of something happening."

"The janitor found her last night. All I can say is what I've been told. Why don't you come by the office later. There may be more information by then."

"Okay, I'll see you shortly. But I want you to know that I'm not very confident that an investigation will do any good. My impression of the police–and the university–is that a perfunctory investigation will take place and it'll find that it was truly an accident: case closed."

"We'll talk when you get here."

Maggie tried calling Sam, but, as usual, the phone was unplugged. She paced the floor, alternately giving way to bouts of rage and collapsing into tears. There was no way she could envision Doris falling into the pool. She was a Red Cross safety instructor; she was an experienced swimmer; she taught swimming! And what the hell was she doing at the pool at that time? It didn't make sense.

Maggie's ever-present guilt indicator was on high alert. She was supposed to help Doris but she had managed to do nothing but initiate an internal grievance review. Big deal! Now, all that happened to Doris would be set aside and the "old boys" could get on with business as usual. Well, not if she could prevent it. She owed at least that much to Doris.

She dressed, gathered her books, and left for campus.

....

Jessie wasn't in her office and Maggie had an hour before her first class of the day. She stopped in the department office where she found Louise, red-eyed, with tears cascading down her cheeks.

"Oh, Maggie, I can't stop crying. I just heard about Doris. I knew her. She taught my children how to swim and I took care of her dog when she was of town. She was like a daughter to me. I can't believe she's dead."

Just then, Charles came out of his office and looked at Louise. "Why don't you take the day off. I'm sure we can survive without you for a day. You won't get any work done anyway when you're so upset."

Charles was a caring person, but somewhat clumsy in personal relations. He couldn't stand confrontations and it was obvious to Maggie that he certainly couldn't handle weeping women. Many people thought that his wife had perfected the technique of weeping in order to get Charles to agree with her.

Louise blew her nose, and dried her eyes. "No, I'm better off here. If I went home I'd just keep thinking about it. Besides, the preliminary schedule for next year is due when we get back from Thanksgiving Break and you'll just mess it up if you handle it."

Louise had been department secretary for fifteen years; she had worked for three chairs in that period and had become indispensable to them. Schedules, finances, reports–all were done under her watchful eye. It was clear to Maggie that Charles depended on Louise to tell him what their financial situation was as he never looked at a spreadsheet—numbers weren't his forte, he was fond of saying at department meetings.

Maggie left the office and walked down to the lounge where people were gathered around the coffeepot talking about Doris's death. Toby was still wearing his jacket with the tear in the back; in fact, it was such a familiar sight that it looked right. He looked stunned as if he couldn't quite understand what was going on. Doug, in typical fashion, picked up on the question of Doris's sexual orientation, asking, "She was a lesbian, wasn't she?", as if that were relevant to her death.

"What the hell does that matter?" fumed Ben. "Do you think lesbians drown more frequently than straights?"

"No, I was just saying …"

"Yeah, I know what you were just saying. That's what a lot of people are going to be 'just saying.' As if the death of a lesbian isn't as tragic as the death of a straight woman. And besides, we don't know if she even was a lesbian–although everyone seems to assume that if a woman is an athlete she must be gay. Maggie, you knew her. What do you make of all this?"

"Well, I don't know if she was a lesbian or not, but I find it hard to believe it was an accident. But I don't have any more information than you have, except to know that she was being sexually harassed by guys in her department. The lesbian-baiting was pretty strong with those guys; in fact, I don't know how she could work in such a hostile environment."

"Why do people care if she was a lesbian?" asked Toby. "What does it bloody matter what one's sex life is like. Why, in my classes when we talk about homosexuality the students don't seem to think it matters who has sex with whom–certainly different than when I started teaching here. Back then, the very mention of homosexuality would send shivers down their spines. They couldn't even discuss the bloody issue without indicating their distaste. But now young people seem more accepting of differences."

"Yes, but there are still enough people around to pass legislation against same-sex marriages and granting partner benefits to gays. And, unfortunately, the Athletics Department is filled with people like that," replied Ben.

Toby seemed genuinely perplexed. He was a gentle soul; some considered him "pathologically tolerant", but everyone was willing to overlook his eccentricities–and there were many–because of his genuine tolerance of the flaws of others.

Felipe, on the other hand, had no tolerance for the flaws of others–or even for their virtues. Maggie, in her limited interactions with him had concluded that he was quick to judge and even quicker to condemn. Anyone who didn't agree with him was a fool; anyone who criticized his positions was ignorant; and anyone he didn't like wasn't worthy of his attention. One of his favorite words to describe the work, or value, of a colleague was "piffle"; he used the term so often, that Maggie heard some of his colleagues calling him "Dr. Piffle"–although only behind his back. Unfortunately, he was bright and also quite often right. But his general demeanor made it difficult for those who agreed with him to actually agree with him, leading to strange arguments in department meetings. People, who before the meeting had indicated their approval of a proposal, would actually argue against it once Felipe claimed that anyone who disagreed was an idiot. That was enough to get people like Ben to mount as many arguments as was possible to marshal on the spot. This usually resulted in a tabling of the issue until a later date, an action which annoyed both sides of the issue.

Although Felipe was present at the discussion of Doris's death, he was silent, giving the impression that it didn't deserve his attention. Ben, as usual, rose to the challenge and tried to draw Felipe into the discussion.

"So, what do you think, Felipe?" he asked.

"About what? I didn't know her."

"About a person's sexual orientation. Do you think it matters? Do you agree with Toby that students today are more tolerant of gays than they were years ago?"

"I'm not interested in such things. I have more important things to do."

With that, Felipe took his coffee cup and left the office. Ben smiled, apparently satisfied that he had precipitated Felipe's removal from the room.

Maggie also smiled. It was clear that people like Felipe wouldn't be allies in a fight against sexual harassment. In fact, it wasn't clear that he would recognize it when he came up against it. But, the good point was that people like Felipe most likely wouldn't engage in sexual harassment—"there were more important things to do."

The conversation drifted into other issues: the new computers, and Felipe's proposed cognitive science program which was coming up again at the department meeting that week.

Maggie looked at the clock and realized that if she wanted to see Jessie before her class, she had better see her now. With a wave to the others, she left, after washing her coffee cup and putting it back in the cabinet. She was one of the few who cleaned up after themselves. Old habits die hard, especially those that were drilled into you by a mother obsessed with neatness.

Jessie greeted Maggie with a hug. "Are you all right?" she asked.

"Well, I'm better than I was this morning. I still can't believe it. You know I'm a fan of mystery novels and this is something that I would read about in one of them. But I can't believe it's actually happened."

"Wait a minute. We don't know what happened. It may turn out that It was simply an accident."

Maggie realized that Jessie was just trying to keep her from running off half-cocked. "I know, I know," replied Maggie. "But I just can't get Doris's face out of my mind. She was scared—she really thought her life was in danger. And then this happens? Coincidence? Perhaps. But I'm afraid that no one will even consider the possibility that it was anything but an accident. I know what you're saying. I won't go off half-cocked.

"But, I do need your advice on a related matter. The grievance that I worked on with Doris is still pending. I'd like it to continue even though she's no longer here. I think it raises an important issue and I'd like to have some resolution on it. In fact, if they won't continue the grievance—if they call it moot—I'm thinking of going public, raising the issue in the press. What do you think?"

Jessie looked at her and smiled. "Of course, go ahead with the grievance. You know what I'd say about going to the press prematurely, but you should also know that I'll support you in whatever you do. Just be aware that there are consequences to what you do and be sure you're willing to take that risk."

....

Dear Sam,

I tried to call you this morning but you were out or had your phone unplugged again. Doris is dead. They're saying it's an accident, but I don't believe it. She supposedly fell in the pool and drowned. That's ridiculous—she was a fucking swimming coach. I feel terrible— should have seen it coming. I should have realized that she was in danger. I feel awful. Everyone is talking about it, but they all accept that it was an accident. A "tragedy" they're saying. Tragedy, my ass. I'm convinced it wasn't an accident, but I don't know how to convince anyone of that. Even Jessie thinks it was probably an accident.

I'll call you later. Plug your phone in!
Love, Maggie

Chapter 14

Maggie spent Thanksgiving day with Jessie and her husband Mark, a retired English professor. The dinner, as usual, was delicious, but the mood was somber. The talk kept returning to Doris, with Maggie protesting that her death couldn't have been an accident, and Jessie maintaining a "wait-and-see" attitude.

That evening Maggie called Sam. She needed to hear the calm voice that always helped to settle her soul, that helped her to realize that no matter how bad things became there was someone who understood her, who stood by her, who loved her.

She spent the rest of the weekend trying to work on her manuscript but found herself going back over the last few weeks, trying to make sense of Doris's death. Was there something she had missed? Should she have taken Doris's fears more seriously?

Her mind kept refusing to stay on task until she finally gave up and spent all of Sunday watching movies at home. None of them were memorable, but that didn't matter— they had succeeded in taking her mind off Doris for a while.

....

On Monday morning, Maggie kept her appointment with Dean Morris.

"Please have a seat. Dean Morris will be with you in a minute." The woman at the desk smiled at Maggie, then turned to her computer to continue with her work. The reception area of the Dean's office was spacious, with deep oak furniture and mauve trimmings. The paintings on the wall were obviously selected to go with the décor: pretty pictures of pastel flowers and pastoral scenes. There was a feminine touch to the extras that were strategically placed around the room. A plant here, a piece of pottery there. Even the scarf that the secretary wore seemed to blend into the design of the room—mauve background, with moss green and pale yellow flowers. Very soothing, but somehow off-putting. Maggie felt that she was in the waiting room of some corporate executive catering to helping rich widows invest their money. That was probably an unfair judgment. Maggie had never been in a corporate executive's office and therefore had no idea of their reception rooms. But she did know about deans' offices. Typically they had some books or professional publications on display. Here there were none. But then in this part of the university the main goal was for your teams to win–forget about publications and research.

But one thing Maggie had already learned in her short time at Claxton: each time a new administrator took over, the office was redecorated. Sometimes that was simply a matter of changing the color of the walls, or hanging different paintings. But sometimes, as had just happened in the education dean's office, it was a complete remodeling with walls removed and cabinets built into other walls, a new carpet installed, a complete paint job, and new furniture. There always seemed to be money available for such remodeling, even though faculty offices were furnished with desks and bookcases that were new in the 1960s. But, of course, faculty didn't have to deal with public impressions. In fact, as far as the public was concerned, it was only fitting that academics had shabbily furnished offices;   after all, they just think, write, and talk. You don't need special surroundings to do that.

After 10 minutes, the secretary called over to Maggie, "You may go in now." Maggie gathered her coat and books and entered the Dean's office. It, too, was apportioned in mauve and oak, and the bookcases, which would typically house books, were filled with dainty tea sets. Maggie found all this surprising as most of the people in this dean's college were athletes who, she thought, would find these surroundings uncomfortable. But, what did she know!

Dean Morris was a small, attractive woman with short gray hair cut in a severe bob. She motioned to Maggie to take a seat at the large oak table and offered her some coffee.

"No, thanks; I've already had too much coffee this morning."

Morris looked at Maggie, practiced concern painted on her face. "I'm sure you're as upset about Doris's death as we all are here. Such a lovely woman, such a tragic accident. Though I've told people that it's always risky to use the facilities after hours. You never know when something will go wrong and then there is no one around to help. But, enough of that. What is it you wanted to see me about?"

"The grievance that Doris filed against the department. She hadn't gotten a response from your office and I'd like to pursue the issue on her behalf. She thought, as I do, that the issue was one that deserves a response. The harassment that she experienced wasn't unique to her, but others are afraid to complain."

"I think the issue is dead—after all, we can hardly pursue a grievance without the grievant." Dean Morris smiled sympathetically, assuming that her answer clearly put an end to the discussion.

"But you could investigate the allegations she made. If she was harassed, if she was treated differently than others in the department, surely that could be determined and prevented from occurring in the future. I see it as an opportunity for you—and the administration—to make sure that there isn't a 'chilling workplace environment,' as it's called."

Maggie could tell from the look on the Dean's face that the reference to the sexual harassment legal language was disturbing. Even if nothing came from this meeting, Maggie had wanted it known that she was aware of the law regarding this issue and that she would pursue it, if necessary.

"Well, I will certainly look into what the university's responsibility is in a situation like this and I'll get back to you. I appreciate your concern about Doris. We are all devastated by her death."

It was clear to Maggie that she was being dismissed. Taking Jessie's advice, she didn't push Morris any further, but thanked her for her time and left.

....

Since she had no classes that day, she next went to the police department. She asked the clerk on duty to speak to the officer in charge of the investigation, only to be told that there was no ongoing investigation. At this point, Maggie's resolve to keep her temper disappeared. She sharply retorted that surely it must be standard procedure to conduct an investigation into any questionable death, at which time the clerk said that she would have an officer come down to talk to Maggie.

It took 20 minutes for anyone to appear, during which time Maggie alternated between pacing, and sitting and fidgeting. When finally someone appeared, it was the same red-headed officer she and Doris had talked to before.

"Well, now will you take her complaints seriously?" Maggie blurted out. "At least find out if her death was truly an accident. Did they do an autopsy? Don't you find it strange that a swimming instructor–someone with years of experience, someone who taught life saving for the Red Cross, someone who had been a champion swimmer"–Maggie didn't know this, but tossed it in for emphasis–"would drown? Surely, there are some questions you have about her death. Or is the university pressuring your department to leave it alone to avoid the publicity?"

Maggie was on a roll and would have continued with even more accusations of conspiracy, but the officer put up his hand, with palms outward. "Look, let's start all over. Let me introduce myself–I'm Jerry Fitzgerald–and I can assure you that there has been no pressure not to investigate the case. We take every accidental death as a potential homicide until we have done a complete investigation. I remember your friend. She was obviously scared, and I believed her story; but there was no evidence to support it. We need something to go on before we can order an investigation."

"Well, I hope you have enough to go on now. I mean, what was she doing in the pool area at night? She was an excellent swimmer, knew all the precautions about safety around water. I don't even know what time she died, do you?"

Fitzgerald took out a folder and pulled out a page. "It looks as if TOD was between 8:00 and 10:00 p.m."

"That in itself is strange. She wasn't a night person; why would she be in the pool at that hour? She was usually in bed by 10:00. When I had to reach her I knew to call before 10:00 unless it was an emergency. Don't you find that strange? I certainly do!"

"Look, I'm not trying to stonewall you here. We will–we are–looking into this. Why don't you give me your number in case we have any questions to ask."

Maggie gave him her numbers–cell phone, home, and office–and got up to leave. As she reached the door, she turned and pleaded, "Please, for her sake and mine, don't let this drop."

....

Dear Sam,

Thanks for your concern, but I am being careful. I met with the Dean yesterday and I was right—it looks like they're not going to pursue the grievance. I didn't create a scene; I just wanted to hear her say that the issue was closed so that I can pursue other avenues. And the other avenues are all perfectly legal. I can certainly speak to the police again, although that hasn't been very productive, and I can certainly discuss certain things with the student newspaper. I won't be saying anything to break confidentiality, just calling attention to certain facts that are publicly known.

I did take your advice and talked to Jessie. You're right: she thinks I should be careful, but for different reasons than you. She's not worried about my safety, just my career! But I think at the end of our talk, she was supportive. At least, that's the way I saw it.

On a lighter note, I went out for drinks with friends last Friday. We went to the Penguin, one of the few bars that doesn't cater to students. There's a new faculty member in the Social Studies Department this year who is 500 pounds! I've never seen someone so large. He's very bright, with a rather sharp personality. But more striking are his manners. The bar has a "happy hour" on Fridays, and provides food along with discounted drinks. This guy ordered a soft drink and emptied the trays of food onto his plate. And I mean trays. He single-handedly finished off all the shrimp and stuffed mushrooms that they had on the buffet table. The servers graciously said nothing but went and replenished the trays, at which point this guy asked other people at the table to get him some more food as it was too difficult for him to get up from the table. Nick Marzetti, Sarah Lowell's husband, called him an insensitive pig and told him to "fuck off." No one came to this guy's defense and he spent the rest of the evening sulking—and eating. I never did catch his name, but I don't plan on seeing him again so I guess I don't need to know it.

So don't worry. I'll give you a call this weekend and you'll be able to hear my cheerful voice telling you that all is well.

Miss you,
Love, Maggie

Chapter 15

"Okay, let's get down to business. As you should remember, at the last meeting we decided to invite Nikki Dionetti for our January program. We need to finalize the details before the end of the semester. Brandy and I have been working on the arrangements and it's all set. Dionetti arrives on a Wednesday and will give a public talk that evening in the Auditorium; she leaves the next day at noon. We need someone to pick her up and take her back to the airport. Any volunteers?"

Maggie looked around the table, trying to determine if someone would volunteer before she did. Seeing no obvious signs of acquiescence, she volunteered. Jessie laughed. "See, it always works. The newcomer hasn't yet learned how to outwait the others. Thanks, Maggie, but you shouldn't have to make both trips. Anyone else?"

Sarah, agreeing to take Dionetti back to the airport, asked what they were paying her.

"$35,000," Jessie replied. "$10,000 from us and the extra $25,000 comes from the various deans and the Provost."

"What else is she going to be doing? $35,000 for one talk is a lot of money. Is she willing to meet with students, go to classes, things like that?"

"Unfortunately, the deal is $35,000 for a lecture–more if you want more," replied Jessie.

Sarah shook her head. "I remember when people went on lecture tours to get their message out–not to get rich. The commodification of ideas has finally gotten to feminists. 'If you can't beat them, join them' is now the watchword of so-called feminists and leftists. I'm sorry, but it pisses me off."

Jessie nodded. "I agree with you, but what can we do. All the people who would attract an audience are asking these outrageous fees. If we want to put on an event that will get attention and attract an audience, we're stuck paying ransom to these so-called stars. And the administration judges the worthiness of our program by the number of people it serves–both in terms of students in our classes and attendance at our events. Remember, we started out with a closet as our office and an unpaid coordinator. We got our office, such as it is, and the half-time director position because we convinced them there was a need and an interest. We're still continually having to prove ourselves in order to survive."

This seemed to be a continuing issue. Everyone indicated agreement in principle, but most voted on the side of practicality when the two clashed. The old-timers reminded the others that the Women's Center–which is where they were meeting–had never been approved by the administration. Jessie, when she took over the women's studies directorship, simply had a sign made saying 'Women's Center' and had it placed on the door of their meeting room. Since it was the first year for the new Provost, she invited him to preside over the opening of the Women's Center–which he graciously did. Now, it was a *fait accompli*– but without a paper trail.

Naomi Sloan, the chair of the Social Studies Department, chimed in saying, "Well, it's done for this year, so let's go on to the rest of the agenda. We can decide at a later meeting what we're going to do in the future."

The rest of the meeting was devoted to determining the next year's schedule of courses. Since the Women's Studies courses were given under the auspices of other departments, determining schedules was a more complex process. The offering, and the timing, of the courses had to be approved by both Women's Studies and the home department, and pleasing both parties often required the subtle hand of a magician.

"We have a few more minutes. Anything else you want to talk about?" asked Jessie.

Maggie looked around the table. She knew these people. Why weren't they talking about Doris's death? Seeing Brandy prepare to speak, she sat back, expecting the issue to finally be raised. However, she was disappointed.

Brandy replied to Jessie's question. "I'd like to know more about that English prof's manuscript. Is it still missin? Did the police actually investigate? Why aren't people supportin' him?"

Jessie looked around. She responded by pointing out that while it was true that Aemilia Lanyer, the subject of Grimsky's manuscript, was a minor author and perhaps not deserving of the attention that Grimsky was giving her, it was also true that he was raising an important issue about the invisibility of the achievements of women throughout history. However, she cautioned about jumping to the conclusion that it was stolen.

"No one has yet found evidence that it was stolen, and certainly no evidence that it was stolen by Andrews. If you have seen Grimsky's office, you know it's very likely in there under some pile of papers, or magazines, or whatever he has in there. People aren't supporting him because he's eccentric and prickly. That's my take on it."

Maggie's irritation got the best of her. "Isn't anyone interested in what happened to Doris Redden? The woman is dead, under very suspicious conditions."

Brandy looked at her. "Of course, it's terrible. But what can we say. It's a tragic accident."

"Well, it's not yet clear that it was an accident. There's an investigation going on. And, in my opinion, I don't think it was an accident."

Sarah's interest was piqued. "Are you saying she was killed?"

"I don't know that. But it just doesn't make sense to me. The woman's being harassed and then she drowns—a swimming instructor drowns?"

People around the table looked at Maggie, clearly uncomfortable, not sure what to say. They started to leave, citing classes and meetings to attend.

Jessie adjourned the meeting, and, agreeing to meet with Maggie the next day to hear about the talks with Dean Morris and Officer Fitzgerald, gave her a hug as Maggie ran off to classes.

....

That evening Maggie and Gail took in a movie. After pumping Maggie on her suspicions about Doris's death and getting nothing but, "It just feels wrong," Gail turned to her reaction to the movie they had just seen.

"That was a waste." Gail was clearly unhappy with the movie they had just seen. She and Maggie were sitting in a booth at a local diner. It was a Thursday night and parking places were scarce. They had decided to leave the car where it was and walk to the restaurant, which was situated next to the theater. Gail was still expounding on the defects of the movie. "What a stupid plot; and the acting–I've seen better acting at high school plays. And can you believe that music? I could hardly sit through it."

Gail was a steadfast Stones fan. One might even call her a "groupie," except she didn't travel with them–though she made it clear to Maggie that she would have slept with Mick Jaggar if given the chance. In Maggie's eyes, Gail's adulation of Jagger had all the earmarks of an adolescent crush. Not only did she know all his albums, but she was up on his personal life, too. She could tell you whom he had slept with and when; what his childhood had been like; why his marriage to Bianca had failed. But she did know her rock and roll, and she could sing. At a party a few weeks earlier, she had spontaneously entertained everyone with her renditions of "You Can't Always Get What You Want" and "Honky Tonk Women."

That was Gail at her best: witty and fun loving. If she could have maintained that persona in her professional life she would have found life more satisfying. But it was only at those social occasions that she seemed to relax, and yet her general antagonism prevented her from being invited to many of those occasions. Was this an example of Catch 22? Or just an example of human frailty? So, Gail, a bright, sensitive woman, built a harder and harder shell around herself, and spent more time alone or at the Casino, where she was a steady visitor to the slot machines.

After Gail finished her diatribe against the movie, with which Maggie agreed, although she hadn't had a chance to voice her opinion, they ordered drinks: wine for Maggie and a diet Coke for Gail.

Gail then proceeded to report on the picketing she had done the other day. The local newspaper had reported that the Klan was making an appearance in Hemlock, a small town about 15 miles away to protest the town's newly approved non-discrimination resolution. She had asked other people to join her but the consensus was that it was better not to give the Klan any attention. The thought was that if the Klan spoke to a gathering of five the press wouldn't cover it; but if a crowd appeared to picket the event, it would attract the press and give the Klan more publicity. Maggie hadn't heard about the picketing and was therefore saved from having to debate the issue with Gail. But Gail had stood outside the courthouse, all alone, waving a sign she had painted for the occasion: "The Klan is Un-American." The only people who were there to listen to the talk were the five members of the Klan, but it was typical of Gail: she didn't shy away from confrontation of any sort and was led by her firmly established principles. While Maggie didn't always agree with her "principles", she admired Gail's courage. Not many people would be comfortable being a one-person picket line.

They parted, promising to get together again soon, and Maggie returned home to prepare her classes for the next day. Her classes were going well–too well. She was devoting more time than usual to her lectures and class activities in order to keep the students interested in what most of them would consider "irrelevant" issues, such as: when, if ever, are we responsible for our actions?; can we explain human experience without positing the existence of a soul?; what, if anything, can we really know? These were standard issues in an introductory philosophy course and the challenge was to present them in such a way that students could see the relevance to their lives. Maggie spent much time plowing through newspaper articles, TV programs, music and movies to find examples to illustrate the issues they were discussing in class. So, for example, the case of the father who put his two sons in a foundry furnace because God told him to was used to raise the question of conditions of responsibility–as well as issues of religious belief; the movie "Blade Runner" was used to raise the possibility of thinking and feeling robots; popular music was used to illustrate the values embedded in the lyrics.

To do this, required keeping up with popular culture–at least enough to be only slightly behind where the students were. This didn't require much sacrifice on Maggie's part as she was a movie buff and didn't mind the occasional evening spent watching TV programs or listening to albums recommended by her students. In fact, she looked askance at her colleagues who criticized popular culture without knowing anything about it. She was both amazed and amused by the number of her colleagues who only watched PBS, who never went to the movies, and who only listened to so-called "classical" music–and then criticized the students for being too narrow. Maggie was a follower of Mill who argued that a necessary condition for anyone to judge the superiority of one type of experience over another was to have genuinely experienced both types.

But all this emphasis on teaching and the time spent on Doris's case had put a dent in her own writing. Her article on friendship was not much further along than when she had arrived at Claxton. She would have to carve out specific time in her schedule for writing.

....

Dear Sam,

I actually took time off in the middle of the week to see a movie with Gail. It was like playing hooky in my childhood, and it felt good. One of the things I learned from her tonight was the "monkey bones" incident. This place is quite funny—things happen here that you would only read in books written by British academics about university life. There's a physical anthropology prof who does research on primates. She acquired—no one knows how—some bones (I'm sure there's a more technically correct description, but she just calls them monkey bones) which she kept in the refrigerator of the anthropology lab. Unfortunately, we had a power outage a few weeks ago and for some reason the refrigerator didn't start up when the power came back on. People started complaining about a "funny" smell on the third floor and when the janitor investigated he found it was coming from the refrigerator. The monkey bones had thawed and were decomposing. That's not the funny part, though. That comes next. The prof then had to "clean" the bones, which I guess involves getting rid of the rotting flesh and getting down to clean bones. She decided to boil the bones in a crock pot and used the third floor women's bathroom, which caused an uproar among the women on that floor. She then decided to send the bones down to the state agricultural research center where they use bugs—yes, real bugs—to eat the rotting flesh. (This is really gross.) She just got an angry call from them asking where she got the bones. It seems their bugs all died after eating them! Anyway, the bones are no longer here so I guess we're all safe from what people are now calling "the killer bones."

On a more serious note, I'm meeting tomorrow with Jessie to bring her up to date on my talks with Morris and Fitzgerald. Nothing much to report, though. Doris's memorial service is scheduled for January, after we get back from the Christmas break. I'm curious as to who will be there from her department.

Well, just another week and I'll be in New York. Did you find out what Kristi's kids want? I haven't had time to do any shopping here, but, unless you've already bought their presents, we'll have time to do it when I get there.

Love, Maggie

Chapter 16

"Come in, come in, let me get a look at you. You look wonderful," said Selma, as she gave Maggie a big hug. Selma ran a boarding house in Manhattan, or as she preferred to say, "took in friends." In truth, she had been Maggie's landlady for four years in New York. She was a large, but not fat, woman in her sixties who loved taking care of people, especially young people starting out in their careers. She came from Iowa, where her father had taught religion at Iowa State and her mother had been a grade school teacher. She had come to New York to study ballet, but discovered that while she starred on the Iowa stage, she was just another dancer in New York. She met and married Saul, who started out as a "rag man"–a textile salesman–and later owned his own company. She was widowed and had inherited the old brownstone in lower Manhattan when her husband of 20 years died. She had also inherited half of his textile company, which she gratefully let his partner run, allowing her to receive a sizeable check each month and time to devote to her "friends" and their lives.

Maggie always visited Selma on her trips to the city for Selma had indeed been a friend when Maggie was a lonely student away from home the first time. After being released from Selma's embrace, she sat down at the kitchen table, drinking tea and eating Selma's homemade cookies. Maggie asked, "How have you been?"

"How could I be–I'm getting old. My back hurts, I don't sleep well, my stomach has been acting up–but you know me, I don't complain."

Maggie smiled. "Who's in my old room?"

"Ah, your room–what a story! A nice young man came by the other day and would you believe–he's from Iowa! He's the son of friends of my brother in Ames. I met them once when I was visiting Willie and Arlene. That was right after my husband died. We went to a concert that Willie had tickets for–Mozart mainly, I think. That famous violinist was playing–what's his name? Itzhak Perlman, that's it–and he got sick

81

over dinner. No, not Perlman, this boy's father. It turned out he had an inflamed appendix and Willie had to drive him to the emergency room that night. He was a musician, oboe, I think—I forget his name, but he played with the Ames city orchestra—you know the conductor, Jonathan Merrill? No? Well, he's not really that well known. He—this boy's father, not Merrill—had married this woman from Sweden. Nice woman, but dark hair, not like most Swedish people. She was a musician, too. I don't know what she played though. Her father was a famous doctor in Sweden and she came over here to study and met her husband and had, I think, two children. The daughter was born with a deformed spine and had to have surgery as an infant and again later on. She's okay now, but walks with a limp. But it was a good thing that her grandfather was a doctor in Sweden, because he came over to supervise the medical treatments. Anyway, they also had a son who's in your old room now. He's got a girlfriend—I think he met her in one of his classes. He's not a musician; he wants to be a lawyer and she's studying to be a teacher like her parents. I think her mother teaches high school English and he teaches history, the father, that is. He's a vegetarian, this young man, so I'm learning new recipes."

Maggie was used to these rambling answers to her questions and she had learned to simply let Selma finally come to the point no matter how long it took her. That is, when there was a point. Sometimes something in the conversation would just set Selma off—usually something about Iowa—and she would just go on for what seemed like ages, describing some event or person that the conversation reminded her of. She had been in New York for almost 40 years, but her heart was still in Iowa. Maggie realized this and, even though she couldn't imagine anyone wanting to live in Iowa, she listened politely to Selma's stories. It was the least she could do for this woman who had made her transition to independence so smooth.

"So, how long are you going to be in town?" Selma asked.

"I've got two weeks before I have to get back. That'll give me a few days to prepare for my next semester's classes. I'm planning on just relaxing and hanging out while I'm here. Of course, I'll probably use the library a few times while I'm here. The library there doesn't have all the journals I need—although they're pretty good at getting them for me. This electronic stuff really makes a difference—you can pretty much download any article you want; and if you can't, the library can."

"Typical Maggie! You never could just relax. I remember how you spent your weekends in your room working away on your computer, or at the library. I was so worried you'd never meet a nice man and get married. You're not married yet, are you? Such a waste! You should get out more, meet more people. Lots of women have careers these days and still get married and raise a family."

This was a familiar tune, sung by Selma over the years. While she had no children, she had a marriage that lasted for 25 years, and, to hear her tell, it was a marriage made in heaven. No fights, no disagreements, just love and companionship. Maggie realized that Selma just wanted the same for her and therefore didn't take offense at what ordinarily would have gotten her angry.

It was funny, though; when Maggie's mother made the same remarks, it did get her angry. She tried to respond to her mother with the same understanding she brought to Selma's comments, but somehow found herself responding as she did when a child. Perhaps, the mother-child relationship is too deeply implanted to be modified by an act of will. Maggie's rational self couldn't accept this: she should be able to control her actions once she was aware of what was happening. And she was aware; but, try as she might, she never succeeded in maintaining that control for more than a few minutes when listening to her mother comment on her "life style."

"So, where are you staying? Aren't you going to visit your mother?" Selma, not having children of her own, had informally adopted many of the students who had lived with her. She felt absolutely no reluctance in asking personal questions and giving unasked for advice. It was a testament to the fondness these young people had for her that they didn't rebel.

"I'm staying with Sam, and yes, I'll be spending a few days with the family. You don't have to remind me to be a good daughter!" Maggie smiled as she said this and Selma nodded her approval.

"Well, I've got to get going. Thanks for the tea—and the cookies. I've missed your rugelach. The ones they sell in the stores just aren't the same."

"Of course not, they don't use real butter. Oh, it was so good to see you. You look wonderful–though you could use a haircut. But I guess that's the style now for young women–long, messy hair. It's sexy, right?"

"Enough, I'm leaving; criticism I can get from my mother," laughed Maggie.

The two women hugged, and Maggie could hear Selma calling down to her as she left the apartment: "Take the No. 9 bus; the No. 12 doesn't run on the weekend. And button your coat; it's cold out!"

Maggie nodded and, with a smile, waved goodbye.

....

The next two weeks sped by with friends and a three day holiday visit with her family in Waltham, a town about 10 miles northwest of Boston. The house was in an Upper-Middle-class neighborhood that had once been the domain of physicians, and was therefore called "Pill Hill." The physicians had long ago departed to the new pricier developments, and Pill Hill was now populated by teachers, small business owners, and middle-level executives. The really rich people didn't live in Waltham.

Maggie hadn't grown up in Waltham. When she was a child, her family had lived in New York. Her father, Paul, had done well in the real estate business. Her mother was a stay-at-home mom who devoted her time and attention to raising Maggie. When Paul retired, the family moved to Waltham to be near Maggie's mother's family in Boston. And now, for Maggie's visit, the whole family was present, and, as usual, she had to suffer visits from aunts, uncles, and neighbors–none of whom were really interested in what she was doing, but all were interested in whom she was "seeing."

Her mother had met Sam and knew that they lived together, but told friends that, given the new living arrangements young people had these days, Maggie and Sam were just good friends sharing expenses. Maggie didn't volunteer any more information about their relationship, content to concentrate on getting along with her mother for the few times she visited.

Years ago Maggie had realized that mentioning that she was studying, and then teaching, philosophy just resulted in people asking about her philosophy of life; or else they confused it with psychology and jokingly asked if she was psychoanalyzing everything they said. She started claiming that she was a mathematician, and nobody said anything! For once, math anxiety served a good purpose.

Vivian, Maggie's mother, was clearly proud of her daughter, but often remarked that she wished Maggie was more outgoing–and married, of course. Sometimes she appeared actually embarrassed by Maggie, as when Maggie had explained what epistemology was to a neighbor and hadn't used any big words. All that education and she spoke like a regular person!

But this visit went well. Maggie and Vivian were both on good behavior and the three days went by without incident. Paul had died six years ago; he had always been the mediator between the two women so it was a good sign that they could finally spend some time together without incident or mediation.

The rest of the time was spent in New York with Sam and friends. They went to the theater–Maggie didn't think there was anything derivative about the plays, but then she didn't know what to look for– and partied and ate good food, and, in general, had a good time.

They belatedly celebrated Wayne and Kristi's wedding, and she visited with Gwen, who was still despondent about the divorce she had initiated. Not knowing what to say to console Gwen, Maggie resorted to the technique she had found most useful–she listened. After two hours of listening to Gwen, and two bottles of wine, most of which Gwen had drunk, Maggie realized that Gwen was beginning to see a future for herself without Tim. In fact, the more she talked the more she remembered things about Tim she had never liked.

Maggie left feeling somewhat guilty. Tim was her friend, too. Where Gwen had started the evening extolling all his virtues, what had buoyed her up was the remembrance, exaggerated in Maggie's opinion, of all his faults. But at least Maggie could feel she had served a purpose with her visit with Gwen. And since she hadn't indicated that she agreed with Gwen, she really hadn't been disloyal to Tim and therefore had nothing to feel guilty about.

Having alleviated her guilt, she went home determined to spend a quiet, romantic evening with Sam. They had planned to spend many quiet evenings at home, but somehow the two weeks had gone by in a flurry of activities that left them exhausted.

"Why," she wondered, "did two weeks seem so long in anticipation when it seemed so short in reality."

They had attended the theater twice—once to the award-winning musical *Billy Elliot*, and then to an Off-Broadway production of *Ruined*, about women in the war-torn Congo. Maggie was proud to be able to show off her newly acquired ability to analyze a production beyond its plot—although she had to admit that that was still what interested her most.

They had dined with friends, leading Maggie to complain that they were eating out too often. Sam, however, had reminded her that being invited to dinner at someone's home should be seen as an honor. The fact that friends wanted to prepare food rather than make a reservation in a restaurant showed that they wanted to do something special for her.

They had spent time casually browsing through art galleries, looking at the works of fellow artists, commenting on the pros and cons of each display. They had walked the streets of the city, smiling as they revisited places they had fond memories of, and frowning as they viewed the new trendy shops in areas that had once been lively ethnic neighborhoods.

And they had shopped. Maggie, not one to care about the latest fashions, found styles in New York that would probably never reach the Midwest. Avoiding the more *avant-garde,* she chose outfits that would blend into the Michigan dress style—but with a flair.

Maggie had planned to spend New Year's Eve alone with Sam, but pressure from friends won the day and they partied until the wee hours, long after the ball had dropped in Times Square.

Her plans for long evenings spent with Sam sharing their feelings and thoughts had become evenings spent with friends, catching up on the events in their lives. But tonight the phone would be turned off, Sam would do the cooking—the famous paella, Sam-style— they would listen to their favorite romantic CDs, and they would spend the rest of the evening in bed, making up for lost time.

....

The last day of Maggie's visit was spent saying goodbye to friends—and family, via phone. Since her plane was leaving early in the morning, she had already packed and was enjoying a glass of Cabernet when Sam asked her what her plans were.

"What do you mean?"

"Well, are you going to stay there another year? Are you looking for jobs here?"

"I don't know yet about next year. I've been told that my reappointment was sent forward, and I don't expect any problems higher up. But I've been so busy I haven't had time to even think about looking. It's not so easy getting jobs in philosophy these days. The emphasis is all on pre-professional or vocational programs. Even at Claxton the new money is going into engineering and health science programs. Liberal arts is kept on to be able to say it's a university and not a trade school. And the new degrees are just as bad. You can get a degree in anything that 'sells'—a bachelor of science in casino management, or auto design. But that's not what you're talking about, is it?"

"No. But it's clear: you're staying another year."

"Yeah, I guess I am. What's this all about? You knew I was taking the job—a tenure-track job. We talked about it last year. I know this first year has been hard, but I'm getting the swing of it and once I get some more articles published I should get a raise, if not a promotion, so I'll be able to afford more visits. They've promised me a Tuesday/Thursday schedule for next year which would give me long weekends for travel. And, you know, you could come visit me. The Midwest isn't the wasteland you think it is. Of course, it's not New York, but then no other place is either. So what's this about?"

"What's it about! I miss you; that's what it's about. I read your letters and wish you were here to tell me about everything that's happening. But, you're right. I could take some time off and go out there. I don't even have to take time off. I can take my work with me."

Sam was struggling to stay calm, not wanting to spoil what had been a wonderful two weeks.

"I can't ask you to give up your place here and come live with me. I don't know how long I'll be there. But you could come and stay for long periods. I could get a bigger place and you could work from there and…."

Maggie's voice faded off, trying to hide the tears she felt forming.

"Let's not make any definite plans now. As long as you still feel the same way, I'm satisfied. And I will come and visit–as soon as the snow is gone."

Maggie smiled. "Yes, I still feel the same way. And the snow should be gone by April. They tell me that spring is really lovely there."

Chapter 17

The flight back to Michigan went smoothly, arriving on time. She was seated by a window and could avoid being disturbed every time a seatmate had to go to the bathroom. Fortunately, she was not very tall and didn't have to scrunch her knees to her chest as her seatmate was doing. But not only was he tall, he was big–so big that she had to huddle herself against the window in order to avoid too much physical contact with him.

The time on the flight allowed her to revisit the last two weeks. She recalled the many delightful hours with friends, the pleasant visit with Selma, and the hectic, but warm time spent with her mother. The conversation with Sam the previous night troubled her, although she felt good about its resolution: she would spend the summer in New York, and Sam would visit later in the year. But could this be a long-term adjustment? Would staying in Michigan prove to be too much a strain on their relationship? Well, she would have to deal with that situation when it arose. For now, things seemed to be okay.

....

It was ten thirty when she arrived at her apartment, cold, hungry, and tired. She turned up the heat, made herself a plate of stale crackers and peanut butter, curled up in a blanket on the couch, and fell asleep with the TV turned to an old episode of *Law and Order*.

She spent Monday morning refurbishing her food supply and making last minute preparations for her classes. She was still thinking of the talk she and Sam had had on their last night together. Well, the issue of her staying on another year may be moot. She was about to pursue a course of action, against the advice of Jessie. Everyone was treating Doris's death as a tragic accident, but she wasn't convinced. She had no evidence, just a feeling, but she had decided to push an investigation in whatever way she could. If that affected her reappointment, so be it. If she wasn't reappointed, she'd simply return to New York!

....

It was a typical January day–cold and gray. Maggie was used to the cold, having grown up in the Northeast, but she wasn't used to the constant gray gloom that settled over everything, making even getting out of bed in the morning a major achievement. She had bought some of the special light bulbs that were supposed to provide the benefits of sunshine, but even though she sat in her little kitchen every morning under those lights while she had her coffee and read the paper, she saw no difference in her mood.

It was the day of Doris's memorial. Maggie was sitting in Jessie's office, trying not to think about the service scheduled for the afternoon. She used the time to report on her trip to New York and listen to Jessie's description of her two week visit with grandchildren in North Carolina.

Jessie listened patiently as Maggie predicted that nothing would come of any investigation into Doris's death. Jessie, to Maggie's surprise, agreed. They sat, sipping coffee, trying to think of what could be done to push either the university or the police to action but, aside from going to the press, could think of nothing. Maggie was all for going public, but Jessie was again warning her of the consequences.

After getting nowhere after 15 minutes, Maggie changed the subject. "Tell me about Harriet Taylor–John Stuart Mill's wife. You mentioned her before as one of the women whose work's been ignored. She was never mentioned in any of my philosophy classes, although J. S. Mill was widely taught. And all I know of her is her influence on Mill's views on women."

"That's not surprising. She's come into her own with the women's movement, but she's still not considered a philosopher worthy of reading. Sometimes, our feminist sisters are too anxious to consider as a philosopher any woman who's ever written something, and that feeds into the backlash against feminist studies. But I think Taylor is an exception. I think she is worthy of reading. If you take J. S. Mill's views on her work, she was brilliant. In his *Autobiography*, he claims that she is the most brilliant person he ever knew, and that without her he would never have been able to accomplish what he had. Many of his peers at the time thought that Mill was overly generous with his praise, attributing it to his love for Harriet. She wrote for social and political magazines, mostly on social issues, but there is a whole slew of letters between Mill and Taylor that, at least in my eyes, speaks to a genuine collaboration. She was certainly influential on Mill's views on women–*The Subjection of Women* shows that. In her own writings, though, she goes further than Mill, arguing that women, in the 19th century, should have the vote, and be admitted into the professions. Mill, as enlightened as he was, was a man of his time in that he thought women, even after education, would prefer to be wives and mothers. And on political issues, Taylor was much more impressed with the rise of socialism on the continent at that time. On this issue, she wasn't as influential on Mill as on the women's issue.

"It's difficult to know if their, what we could call today, 'life style' was an issue at the time. She was married to John Taylor and lived with him and their children until his death, even though her relationship with Mill and much of their collaboration occurred during this period. She married Mill after her husband's death, and died shortly after. Some historians think she was considered 'uppity' by the intellectuals of the time, such as Thomas Carlyle, who seems to have resented her influence on Mill; others claim that she was a minor thinker, riding on Mill's large coattails. In any event, she was one of that large group of women who have been invisible throughout history. I'll leave it up to you to decide whether she lives up to Mill's judgment of her; but keep in mind, not all the men whose work has survived merit reading today!"

....

Maggie wasn't looking forward to meeting Doris's sister, Helen Carpenter. Helen had called her and wanted to meet. Maggie wasn't sure what she would say. Should she tell her the suspicions she had? Would it be easier for her to believe that her sister had died from an accident or that she had been murdered–especially since Maggie had no proof, just a feeling? Well, there was no sense in worrying about that now. She would just have to follow Helen's lead, wherever it led.

The service was set for 2:00 p.m. in the Auditorium. The room accommodated 200 people, but less than half the seats were filled. The administrative staff was present, as were members of the Women's Studies department. Some members of the Athletics Department were present, but not the chair. And, of course, Doris's family–her sister, her sister's husband, and her mother. But most noticeable was the large contingent of Doris's students, men and women.

There were the usual speeches from the administration attesting to what an asset she was to the university; members of her department spoke of her contribution to the swimming program; and students spoke of her commitment to their success in the program. One of the young women, with tears in her eyes and a catch in her voice, told how Doris had fought to get adequate support for the women's swimming program. She also made a vague reference to the troubles that Doris had with some of her colleagues in the department, but stopped short of specificity.

All in all, it was a fitting tribute to Doris; her mother, for example, seemed pleased that Doris was so well-liked and respected, although Helen sat expressionless throughout the service.

The service was finished by 4:00, and Maggie and Helen had found a quiet spot at *Isis* to have their talk.

"It's good to finally meet you. Doris talked a lot about the help you gave her. I know she was frightened these past few months, but I felt better knowing that she had you in her corner." Helen was a thin woman in her late 50's. She fought to maintain her composure. As the older sister, she had always felt responsible for Doris and her death had already taken its toll on her. She was pale, red-eyed, and, by the way her gray wool dress hung on her, had recently lost weight.

"Well, I wish I could have done more. I'm still trying to get Dean Morris, her dean, to deal with the sexual harassment Doris was experiencing, but I think they're going to simply file it away, never to be seen again," replied Maggie.

"The thing I don't understand is how this could have happened. She was always so careful around water. That's why we were so surprised when she decided to become a swimming coach. She almost drowned when she was about five. We lived in Wisconsin at the time and had a cottage on a small lake. She wandered off one afternoon and by chance my mother decided to go down to the lake to pick some flowers. She saw Doris floating face down, in the water and managed to pull her out and use CPR–my mother was a nurse. Well, Doris survived, and we were sure she would never go near the water again. But she always had a strong personality.

"When she was born she was allergic to almost everything: milk, wheat, you name it. We didn't think she'd make it beyond the first year. As she got older, she could monitor her food intake herself and I know it was embarrassing for her when she would go to parties and had to check on the ingredients before she would eat anything. I remember one time she went out with friends to a Chinese restaurant and ordered chicken lo mein. She immediately had trouble breathing. If she hadn't had her medicine–her epinephrine–with her I'm not sure she would have survived the trip to the ER. But she did and everything turned out okay. It seems that the sauce for the lo mein had some shrimp in it and she was terribly allergic to shrimp, in fact, to all shellfish. But that's beside the point. I guess the point is that she was used to being super careful–about what she ate and around water. It's just hard to believe that she would drown."

At this point, Maggie had to make a decision. Should she share her doubts with Helen? Would that be fair? Wouldn't it be easier for Doris's family to just accept her death as an accident? But would that be fair to Doris?

"Have you got the results of the autopsy?" Maggie asked. "I think that's standard procedure for even accidental deaths, but perhaps they have to have the family's permission."

"Yes; they say that she somehow hit her head and fell into the pool."

Maggie said nothing for what seemed like an hour to Helen, who responded, "Are you trying to tell me something?"

Maggie just looked at her and simply said, "I just think it's a good idea to get as much information as you can."

....

Dear Sam,

Doris's memorial service was held today. It was a small gathering: the usual administrators who have to make an appearance, the family, some faculty and students. Of course, the chair of her department wasn't there.

I haven't met the guy, but from what I've heard—not just from Doris, but from other women—he's a real jerk. He's been chair for more than twenty years and obviously thinks he's set for life. Chairs do get a pretty hefty stipend—about $30,000 in addition to their base salary—so it can be a pretty cushy job.

Anyway, I met Doris's sister, Helen. She's as puzzled as I am about how Doris could have drowned. But the family is grieving so much I felt uncomfortable sharing my doubts. What if I'm wrong? Is it fair to raise their suspicions when it may turn out to be nothing?

I really feel that I'm in over my head. But I just can't shake the feeling that something isn't right. Maybe it's remembering how frightened Doris was when I last saw her. Or maybe I'm just overreacting to the treatment she received in her department. I realize I may be trying to assuage my guilt at not being able to help her, but I think the issue is so important that I can't let it go. Anyway, I needn't tell you that. I just wish you were here to help me. I need your sane, sensible presence to keep me from going over the top on this. Your advice is always practical as well as principled.

It's now 1 a.m. and I have to get some sleep. I didn't sleep well last night— anticipation, I guess—and it showed in my classes today. I felt like a robot might feel going through the motions. (Of course, that assumes that robots can feel—an interesting question to ponder some other time.)

But enough about here. What's going on there? Any word on an exhibit? Keep me posted on what you're doing.

Love, Maggie

Chapter 18

Maggie was at her favorite table at *Isis:* the one in the back with a lamp on it. Again, it was quiet with a few regulars at their tables, drinking coffee or, more likely, lattes or cappuccinos; and while many of her friends now knew where she hid out, they were respectful of her privacy and didn't bother her. She had managed to block out two mornings a week to work on her manuscript and was well on her way to finishing close to her self-imposed deadline.

Deep into a defense of Nietzsche, a philosopher largely ignored by her fellow philosophers, and his view on friendship: "It is not a lack of love, but a lack of friendship that makes unhappy marriages", she was brought back to the present by the persistent ringing of her cell phone. It was Officer Fitzgerald with a request for her to come down to the station.

There went her plans to finish the Nietzsche section, but this was more important. She packed up her laptop, books, and papers and drove downtown to the station.

"Thanks for coming in." Fitzgerald showed Maggie to one of the chair in the small interrogation room. "We have some questions. The family has gone back home and we haven't been able to contact them yet, so I thought you might have some information about her health since you seemed to be close to her. We have some results from the autopsy. It shows a small bump on her head, but the ME doesn't think that was sufficient to knock her out. What was puzzling, though, is that she didn't drown—she was dead before she hit the water. They're checking to see if she had any heart problems, or anything else that caused her death."

"I don't know much about her health, but she certainly seemed healthy. Her sister told me about some allergy problems she had but nothing about heart problems."

"What kind of allergy problems?" asked Fitzgerald,

"I think she said she was allergic to milk and wheat products when she was a child–oh, and she was allergic to shellfish."

"How allergic?" he asked. Seeing puzzlement on Maggie's face, he added, "Was the reaction to shellfish more likely to cause slight distress rather than respiratory failure?"

"No, I think it was a severe reaction. Helen, her sister, told me of an incident when Doris had to be taken to the ER because some food she ate had been 'touched' by shrimp. So I think she was seriously allergic to shellfish, certainly to shrimp. Why do you ask? What have you found out?"

"That's all I can say at this time, except that we are looking into it further. You've been very helpful."

It was clear that this was the cue for Maggie to leave. But she remained seated. "You know something else that you're not telling me," she said, sitting forward in the chair, eyes blazing. "I think I deserve to know what you've found out. I'm the one who's been pushing you to investigate this as something other than an accident, and now that you've found something you're not going to tell me?"

Maggie was building up to a full-blown scene and Fitzgerald wasn't up to handling it. He put on his official mask and gave the usual response: "That's all I'm at liberty to say at this point. We'll keep you posted on any future developments."

Maggie rose, gathered her purse, and with a shaking voice said, "Well, I wonder if the campus newspaper would be interested in the story of a beloved teacher who might have been murdered!" and left the room.

She was still shaking when she reached her car and sat for a good five minutes before she felt calm enough to drive. She would go to the paper with the story. She would frame it as a "possibility"–a friend puzzled about Doris's death. She would be careful not to make any claims she could not support. In fact, she wouldn't have to make any claims, just ask questions. The student reporters were always anxious to do "investigative reporting" and this would be a good experience for them. Didn't she remember one of her students telling her that he wrote for the paper? That might be the way to get them interested.

All of this was running through her mind as she drove back to campus. She considered going back to *Isis*, but knew she wouldn't be able to concentrate on her manuscript. She didn't want to go home–she would just raid the refrigerator out of frustration. She decided to go up to her office and track down her student reporter.

She took out the gradebook from her briefcase and tried to remember who the reporter was. She had more than 150 students, but she seemed to remember that he had made some comments in class that impressed her. Now if she could just remember what they were she could narrow down the class he would have been in.

Ah, yes, she remembered. He had criticized the view that we should never make judgments about cultures other than our own. He had pointed out that, if carried to its logical conclusion, a very small minority group in a culture should never even criticize the dominant culture. When Maggie had agreed that was a problem, he had gone on to list places where women were treated as inferior to men and that this view would require us to make no judgments of that treatment. Since this was an issue of great importance to her, she used his comment to provide a fuller analysis of the position and its criticisms. So, he had to have been in her social philosophy class, where they were discussing various forms of relativism. That narrowed it down considerably and she was able to determine that it was David who was the reporter.

Now she had to calm down and think through what she was proposing to do. Was it appropriate–ethical–to engage a student in what she was doing? Was it too early to go public? Should she give the police another push before going public? And what about the internal grievance? She hadn't heard anything official from Dean Morris; perhaps she should give her a call.

Maggie didn't have a chance to call Morris before Leo knocked on her door. "Hi, Maggie. Here's that Hume reference you were looking for. How's the article going?"

"Oh, slowly. I need to find time to finish it. The Hume quote will help, though, and maybe I can send it off before Spring Break. I don't know how you do it, Leo. I'm so swamped with classes I can't find time to write."

"Don't worry, it gets easier. After all, this is your first year here. It always takes time to figure out what works with new students. One thing I do that works is to be completely out of touch at certain times. I only teach afternoon classes so mornings are writing times, except for the occasional meeting. My wife knows that I'm not to be disturbed when I'm writing–except for emergencies."

"Yeah, I've trying to do that now. Putting aside those times I don't teach to do my writing. I'm anxious to finish as I have another piece in mind I want to get to: the difference in views on friendship between men and women. But first things first. Thanks again for the reference."

Finally, Maggie dialed Morris' number, only to be told that Dean Morris was at a meeting and would Maggie please call back. It was now 4:55 p.m. and Maggie was in no frame of mind to work, or to do anything that required the use of more than two brain cells. So she called Naomi to see if she wanted to go out for a drink. As usual, Naomi accepted the invitation.

She had met Naomi Sloan at the Women's Studies meetings and they met for drinks at least once a week. Maggie typically found Naomi in her office after five, anxious to take a break before returning to do some more administrative work. Since Maggie wasn't interested in heading home right away, she often suggested going out for a drink, to which Naomi quickly agreed. Both seemed to need a "little something" to relax them after a hectic day.

Naomi was a tall, slim woman with an excess of nervous energy, constantly running her fingers through her hair, making sure that every fiber of her short curly hair was in place. Even when seated, her legs were in constant movement. She was married to Steve, who was a commodity trader at the Mercantile Exchange in Chicago. They saw each other twice a month, once when she visited him and once when he visited her. They were a devoted couple, but people joked that the success of their marriage was due to the infrequency of their visits.

Naomi, as chair of a large, rather dysfunctional department, was always dealing with a crisis. She was usually found in her office at 7:00 a.m. and was often still there at 10:00 p.m. She claimed, and Maggie believed her, that she got more work done before 8:00 a.m. and after 5:00 p.m. than she did in the rest of the day, which seemed to be spent resolving disagreements among faculty and fighting the administration on policies that seemed to make no sense to her.

On this Maggie agreed. Having come from a small private college Maggie had seen governance by fiat, but somehow she had expected something different at a large state university. While it's true the

President couldn't just make decisions on a whim–after all, there were procedures in place–the decisions seemed to be made as far away as possible from the people it would affect. So, if the decision had to do with how secretaries handled travel vouchers, secretaries weren't consulted; if the decision had to do with the hours of computer services for faculty, faculty weren't notified!

They left the building and headed to *Willows*, intending only to have one glass of wine, but ended up sharing appetizers and more wine. Maggie, usually a one glass drinker, was so exhausted from her frustrating day that she knew she wouldn't be good for any work that evening; and it was so nice to just sit back, relax, have another drink, and listen to Naomi's problems!

By the time Maggie arrived home, she was pleasantly light-headed and, lying down on the couch/bed listening to a favorite recording of "Nina Simone at Montreux," she fell asleep, only to be awakened by Sam's call at 11. Since it was obvious that Maggie was still half-asleep, the call was short with Sam laughing at Maggie's inebriation.

Chapter 19

The next few days passed uneventfully. Dean Morris was "unavailable" whenever Maggie called; Maggie was reluctant to involve her student reporter, David, in going public; and she had heard nothing more from Officer Fitzgerald. Fortunately, Maggie was busy grading student papers so she had little time to set any plans in motion. She did, however, contact Doris's sister. She used the pretext to report on her visit with Fitzgerald. When Helen again expressed her bafflement at the "accident," Maggie took the opportunity to raise the issue of further tests.

"Do you know if they did a tox screen? You know, test what she had eaten or taken that evening."

Helen misunderstood Maggie's intentions and angrily replied, "She didn't do drugs! She was very careful about what she put in her body. In fact, she was sometimes fanatical about her food, avoiding anything that would possibly cause an allergic reaction, including alcohol. I can't imagine she would have done any drugs."

"No, that's not what I meant. I was thinking more of something she might have unknowingly eaten. Something that might have triggered an allergic reaction. It just seems that something caused her death before she hit the water. Look, I'm not doing this very well. I may as well be blunt—my attempts at subtlety are obviously not working. Given the hostility toward her in her department, I'm starting to wonder if there was any so-called foul play. Maybe I've read too many mystery stories, but I can't help but wonder what happened that night. I just don't buy the 'accident' story."

"Would a tox screen—is that what it's called?—tell us that? Don't they automatically do that when they do an autopsy?"

Maggie paused. "I thought so, but I'm not sure. Fitzgerald didn't mention anything about a toxicology report. But I'm pretty sure they can tell what she ate, and when. I don't know that they'll find anything, but at least it would rule out some things."

"Well, okay. I'll call Fitzgerald. I'm sorry I flew off the handle before. I know you're trying to help, and we all appreciate it. I'm just starting to understand the pressure she had been under these past few months. I knew something was wrong, but I just attributed it to overwork. I kept telling her not to worry, to get more sleep, not to be such a perfectionist, to say 'no' to extra work, to make more of an effort to fit in. I had no idea the atmosphere there was so bad."

"I'm sure she didn't want to worry you. She was actually looking forward to presenting her case to the grievance committee; we both thought she had a strong case."

"I'm going to call Fitzgerald now," Helen said. "Thanks for calling. Keep in touch."

....

That afternoon, after her classes, Maggie walked over to Dean Morris' office and announced that she had to see the Dean. When told that the Dean was at a meeting, Maggie sat herself down on one of the plush, newly upholstered mauve chairs, and said, "I'll wait."

She had wisely brought along a journal to read, expecting to be kept waiting. It was close to five when the Dean opened the door to her office and came out to speak to Maggie. It was clear that she had been in her office the whole time, but tact won the day and Maggie said nothing.

"I'm so sorry to have kept you waiting. Please come in–although I don't have much time right now. Perhaps you could make an appointment?"

Maggie smiled, she wasn't going to fall into that trap! "This won't take long. I just wanted to know your decision about going ahead with Doris's grievance."

"Oh, yes. Well, I've spoken to the senior officers and legal counsel and they all agree that it would be most unusual–and inappropriate–to pursue the grievance in light of the circumstances. You understand, of course."

"Yes, I understand–rules, right? Well, I just wanted to be sure that there was a final decision. Thanks for your time."

With that, Maggie turned and left the office. Now she knew what she had to do.

....

After class the next day, Maggie took David aside and asked if he would stop by her office later. David looked concerned. Fortunately, he didn't have long to wait for his meeting with Maggie. He entered her office—the door was seldom closed—and started apologizing for his essay. He explained that he had tried to be creative, but realized now that philosophers were more interested in argumentation than creativity. He could see ways to improve his essay. He was aiming for an A in the class and hoped that he hadn't messed up.

Maggie gave him a puzzled looked. "No, your essay is fine—quite creative. Don't be so critical of your work. That's not why I asked you here. Please, sit down. Relax."

David took a seat on the only chair available. He was a chubby young man, with a perpetual frown on his face. "You're a reporter on the campus paper, right?" Maggie asked. When David nodded, Maggie went on. "I'm sure you've heard of the death of one of the women in Athletics. Well, I've spoken to the police. It's been ruled an accident, and I was wondering if you—or your paper—would be interested in following up on the story. I'm going to be up-front with you. I have questions about it being an accident and I don't think the university, or the police, is taking it seriously enough. It may actually have been an accident—I don't have any information to the contrary. But I thought if someone other than me pushed for details, they might take the case more seriously. There's no pressure, David. If this is a bad idea, or if you don't want to do it, no problem. Please believe me on that. I'll certainly understand if you aren't interested."

"Wow! That's a great idea! We're always like looking for things to 'investigate' and this would be major. Let me talk to my editor and see if she has like any ideas on how to go about it."

"Thanks. Let me know what you decide."

When David left, Maggie closed her door, put her head down on the desk, and cried. She hadn't realized how wound up she was. If he had turned her down, what would she have done? And will this backfire? Well, no sense worrying about that; she had started something and would just have to see where it led.

....

That evening Maggie was scheduled to attend a department lecture by Leo on Hume's "Causal Realism." She felt drained but was committed to supporting her colleagues' research projects, so after a quick dinner of scrambled eggs and toast she set off for the lecture hall. The talk was not very well attended, but greatly appreciated by those who were there. Charles and Toby, as usual, were there, as were Ben and Henry. Doug was probably at the bar plying his charms on the young women there and Felipe was so busy with his cognitive science proposal that he seldom came to campus functions. And then there was Barbara. No one expected her to attend any of these lectures; in fact, they would have been surprised if she had shown up! Some of Leo's advanced students were present, taking copious notes as Leo spoke.

Maggie felt that Leo was persuasive in his argument that Hume had a realist analysis of causality, although that position was largely rejected by many Hume scholars. Toby's questions, which were really mini-lectures, generated an interesting discussion and were adequately answered by Leo. Henry's comments about the adequacy of the "translation" Leo used–yes, Hume wrote in English, but there were always controversies about which edition of his work was the "best"!– were politely received by Leo, who promised to look at other editions. All in all, it was a pleasant evening.

....

Dear Sam,

Another weird episode from this place. One of the women I've met from the Business Department told me about a departmental election they had last week. They have a procedure of nominating people for the next chair position at one meeting and then having a box in the department office where people can put their ballots. The voting was to go on until 5:00 p.m. of the next day. It was a very contentious election, and when she and some others went to vote at the last minute, the box was missing. It was later found in one of the candidates' office! Well, the whole election had to be done over and, to no one's surprise, that candidate lost! It's hard to imagine what he thought he could accomplish—but it's not clear he was thinking.

I wonder if these sorts of things happened back at Bennett. Maybe I was just too out of the loop to know what was going on, or maybe I was too naïve. But I'm constantly amazed at the antics of people here. I wonder if it's typical of most universities. It sure gives one a different perspective on the effect of education if these super-educated people behave no better than adolescents at their worst.

I think I'm coming down with something, so I'm going to take a warm bath and get to bed early. I'll speak to you this weekend.

Love, Maggie

Chapter 20

The next day Maggie awoke with a dull headache and a sore throat. The day was gray, with clouds threatening snow. She would have loved to stay in bed, but had a class at nine. She hated to cancel classes as it upset her finely tuned schedule for the semester. Like many professors, her ego made it difficult for her to consider leaving out a section of the syllabus. After all, it had been created to include all the things she thought were important for students to learn. That they would miss out on something she wanted to impart to them before they finished the course was painful! How could she make that decision?

Of course, not all professors felt this way. She had learned the other day of a man in the Political Science Department who, two-thirds of the way through the semester, had cancelled the rest of the sessions on the grounds that they had been such good students they had already covered everything in the syllabus. The idea that more material in the course might have been appropriate never occurred to him. He probably wanted to spend the freed-up time working on his latest book. To Maggie the most remarkable thing was that he got away with it.

After showering and taking some aspirin, Maggie felt at least presentable to head up to campus. Her class went well; she was very good at using small groups in class, which allowed her to simply facilitate and focus the discussion. She was packing up to return home after her class when she received a call from Officer Fitzgerald.

At any other time, she would have welcomed the call as it might involve some new information. Today, all she wanted was to return to bed, pull the covers over her head, and sleep.

"Good morning, Dr. Bell. I hope I'm not disturbing you." Fitzgerald sounded more formal than usual, which immediately put Maggie on alert.

"No, not at all. What can I do for you?"

"I think you've already done it. We've had a visit from a reporter from the campus paper. Seems there's an interest in the Doris Redden case. Your influence, perhaps?"

"Well, I did speak to a student of mine who's on the staff. But, listen, I did warn you that I wouldn't let go. And besides I think I'm perfectly within my rights to discuss the case with other people."

"Don't go getting defensive. You're not in trouble. In fact, I do have some more information. Can you come down to the station today?"

"I'm on my way!"

All of a sudden, Maggie's headache seemed to disappear. She packed up her papers and headed out to the parking lot. She waved at Louise as she passed the department office, but did not stop to talk. She was usually anxious to hear Louise's latest complaints about the administration, but not today.

She parked in front of the police station and found Fitzgerald at the front desk, talking to the clerk. When he saw Maggie, he waved her to accompany him to his office.

"What have you found out?" asked Maggie.

"Whoa! Slow down. No 'How are you Officer Fitzgerald?' No preliminaries?"

"How are you Officer Fitzgerald? What have you found out?"

Fitzgerald laughed. "Okay, you win. We got a call from Mrs. Carpenter—I assume you spoke with her—asking us for the results of the tox screen. Well, I have the results here. You'll be disappointed to hear that there was nothing problematic about the results. In fact it confirms what we thought all along. There was no indication of poisoning, but when we learned of her allergies the ME did some further testing. She obviously had eaten a dinner containing shrimp before she went to the pool. Since she was allergic, she had a severe allergic reaction, which caused her death. Her falling into the pool was unrelated to her death—she just happened to be there when she had the reaction. The medical examiner has officially called the death respiratory failure due to an allergic reaction. Case closed."

Fitzgerald leaned back in his chair, arms behind his head, and looked at Maggie. "So, all your suspicions should be laid to rest and you can go back to life as usual."

"Are you serious? This doesn't make sense. She wouldn't have eaten shrimp, and even if she had shrimp for dinner, the reaction would've been immediate–she wouldn't have had time to get to the pool before the reaction set in. And if the reaction was severe enough to cause respiratory failure she would've died at dinner not in the pool. Besides, she always carried around her medicine so even if she had unknowingly eaten shrimp, she would've used the medicine as soon as she felt a reaction. This doesn't hold together. There are too many questions."

Maggie was out of her chair, pacing around the room, raising her voice with each word. "You can't accept that verdict. You've got to do more." She was almost in tears, realizing that her words were falling on deaf ears. It was clear that Fitzgerald was unswayed by the logic of her argument and that he would do nothing more.

"Look, I'm really sorry about your friend's death. There's just nothing more we can do. The case is officially closed, and even if I wanted to open it, I'd need something more than your suspicions. You need to accept the fact that your friend died of respiratory failure– nothing more nefarious than that. Go home, get some rest."

"So nothing I said raises any suspicions for you? You're content to believe it was purely accidental that a woman who had lived with allergies all her life, and who had *always* been careful about what she ate and knew how to treat an emergency, just eats something she shouldn't, doesn't use her medication, and dies–how many hours later? In fact, when did she eat and when did she die? Do you know that?"

"Dr. Bell, drop it. It's over. I'm sorry."

Maggie looked at him, shook her head, and left the room. When she arrived home she realized that her headache was back and that she was exhausted. She felt as if she had run the Boston Marathon. She undressed, closed the shades, and curled up under the covers to sleep for the rest of the day.

....

Dear Sam,

I need your sane, calm advice–and your arms around me. I don't remember ever feeling so low, and yet so angry. I know I should just let Doris's death go, but I can't. I try. I've gone out to the movies with Gail, I've had dinner with Sarah and Olympia, I'm working on a committee with Ben trying to establish a diversity requirement in the curriculum, but I can't shake the feeling that there was something wrong about Doris's death. The Dean told me that the university isn't going to do anything about the grievance that Doris had filed and the police told me that the case is closed: it was an accident caused by an allergic reaction to some shrimp she ate. When I pointed out all the problems involved in that conclusion, Fitzgerald—you remember him, the cop who was handling the Case— just looked at me as if I were an emotional female and told me to go home and get some rest.

I don't know what else to do. But I did talk to one of my students, who's a reporter for the campus paper. Maybe they'll be able to get farther than I did.

I miss you. Do you think you could come out here for our Spring Break? It's a strange time for a break as it's only four weeks before the end of the semester, but the weather should be a little better by then and I promise I won't be working the whole time!

Love, Maggie

Chapter 21

"Hi, Dr. Bell. Do you have a few minutes?"

"Come in, David. I want to thank you for speaking to the police. It didn't budge them, but at least it got their attention."

"That's what I wanted to talk to you about. One of our staff guys covered that memorial thing last month. He remembered someone like making some comments about like some trouble that lady had in the department. We'd like to follow up on that. Do you like know anything about that?"

Maggie couldn't stop herself from responding: "Please don't use 'like' so much! As for your question, all I can say is that there was an official complaint filed by Dr. Redden–that's public information. But now that she's dead, there's no further investigation."

"Well, we can use the Freedom of Information Act to get more information. We've been like–sorry–we've been successful in the past that way."

"Good idea. Let me know how that turns out."

David gathered his backpack and left the office as on a mission. It seemed that the possibility of doing investigative reporting had caught fire with David and the editorial staff of the paper.

Maggie considered whether she should have given more information to David. After all, he would find out that she had been working with Doris on the complaint. But she was still reluctant to influence him and the paper; let them discover the facts on their own. Then, if they had questions about the official grievance she could be more specific. But deep in her heart she desperately wanted to share her suspicions of Doris's colleagues. She would have to be especially careful not to interfere in David's investigative reporting.

....

That afternoon Maggie attended a department meeting where plans were being made to interview a candidate for a replacement for

Leo, who would be on a sabbatical leave the following year. Most of the department was there—in fact, everyone but Barbara. The schedule of interviews was set and the item for discussion was dinner: who would accompany the candidate to dinner that evening? Leo, of course, volunteered and everyone looked at Henry as the next logical person because of his interest in 17th century philosophers. However, when Henry said he had a previous appointment and couldn't attend the dinner, Toby volunteered to join Leo.

"Fine, that's set then," said Charles. "I'll make reservations at *Willows* and tell them to put the tab on the department's account. Remember, the university won't pay for alcohol, so the wine is on you."

Henry looked up. "Since when does the department pay for these dinners?" he asked.

"We've always done that. We pay for the candidate and two others. Obviously, you haven't volunteered before." Charles's usually calm voice had an edge to it. It was frustrating to deal with Henry, who seldom knew what was going on.

"Oh, well, in that case, I'll go."

Toby, in a typical attempt to fend off an escalation of tempers, volunteered to step down and let Henry go in his place, but Charles wouldn't hear of it. "No, we'll pay for three others this time," he bellowed, glaring at Henry.

Henry seemed oblivious of the impression he had given and simply asked about the next item on the agenda. Maggie, who found Henry and his excessive concern with trivial matters annoying, was amazed that he couldn't see how the others regarded him. To be self-interested was not unusual, but to be so blatant about it was.

The next item on the agenda was a discussion of Felipe's cognitive science proposal. To Maggie's surprise, Felipe was quite eloquent—and calm—in explaining why the program was needed and how it could be handled without harming the undergraduate program. There were the usual criticisms, most of which had been made before, but Maggie found herself being swayed by Felipe's presentation. No vote was taken at the meeting, but Felipe seemed more optimistic about the outcome than he had before. Perhaps he finally realized that he would get more support by answering the criticisms than by dismissing them as *piffle*.

The rest of the meeting was concerned with the usual request from

Dean Sweeney for information regarding enrollments, which was easily available on-line. Since the Dean's secretary didn't like to bother collecting the information, departments were asked to do the work for her. This annoyed the secretaries, who had enough to do and felt that she was just lazy. There was also the request from the Dean for a defense of why their classes were capped at 50. Since money to his college came primarily from tuition, and not external grants, he was concerned to maximize enrollments at all costs.

When Charles reported this request from the Dean, everyone groaned. "It's the classroom size, dummy!" said Doug. "How many times do we have to tell him that?"

"But we have to be careful about that. We don't want to be moved to larger classrooms in other buildings. We need to keep making the point about quality of instruction. How are we going to elicit discussion in class with so many students? It's difficult enough as it is. With more than 50 it'll be impossible." This came from Leo, who used the Socratic method of discussion in his classes.

"Well, I can handle an auditorium so I don't care how large you make my classes," volunteered Doug, who taught logic to freshmen. His charisma had made him a very popular teacher, and there were always students begging to get into his filled classes. There wasn't much discussion in his classes, but his lectures were well prepared and kept the attention of the room. The rumor was that he used sexual innuendos in his examples of logical fallacies, which endeared him to most students, but resulted in complaints from some of the women about his sexism.

"Yes, but you don't have to grade papers and essay exams. You have an assistant who does the grading for you. Even if I could generate discussions in a class of 100, I'd never be able to grade the exams and papers that I give," replied Leo.

"Well, change your requirements. Give multiple-choice exams, and omit the papers."

At this point, Leo's face started to turn a startling shade of red. He was fair-haired and fair-skinned, and any emotion easily showed on his face. But rarely did it reach that stage of red. "That's academically irresponsible. I'm not even going to respond to such a suggestion."

At this point Henry jumped in. "Of course it's academically

irresponsible. We should limit our classes to 10 so that we can let in only the best students. Then we'd have good discussions."

"Oh, my God," sighed Charles.

Leo looked at Henry and was about to say something when Ben interrupted, saying, "I think we're getting off the point. I agree with Leo that we should remind the dean about the limitations of the classrooms, but also stress the need of smaller classes for the pedagogy that's needed in most of our courses. Doug can do what he wants with his classes, but that won't work for most of us."

Charles looked at Maggie. "Maggie, I've been hearing good things about your classes and how you get the students to engage in discussion. Maybe you can give a presentation–not now, of course–on how you do that in a class of 50. Would you be willing?"

"Of course. But I'm not sure I do anything unusual; probably most of you do the same thing. But, sure, I'd be glad to do that."

The meeting ended on that note, and Maggie returned to her office to pack up and head for home. She was meeting some friends for drinks and wanted to check her phone messages at home before she joined them. There were no messages waiting and while she combed her hair and refreshed her lipstick, she thought about Sam. They had yet to confirm plans for Spring Break and Maggie was getting worried. She so wanted Sam to visit, to see where she was living, what she was doing, who her friends were. But if that wasn't possible, she had to make plane reservations to New York and make them soon. Taking one last look to check her hair, she left the apartment and headed to the *Penguin*.

....

Sarah was seated in a booth at the *Penguin* and looked up as Maggie entered. She was wearing a heavy blue sweater which brought out the blue in her eyes, a dark green woolen scarf around her neck, and her parka.

"Where are the others?" asked Maggie. "I thought I'd be late. Have you been waiting long.?"

"No, you're right on time. My meeting ended earlier than expected so I got here a little early. The others will be along–late as usual. Let's order; no sense waiting."

Sarah finally removed her parka, having warmed up sufficiently, and they ordered their drinks: scotch for Maggie, cabernet for Sarah. They were catching up on the week's events when Olympia joined them, followed shortly by Naomi. Merlot for Olympia, chardonnay for Naomi, who, clearly agitated, related the latest administrative idiocy, aimed, she was convinced, at making her life even more complicated.

Her department was conducting searches for five new faculty members and each one had a complication. On one of the searches, the faculty couldn't agree on whom to hire; on two of them, all of the candidates had turned them down; and on the other two, the department had made offers to candidates, who had accepted, but now the administration was claiming that some forms hadn't been properly filled out and was therefore holding up the appointments.

Naomi was fuming. "Don't they realize how difficult it is to get good people to come to a town like this? If we wait much longer, we'll lose these candidates. They probably already have other offers to consider, most likely in better places."

Everyone commiserated and contributed their latest examples of administrative idiocy. They were on a roll when Nina arrived. Dressed in her usual black tights, topped by a fake fur black coat, she looked even taller and thinner than usual.

"I'm sorry I'm so late, but rehearsals went on longer than I'd planned. Oh, I see you didn't wait," she said with a laugh.

Nina was quite particular with her wines and proceeded to interrogate the server with questions about the various wines, turning down a Robert Mondavi merlot as being too old, finally ordering, after examining the label to make sure it was of the right vintage, a Joseph Drouhin pinot noir, a French wine described by Nina as having cherry and licorice undertones.

By the time the drinks were finished, Naomi announced she was hungry and asked if anyone wanted to go out for dinner. All agreed, finished their drinks and headed for *Willows*. The evening had the feel of approaching spring, and the women talked of their plans for the following week as they walked down the street to the restaurant.

Willows was unusually empty for a Friday evening and they were seated right away. More drinks were ordered while the menu was examined. Maggie and Sarah ordered the salmon, Naomi the shellfish pasta, and Olympia the spanikopita, a specialty of the house. Nina took more time to place her order. Questions about the brand of bottled water served and about the preparation of the various dishes were asked and, after the server made many trips to the kitchen, answered. She finally ordered the salmon, but ended up returning it to the kitchen–too dry, and too much rosemary. Since there was nothing else on the menu that appealed to her that evening, she settled for a side dish of broccoli.

Maggie looked at the others to see if they thought Nina's behavior was over the top, but no one seemed surprised so she quietly ate her salmon, which she thought quite good. She noticed that Sarah, too, seemed to be enjoying her meal, as were the others. Naomi announced with each mouthful, "It's delicious," and Olympia claimed about her spanikopita: "It is very good".

When the dessert cart came around, Maggie claimed that she was too full, even though everything looked yummy. Sarah suggested that they all share a Death by Chocolate–a chocolate cake with fudge filling and chocolate ice cream on the side. Everyone agreed, except Olympia who said, "I think I will have the key lime pie."

Throughout the meal, the conversation was light-hearted, with many references to food and other restaurants in the area. Toward the end of the evening talk turned to the young student who was confronting faculty in their classrooms and offices. He was of the opinion that since the university was a public institution anything that went on there was open to the public and could be recorded. He would appear in classes–not necessarily those he was registered for–with a videocamera and attempt to record the sessions. Usually the conversations recorded went as follows: "You can't come in here with that camera," "Oh, yes I can. This is a public place and the public has a right to know what goes on in these classes."

In one instance, the instructor grabbed the camera out of the student's hands and angrily told him to leave the room. This had been caught on the camera, and shown on the Internet via YouTube. The student was filing charges of assault against the instructor–a young woman half his size–and the administration was trying to figure out what to do.

"They'll probably leave her out to hang," opined Sarah. "Anything to avoid negative publicity. It would be too much to expect the President to make a statement defending the integrity of the classroom. The only suggestion that was made by the administration was to lock the door if you didn't want anyone to interfere with your class—but the classroom doors don't have locks! Shows you how much they know about what goes on here."

"I saw the video on YouTube," Maggie added. "It didn't appear to me to be an assault at all. She grabs the camera away, but I didn't see her touch him, except maybe his hands where he was holding the camera. I heard that the downtown police didn't take the assault charge seriously and turned him away."

"Yes, and now he is asking the university to impose some penalty on her," responded Olympia.

"And Sarah is right," chimed in Naomi. "They don't know what to do so they're doing nothing. And that leaves her in limbo, not knowing if there's going to be some kind of reprimand."

"You know this has ramifications for the rest of us. I consider my classroom a 'safe' place where students can say whatever they're comfortable saying. I realize I can't guarantee confidentiality on the part of the other students, but if someone's comfortable giving their views on a controversial issue, or, for example, announcing that they're gay, I certainly don't think anyone has a right to record that—nor unless there was explicit permission granted. So I see this issue as larger than the question of whether or not he was assaulted. In fact, I'm inclined to think he should have been assaulted—although I wouldn't admit that publicly!"

When Maggie was finished talking, Nina looked puzzled. "I hadn't heard about any of this. When did this all take place?"

Everyone looked at her. It was Sarah, however, who replied, "Two weeks ago; it was in the local newspaper and the campus paper—and all over campus. You need to take time out from rehearsals and join the real world."

Nina, nibbling at the pieces of the remaining cake, nodded her agreement.

....

Dear Sam,

I had dinner with the women tonight. I have to admit that that's one of the plusses about this place. I've never before worked in a place where I had like-minded people around. Some are married or with a partner, but they are as willing to spend an evening out as the single women are. That never happened before. The only time I saw any of the married women at Bennett was when there was a social event where husbands were included. Maybe it has to do with children. None of the women that I've met here have young children to rush home to. The only one who seems somewhat restricted is Nina, who dashes home to feed her cats. But we've been somewhat successful in convincing her that they don't really have to eat at 5:00 every evening; they'll be fine if they have to wait until 7:00 or so.

Naomi was in her usual form this evening, relating every administration stupidity she encountered this week. One of the recent fiascos had to do with the new electronic forms for reimbursements. They were devised to cut down on paperwork, but it turned out that you couldn't fill them out on-line. So they had to be printed, filled out, and mailed back by snail mail. It not only didn't save paper, it took more time. Another example of a potentially good idea gone wrong because the people who would be implementing it were never consulted in its development.

A recent squabble had been about the book store's policy for buy-back of textbooks at the end of a semester. Some wise person had decided that the deadline for students to sell books back to the book store was the Friday before final exam week. Obviously, the possibility of students wanting to use their textbooks to study for final exams never entered this person's head.

Enough about the strange doings at Claxton. Have you thought any more about Spring Break? I know you're busy trying to get a show scheduled, so I'm not pushing. But I miss you!

Love, Maggie

Chapter 22

Last night had ended later than Maggie had planned, with more drinks than she should have had. She had planned on sleeping in, but those plans were shot when the phone rang at 7:00 a.m.

"Calm down, Helen, I can't understand you."

"I can't calm down, I'm so angry I wish I knew some good swear words to use. How could they conclude that she ate shrimp. She never ate shrimp. She was always so careful about what she ate, it's impossible to believe she would have eaten shrimp–or anything that could have been near shrimp. You don't understand; she was almost obsessive about it. We used to tease her about it, called her paranoid the way she would question restaurants on their preparations. And anyone who knew her had to know she was allergic to shellfish–she talked about it all the time. No one would have accidentally given her food that had shrimp in it. I *know* she didn't have shrimp for dinner. That autopsy is wrong! I tried to tell that officer the autopsy was mistaken, but he kept saying it had been double-checked and there was shrimp in her system. He just wouldn't listen, treated me like an hysterical woman."

Helen stopped to take a breath and Maggie used that opportunity to interject some hopefully calming words. "I'll try to get them to reopen the case. I have a reporter on one of the newspapers working on it." Not wanting to upset Helen any further, she didn't mention that it was a student reporter for a student paper. But it did seem to have the desired effect. Helen calmed down a bit. They talked about what could be done and after another thirty minutes Helen rang off, asking Maggie to keep her informed.

It was impossible for Maggie to go back to bed even though the apartment was cold and the bed was warm. She quickly showered and dressed, intending to descend on Fitzgerald once again, hoping he was in on a Saturday. As she was leaving the apartment, the phone rang.

As anxious as she was to leave, she couldn't overcome her obsession to answer ringing phones.

"Hello."

"Dr. Bell? This is Officer Fitzgerald. I wonder if I could have a few words with you. Could you come down to the station sometime today?"

He sounded less official than previously, in fact he sounded human!

"Well, yes, I think I could find some time. In fact, I was just on my way out–I could stop in now, before my next appointment. Would that work?"

"Perfect. See you soon."

....

Fitzgerald was waiting at the front desk when Maggie arrived at the station. Somewhat surprised at seeing him there, she started to tease him about being anxious to see her, but as his expression was so serious she just raised her eyebrows in anticipation.

"Come with me, let's go to my office." He led Maggie into his office, indicating a chair for her to use. "I've been reviewing the material we have on Dr. Redden's death. I need more information if I'm to investigate any further. The autopsy is clear: she died of respiratory failure brought on by an anaphylactic reaction to shellfish–shrimp, in particular. There's no question about that. Now, the question is how did she ingest the shrimp. Her sister–yes, Mrs. Carpenter called me– swears that it is not possible that she ate it. If she didn't eat it, I don't understand how it could be found in her system. Do you?"

Maggie put her hands up to her head and pressed hard on her temples. This was a gesture she unconsciously performed when she was confused. It was as if the pressure on the brain helped to pull her thoughts together. Talk about the mind-body connection! She sat that way for a few minutes; Fitzgerald, realizing that she was thinking and not just zoning out, quietly waited for her response.

"You said, 'in her system;' was it part of her dinner?"

Fitzgerald pulled out the autopsy report and turned the pages. Finding the section on the contents of the stomach, he stopped and looked at Maggie. "Yep, it's listed there. It seems she had shrimp and chicken in a salad. But, unofficially–to get you and that reporter kid off my back–give me some background as to why you think there might be foul play."

Maggie sat back, took a deep breath, and proceeded to tell him about the departmental environment that Doris worked in, including the lesbian-baiting and the pressure to get her fired. To her surprise, and admiration, Fitzgerald just sat and took notes–no facial expressions of exasperation or disapproval. Maggie reluctantly thought she might have to reexamine her prejudices against the police.

She got up to leave, having gotten a nod of agreement that he would look into the matter. Maggie suggested that he look into what Doris's activities were the day of her death: where she had dinner, with whom, what she ate, what time she arrived at the pool, was anyone else there, and so forth.

Fitzgerald sat back in his chair, and looking at Maggie said, with dripping sarcasm, "Thank you, Dr. Bell, for teaching me my job. Perhaps you'd like to join the department?"

Somewhat embarrassed, Maggie thanked him and, with an apologetic smile, left the office.

....

Dear Sam,

I so wish you were here. Helen, Doris's sister, called, and she was so upset I could only calm her down by telling her the newspaper was looking into Doris's death–I didn't tell her it was the student paper, though; that might not have impressed her as much. I then met with Fitzgerald. At least this time he seemed to take my suspicions seriously.

I'm meeting with Jessie tomorrow to see if she has any contact with people in the Athletics Department. Maybe they could tell us something about what goes on there. I have the feeling that some people think I've become obsessive about this, but at least Jessie hasn't written me off yet.

I'll be home all weekend, doing laundry and grading papers. Plug in your phone and call me; I need to hear your voice.

Love, Maggie

Chapter 23

"Hi, do you have time for coffee?" Maggie asked as she poked her head through Jessie's door. Jessie had been seated at her desk, reviewing the data on Women's Studies enrollments. She looked more frazzled than usual, most likely due to the pressure on her to prove once again that Women's Studies classes attracted enough students to keep the program alive.

"I don't want coffee, but I have time to talk. What's up?"

Jessie got up from her desk and motioned for Maggie to join her on the old couch in her office. "I haven't seen you this week–that's either good news or bad news. Which is it?"

Maggie laughed. "I guess it's both. I've been busy working on that article on friendship, so that's the good news. And I've been following up on Doris's death–that's either good or bad news, you can decide that. I thought I'd let you know what I've been doing. I've spoken to the police again and the guy in charge of the case–Fitzgerald–has finally agreed to do more investigating. The campus paper is also interested. But I'm not comfortable that they know what to look for. I need your help."

"You know you have it. But when you say the paper is interested–how did that happen?" It was unusual for the student newspaper to latch onto something like this without some outside "help," so Jessie waited for Maggie's response, while Maggie squirmed.

"Well, I did mention it to a student of mine who writes for the paper. I was careful not to put any pressure on him, or to give out any information that wasn't publicly available. I did consider the ethical implications of getting him involved, but I really don't think it was wrong to do so. I presented a possible story to investigate, and he was excited about it–as was the editor. Don't look at me that way; I didn't do anything wrong."

Clearly Maggie was reliving the original reservations she had about getting David involved. Jessie, smiling, just shook her head.

"I didn't say anything. You're defensive because you're not really sure you did the right thing. Maggie, don't be so hard on yourself. You didn't do anything wrong. The only issue with his being a student in your class is that you don't confuse his performance on this matter with his performance in class—and I have every confidence that you won't. Now, tell me how I can help."

Maggie leaned forward and thanked Jessie. "I think we need to find out what Doris did the evening she died. I was wondering if anyone in her department—the women, in particular—heard her say what her plans were. You know, like she was having dinner with someone, or she was checking something out at the pool that night. Were they surprised to hear that she was at the pool that late at night? Was that unusual? Did everyone know that she was allergic to shellfish? Have they heard anyone say anything since her death? I don't know—anything that might help. What bothers me is that her death is attributed to an anaphylactic reaction to shrimp which caused respiratory failure. They say she ate some kind of shrimp salad. But I just can't believe she would knowingly have eaten it. I don't know how else it could be in her system, and Officer Fitzgerald doesn't know—although he did seem interested when I asked him that question—but maybe someone could tell us something about swimming, or about the pool, or the locker room—something that could explain it. So, I thought—with your connections—perhaps you could arrange an informal meeting with some of the women in Athletics. It would be purely voluntary, of course, but, who knows, maybe there's someone who would like to talk about it."

"You think they put shrimp in the water?" Jessie asked with amusement.

"Of course not. But what about food in the locker room? That's not so outrageous. What if someone brought in some crackers and dip and the dip had shrimp in it and Doris accidentally ate some of it. That's not so far-fetched, is it?"

"Yes, it is. Even I know how careful Doris was about what she ate. I can't see her eating something without checking what was in it. But your idea about a meeting is fine. I'll see what I can arrange for next

Friday. It would be better if it were held off-campus; I'll invite people to my home."

"Thanks. I know I'm too wrapped up in this; that's why I come to you. Sam tells me not to do anything without discussing it with you first. I've obviously given an impression of you as a wise woman."

Jessie laughed at that and, rising, gave Maggie a hug before shooing her out of the office.

....

The next week Naomi and Maggie were walking across campus to a Women's Studies meeting, coming from a quick lunch at the student cafeteria. "Why do they have those benches over there?" Maggie asked. "You can't get to them with that fence there."

Naomi laughed, saying, "Why, they do that all the time. It's called 'lack of planning.' They put up those benches outside the library so people could sit and talk and then they put up a fence so no one can get to the benches. Once they repainted the lines in the main parking lot and then the next week re-tarred the whole surface–and then repainted the lines again. Who knows how much money that cost. After a while, you almost expect this idiocy. If something stupid isn't done each month, you worry what they're up to!"

Jessie had called a special meeting of the Women's Studies Board to make plans for their annual retreat, which was going to be held the next day at a rustic lodge Claxton owned and used for nature studies and such occasions as this. It was a time when they could all get together and plan for next year. It was usually well-attended, as it provided a pleasant venue away from campus where people could meet with like-minded others. It was often the only opportunity to get together with those whose schedules didn't match their own.

Jessie scheduled the retreat for the whole day: 10:00 to 5:00. Maggie knew that a good amount of time would be spent catching up and sharing experiences before any serious work could be started. But that was also a major function of such retreats. With everyone so busy, it was important to have a time when people could share their interests and concerns with colleagues who were on the same page, or at least in the same book. That was not to say that there were no disagreements within the group. Maggie was not looking forward to the usual disputes, often rising into outright quarrels, between Sarah and Gail, or the criticisms of Brandy, whom she felt Jessie tried to protect from the others.

....

It was Maggie's first retreat but she had heard that they were usually successful and sometimes fun. It started with the usual passing of the plate of cookies, which had almost become a sacred ceremony. Maggie often wondered what the response would be if Jessie failed to provide food at a meeting. Would they impeach her? Or worse?

When they were settled down with their coffee and cookies, Jessie started by asking how classes were going. In the past, this had resulted in some of the women sharing tales of outright hostility toward them by some of the men in their classes. There seemed to be less of this in recent years, but Jessie always gave them the opportunity for support if they were experiencing trouble in the classroom.

This year the only one who spoke up was Claudia, a new faculty member in the Education Department. She was a young woman just out of graduate school and looked even younger than some of her students, with her long blond hair and tight jeans. She explained that she had trouble with some of the women as well as the men in her classes. They were complaining about her grading being too strict and her lectures too boring. In fact, she had trouble keeping order in the classroom and often resorted to ending class early in order to avoid the chaos. She found the whole experience depressing and was worried how her colleagues would evaluate her for reappointment.

Gail jumped in. "You don't have to put up with that shit. You should report them to the dean."

Sarah disagreed. "Go to your chair first; you want to get the support of your department before you get the dean involved. But, if your chair—who is your chair?—doesn't do anything, then take it to the dean."

"My chair is Brad Kendrick," replied Claudia.

"Oh, well, he's not going to be much help," declared Naomi. "He's on the Council of Chairs and he never says a word. He doesn't even vote—just abstains. I can't see him sticking his neck out for anyone. You need to find someone in your department who will mentor you–you know, give you advice about how to handle those kids."

At this point, Jessie suggested that what was needed was a forum for new faculty–not necessarily only women faculty–on how to handle troublesome students in class. "Women, and some men, need to learn how to show authority in front of an audience. We don't need to become aggressive or arrogant, but we need to exude confidence, otherwise students lose respect. And we can't depend on colleagues in our departments to mentor new faculty; we should sponsor the forum, use our experiences to help them."

Everyone agreed that it was a good idea and Brandy volunteered to take responsibility for setting up the forum in the fall. Of course, as soon as Brandy spoke up, Gail volunteered to work with her. Maggie smiled. It was clear that there was no way Gail was going to let Brandy determine the composition and focus of the forum.

Once that was decided, Jessie turned to the agenda for the retreat. Class schedules for the following year were determined, suggestions for speakers to be brought to campus were discussed, and membership on committees was finalized

After such a productive morning, the group broke for lunch and a walk in the surrounding woods to look for wildflowers and other signs of spring. They found little to indicate that spring was close, except for a few crocuses in areas protected by the trees. When they reconvened, the conversation turned to the young man who had been attempting to videotape classes.

"What's the latest on that case?" asked Maggie.

Sarah brought them up to date. The police had dismissed his complaint, and, as she had predicted, the university did nothing. There was, however, a committee formed to look into the issue. "And we all know how useful these committees are. They'll produce a report, which will most likely be filed away in a safe place–never to be seen again."

"But what about the instructor? I'm assuming there was no disciplinary action taken against her–right?"

"As far as I know, nothing was done. I think the guy is still making noises about being assaulted, but I don't think anyone is taking him seriously."

The rest of the afternoon was spent discussing the various projects underway or in planning stages. It was always interesting to find out what people were working on; sometimes one found others who were doing research on related topics and collaborations were formed.

The retreat ended at five and, while some lingered to enjoy the quiet of the woods, most headed home to their family responsibilities.

....

Dear Sam,

The photos you sent me are fabulous. I'm not surprised that the Julie Saul Gallery offered you a show. That's a great gallery and they obviously recognize talent. The theme of playgrounds works beautifully. When you first told me what you were doing, I have to admit I couldn't visualize it. But now when I see them it's perfectly clear. It's like looking at a microcosm of children at play, including those who are excluded from play. I wish that the exhibit was later–during my Spring Break–but in any event I'll be there for your opening night.

My article is finally finished, at least a first draft. I'll make corrections this weekend, and then send it off. I guess that means I should start on the next one, but I find I'm so busy that I barely have time to keep up with classes. The weather has been warmer and the days aren't so gloomy—both of which help my mood. I can get out and walk without fear of freezing to death or breaking a leg on the ice. Did I always worry about these things before or am I truly getting old? Don't answer!

I went to the Women's Studies retreat today. They hold it in a really nice log house in the woods and we had time to check out the surroundings. The retreat was productive, but the best thing was meeting people I haven't met before. I might be alone in this, but I find Gail to be quite refreshing. It was amusing to see how she got herself on a committee just to make sure that Brandy wasn't in charge. It's a committee on helping people in the classroom, and Gail had previously told me what she thought of Brandy's teaching. I'm just glad she didn't share her opinion at the meeting.

Well, time for bed. I'll check on reservations and let you know what I find.

Love, Maggie

Chapter 24

When Maggie arrived at her office on Monday, she found a message from Sarah, inviting her to spend the weekend at a cottage she and her husband owned up north. Maggie had indicated interest in visiting when she was first told about it, but everyone was so busy that plans were never finalized.

As she prepared to return Sarah's call and beg off, citing too much work, the phone rang. It was Sarah following up on her invitation for the weekend. Sarah presented the doings of the weekend in such a tempting way that, even though Maggie had planned on using the weekend to get things in order before her trip to New York for Sam's exhibit, she accepted.

By Friday, the weather had finally cleared and they were on their way to show Maggie some of the beauties of the state–especially in the spring. Sarah was driving, with Maggie in the passenger seat. Nick was in the back seat, writing on a tablet. Maggie turned to him and said, "You're awfully quiet back there. What are you working on?"

Sarah looked at Maggie and smiled.

"Did I say something funny?" asked Maggie.

"No. Nick, tell Maggie what you're doing."

"I'm updating my list of publications in chronological as well as topical order," replied Nick. "Now if I write two more articles next year I will have twice as many publications as my age." Nick Marzetti was 59, so that meant that he had 116 articles published already.

"What about books?" Maggie mischievously asked. "What's your goal for books?"

"One every five years of my career. Since I started at 30 in the profession, by the time I'm 60 I should have six books published. When I finish this one, I'll have reached that goal–then I have another five years before I have to get another one out."

Maggie looked at Sarah with raised eyebrows. Sarah answered the look with a shrug. "He's nuts, what can I say?"

Nick was a portly, short man, with thinning black hair. He was still handsome, although overly sensitive about his height, his weight, and his hair. He had a great sense of humor–puns coming to him so naturally Maggie wondered if he had memorized a pun for every word in the dictionary. More importantly, he was a prolific writer, greatly respected in his field of contemporary American history. He was president of the Midwest Society of American Historians and a charter member of the Marxist Division of the American Historical Society. He was equally loved and hated–but by different constituencies. His books were used in major universities by progressive social scientists and his work was roundly criticized by those in the mainstream of academia. Sometimes it was hard to decide if he was more pleased by his supporters or by his detractors. He lived for confrontation. And yet he was one of the kindest, most generous men Maggie had known.

In true, but rare, Marxist fashion he cared little for material wealth, known to lend large amounts of money to needy students, who everyone could tell would never pay him back. His only valued possessions beside his books were his clothes. In a paradoxical way, he was a fancy dresser. He always appeared in a suit and tie for classes, never wearing the same suit more than once in a semester. Fortunately, he only taught two days a week, requiring only 30, rather than 45 suits! His sartorial splendor was compromised only once. Being color-blind, he was known to buy whole outfits together–suit, shirt, and tie coordinated by a salesperson. The story was that one day he appeared for class in a new pink suit–nicely coordinated with the appropriately colored shirt and tie. He thought he had bought a cream-colored suit. When people commented on his suit, saying, "What an interesting color," he put the suit away, never to be seen in it again!

When they arrived at the cottage, Sarah quickly turned up the thermostat. While the weather was turning mild, the cottage was still quite chilly, having had the heat turned down for most of the winter. Maggie was shown to the spare bedroom, where she unpacked her few belongings, and then joined the others in the kitchen.

The cottage was more a year-round house than a cottage, with three bedrooms, two bathrooms, a large kitchen/dining area, and a living room which overlooked a small lake. Maggie asked if the lake was good for swimming. Both Sarah and Nick shook their heads; no, it had too muddy a bottom. Sarah told the story of Nick taking some friends and their young daughter out fishing. When they returned, the young girl had jumped out of the boat, intending to help pull it to shore, and found she was knee-deep in mud. She thought it was funny, but the adults were not so amused. After that, children were not allowed to swim in the lake!

But, as Nick was pleased to report, it was great for fishing. And to prove his claim, he volunteered to prepare a fish dinner that evening. Sarah rolled her eyes. "Bass is not the best eating fish," she said. "But bass from this lake, the way I make it, is great," responded Nick.

Maggie kept silent. She had never eaten bass, but was game to try it. How bad could it be?

Nick then spent the next two hours in the kitchen, using every pot and pan available. He and Sarah had made a deal that each one would clean up after their own cooking, since their former deal–one cook, the other clean up–had proved disadvantageous for Sarah.

While Nick cooked, Sarah and Maggie went for a walk. There was still snow on the ground, but the unseasonably mild March weather had greatly reduced the snow banks on the side of the road. Sarah wanted to visit the local cemetery, which was only about a mile away. So off they went, with Maggie thinking this was a strange interest, but becoming used to the fact that anthropologists seemed to find fascination in the oddest things.

When they returned to the cottage, Nick had finished preparing the food and had already set the table. The bass, topped with a spicy tomato sauce, was served with fried potatoes and green beans; it was not something Maggie would order in a restaurant, but was quite edible and the sauce was extremely tasty. Accompanied by a fruit salad for dessert that Sarah had prepared and good conversation, the meal was quite pleasant.

After dinner, the conversation turned to the case of the missing manuscript. Nick had served on a committee with Jonathan Grimsky and found him to be slightly disorganized but generally okay. As Nick pointed out, he at least attended meetings and often had intelligent things to say. But he had a prissy, yet arrogant, way about him that turned people off. They speculated as to whether Grimsky's suspicion of Andrews was reasonable and concluded that, unless there was more animosity between the two men that they were aware of, it was highly unlikely that Andrews had stolen the manuscript.

Since neither Nick nor Sarah knew what the manuscript was about, Maggie took the opportunity to tell them about Aemilia Lanyer. When she was finished, Nick was now convinced that Andrews had stolen the manuscript.

"Why?" asked Maggie.

"We all know that Andrews is a right-wing conservative and a sexist. Surely he'd be opposed to any work pointing out that women had made any significant contributions to culture and therefore he wouldn't want Grimsky's manuscript to be published."

"Wow! That's quite a train of thought–lots of questionable assumptions, don't you think?"

"Not really," replied Nick. "Right-wing conservatives are typically sexist and do their damnedest to maintain the status quo. The status quo is sexist–do you deny that?–so it stands to reason that, given the opportunity, a right-wing conservative would do what he could to protect the status quo–ergo, prevent the publication of this kind of work."

"But, even granting your argument, how could he have done it? He was at a conference in Ohio when the manuscript was found missing."

"Ah, yes; the old 'at a conference' alibi," replied Nick, with a twinkle in his eye. "How do we know he was there the whole time? He could have slipped away, driven home, gone to the office he shares with Grimsky, stolen the manuscript, and then driven back. No one notices someone's temporary absence at these conferences; there are so many places one could be that it's hard to keep track. So, my scenario is possible, isn't it?"

"Possible, yes. But far-fetched. I don't know Andrews and I barely know Grimsky. So I'll reserve judgment for now."

At that point, Sarah rose, saying that she had heard enough speculation and was going to bed. Maggie agreed and they both went off to their rooms, leaving Nick to watch late night TV and fall asleep on the couch.

....

The next morning they all decided to show Maggie around the area, stopping off at some of the wineries later in the day. The cottage was located in an area of rolling hills and lakes. The trees were still bare, but every now and then crocuses could be seen popping up along the road. In more protected areas, a few blue violets and hypatica added color to the landscape. It was a big tourist area and the shops were just starting to open for the season. They visited a few boutiques catering to the trendy rich, and stopped off for lunch at an interesting vegetarian café. The food was delicious. There was a vegetarian ballotine–Maggie didn't know what that was–with artichokes and coarse mustard, "crab" cakes made with tempeh, and served with a sherry sauce, a salad of baby greens, frisse and watercress tossed with shallot and champagne vinaigrette, and a main dish of what seemed to be meat loaf, but was obviously made with tofu and other things. All of this was presented on beautiful platters and described in the most precious of terms: dollops, soupçons, emulsions, and reductions.

After lunch, they visited the area wineries. Wine making was no longer restricted to the great European vineyards; it seemed decent wine could be made anywhere. And they had many adequate samples as they tasted their way through the various wineries. Not being used to so much alcohol, by the time they arrived back at the cottage, Maggie found herself needing a nap.

They spent the evening watching a movie and eating popcorn, after a light dinner of spinach and crab salad. They were planning to leave early the next morning in order to avoid the traffic and so retired early.

Maggie called Sam, relating the adventures of the day, and then read for a while before turning off her light. She was glad she had decided to accept Sarah's invitation; she felt relaxed and ready to meet whatever the next day would present.

Chapter 25

Jessie had scheduled the meeting with the women in Athletics for the coming Friday. Maggie tried to concentrate on her classes and her manuscript, but found her mind wandering to a rehearsal of the coming meeting. After about an hour of preparing in her mind what she would say to these women, she realized she was wasting time. She wasn't going to give a prepared speech; she would be there to listen to what they had to say. Clearly, she needed to exercise some of that discipline she lectured her students–and friends–about. "Focus," she would say when they complained about not being able to concentrate on a project. "Make a list of what you have to do; organize it in temporal priority; and do it!" Well, now she had to take her own advice–focus!

Her classes were all prepared for the week; the "thought papers" her students had handed in last week were all graded, with copious comments on each paper indicating where they needed to add more argumentation and where they had done a good job. She found that, while many students never read the comments, some took them seriously and showed improvement in their subsequent papers.

There was a movement afoot, probably started in the English Department, proposing you have students do a lot of writing, without having to read all of it. They called it the "portfolio" system: students handed in a series of papers, only some of which the instructor would read and comment on. Since the students never knew which papers would be read, the assumption was that they would take all the assignments seriously, and the instructor would not be loaded down with a mountain of grading.

In Maggie's eyes this served two purposes: it allowed lots of writing to be required in large classes, and it certainly made it easier for the instructor. The system was gaining a lot of support from both faculty and administration: faculty because it cut down on their work, and administration because it justified increasing the size of classes. Neither of these reasons appealed to Maggie. It just seemed inappropriate to have students write something without the instructor at least reading, no less commenting on, it. She had no evidence that her method of assigning fewer papers but providing comments–including comments on spelling and grammar–on all of them, was productive of better thinking or writing, but at least she felt more comfortable in doing so.

....

Maggie was pleased at the group assembled in Jessie's living room on Friday evening. All three of the women in the Athletics Department had accepted her invitation to discuss Doris. They were all on adjunct appointments and, in addition to their coaching responsibilities, taught a few classes each semester.

Jessie invited them to sit in the chairs near the fireplace, which, although it was not a cold evening, gave a warm glow to the room and a feeling of comfort and safety. Maggie smiled, as she realized that Jessie was not above manipulating an atmosphere when it would serve her interests. It was important that the women feel comfortable, otherwise the evening would be a waste.

Snacks were placed on the table in front of the loveseat where Maggie was already seated. Maggie rose to introduce herself to the women and offered to get drinks for everyone. Wine, as well as soft drinks and coffee, was served and everyone sat back to get down to business.

"I think you all know why I've invited you here tonight. Maggie and I are puzzled about Doris's accident and we thought that you, having worked with her, could help us sort things out. I think you know that Doris had filed a sexual harassment complaint against the department. We're not in a position to know how she was treated in the department–only what she said to us–but you might have some first-hand information on that. Do you think that she was being treated unfairly?"

Marge, the oldest of the group, spoke first. "I've been here for almost thirteen years and if my husband didn't teach in the Chemistry Department, I'd have shoved this job long ago. It's clearly an old boys' group, but you can survive by doing your job and not getting involved. I used to go to department meetings, just to learn what was going on–

you know, trying to fit in, to show that I was a team player and willing to participate. Well, that stopped after the first year. They would look at me when I entered the room as if I had entered the men's locker room. I got the message! Now I do my job and go home."

Sandy was next to speak. "Well, this is just my second year here and everyone's been friendly enough. I have two small kids so I made it clear when I was hired that I couldn't do any committee work, or things like that, and they said that was fine."

"Of course, that's fine. That's what they want: women to be quiet and go away," Marge said.

"That's not fair. After all, we are adjuncts; we can't vote, so it makes sense that they wouldn't want us on committees or at department meetings." Sandy was an attractive dark-haired young woman, whose spandex outfit clung to every curve she had. Marge looked at her with a mixture of disapproval and sympathy, as if to say: wait until you're no longer young and attractive; then see how they treat you.

It was Bea who piped in: "Kevin used to be an adjunct when he first arrived but he was on important department committees and attended department meetings from the beginning, even before he became coach. In fact, he was quite accepted at those events and, if you check it out, you'll see that he had a very different schedule than the rest of us adjuncts had. He didn't have classes five days a week, spread throughout the day. That was one of Doris's complaints. Her schedule was more like ours than that of the men."

Jessie followed up on Bea's comments, bringing the focus back to Doris. "So you're saying that she was treated differently from the men in the department. Did you notice any outright hostility toward her? You know that she was receiving what seems like hate mail a few months before she died, right?

"She told me about the mail," replied Bea, "and I had seen the pictures on her office door. I knew she had complained to Jack–that's our chair–but as far as I know, nothing was done."

Since Maggie was already convinced that Doris worked in a hostile environment, she wanted to focus the discussion on the evening of Doris's death. But not wanting to seem overly anxious, she just nodded her head in sympathy and offered to get refills. Jessie was quicker on her feet and left to get the drinks.

Maggie took the opportunity to ask about the classes the women taught. Were they like typical classes or more like skill training? The women were glad to talk about each of their areas—tennis for Marge, basketball for Bea, and track for Sandy—in addition to the usual physical education courses they taught. Women's sports didn't have the same status as the men's even though universities were required to have them; thus, the women coaches were on different contracts than the men.

"Well, at least you didn't have to get wet every day," Maggie joked. "I imagine Doris spent most of her time in the pool."

"That's for sure. I remember her when she had long hair. She was constantly worried that between the chlorine in the pool and the hair dryer her hair was getting damaged. That's when she decided to go with short hair that didn't need a hair dryer, but she still insisted on wearing a bathing cap to protect her hair from the chlorine." Marge smiled at the memory. It was clear that she had been fond of Doris.

"But remember how she hated the amount of chlorine they used?" said Bea. "She always complained that it was too high, that it aggravated her sinuses. They wouldn't do anything about it so she bought herself nose plugs, which she used whenever she was in the pool. The kids thought it was a blast—their teacher with nose plugs—but she didn't care how she looked as long as she didn't have to deal with that chlorine."

Maggie looked at Bea and was about to say something when Jessie returned with the drinks. Jessie had overheard the conversation while she was in the kitchen and picked up where Maggie had left off.

"Are hair dryers provided in the locker rooms or do you have to bring your own? I'm assuming that you keep your personal items in your lockers, right?"

Bea responded, "Some people bring in their own dryers, but there are professional ones installed in the locker room. The trouble is that most of the lockers don't lock! So we don't leave anything of value in them. Just some lotions, extra socks, that sort of thing."

"Is the locker room restricted or can anybody go in?" asked Maggie, trying to keep the excitement out of her voice.

"Well, it's open to faculty and students. I guess anyone could come in, but I don't think that's been a problem. And it's locked after hours so you'd need a key to get into the room after five."

"And all the faculty have keys, right?"

"Sure. Even if we're not using the pool that's where we change our clothes, and do things like that."

"Do you know what Doris kept in her locker?" asked Maggie.

Marge looked at Maggie and frowned. "Are you thinking that her death wasn't an accident?"

"I don't know. But you know the official verdict was that she didn't drown, that she died from respiratory failure due to a reaction to shellfish. And I know she was allergic to shellfish and I've heard how careful she was about what she ate, so I don't understand how she could have knowingly eaten shrimp." Maggie had gotten up from her chair and was pacing in front of the fireplace by the time she finished. She took a big breath, sat down, and tried to get her heart beat slowed. She hadn't meant to say all that, but had gotten carried away with her frustration.

The silence that followed Maggie's outburst was broken by Marge. "It's funny. I didn't think much of it at the time, but that afternoon–the Tuesday before Thanksgiving–I ran into Doris in the hall outside her office. We talked about our plans for the long weekend–I was going to visit my son in Detroit, and she was staying in town. She had entered a swimming competition for women over 40 and was going to use the free time to practice. I remember teasing her about 'all work and no play' and she said that this competition was really important to her. She wanted to do well so that they couldn't say she was over-the-hill and use that to not reappoint her. She had laughed and said she wasn't going to work the whole time, though– in fact, she was going to have dinner with someone that evening. She had looked kind of coy, and when I asked her who she was having dinner with, she smiled and said, 'just a friend.' I assumed she had a date with someone and was pleased for her. But I don't know why she would have gone to the pool after a date–unless the date didn't turn out so well."

Sandy, who had been quiet for most of the evening, looked at Marge. "I saw her that evening, too–around seven. I had gone up to the office to get a sweater I had left there. We were going to leave town in the morning–I didn't have any classes on Wednesday, and we were getting an early start on our trip to my parents in Ohio. She was just leaving. She had street clothes on but was headed toward the locker room. I was in a hurry and we just waved at each other. It's funny how I forgot about that."

"Do you know who she was meeting? Was anyone else around?"

"No, I didn't see her with anybody. The building was kind of empty by then. I remember seeing the janitor emptying waste baskets, and–oh, I almost forgot–Kevin was in his office talking to Jack. I remember jokingly telling them to go home, and then I left. My kids were in the car and I was hurrying to get back to them; we were going to the Dairy Queen for a treat."

The rest of the evening was spent sharing remembrances of Doris and her problems in the department. When Jessie asked if they thought Doris had been a lesbian, Marge and Bea claimed that they had never even thought about it; however, Sandy had heard the rumors and considered it a possibility. Maggie thought that perhaps their different responses were due to the generational difference between them; perhaps it was due to a reluctance for Marge and Bea to acknowledge the possibility. Women in athletics always had to deal with lesbian-baiting and many of the older women had made a point of, at least publicly, leading a traditional heterosexual life. The policy of "Don't ask; don't tell" had informally existed way before it was introduced into the military.

After the women left, Maggie stayed behind to help Jessie tidy up. Jessie's husband, Mark, came out of his study to join them in a glass of wine.

"Well, how did it go?' he asked. He was a tall, thin man with white hair and gray eyes. He was wearing what Maggie would have called a short robe, but what he called a "smoking jacket," over gray trousers. He was older than Jessie by about twenty years, but walked with a firm step and erect posture. Together they made a handsome couple and their devotion to each other was obvious. The looks they exchanged and the way they casually touched each other when moving around the kitchen spoke volumes about the nature of their relationship. He had been Jessie's graduate advisor and they had married as soon as she had received her degree. Their two children were grown with children of their own, and Mark was trying to convince Jessie to join him in retirement and spend time traveling and playing with the grandchildren.

"Well, we did get some interesting information," Jessie replied. "But I don't know if it gets us any closer to figuring out what happened."

Maggie was silent. Mark looked at her. "What are you thinking, Maggie?"

"I don't know—I need to think about all this. I also need to go home and get some sleep. Thanks for doing this, Jessie." She hugged Jessie, waved at Mark, and left.

When she arrived home, she found a message from Sam waiting for her. She returned the call and spent the next hour recounting the events of the evening and listening to Sam discuss the preparations being made for the big opening. They discussed plans for Maggie's upcoming visit, trying to cram as much as they could into the two days that she would be in New York. When Maggie hung up, she went straight to bed, falling into an exhausted sleep.

Chapter 26

Maggie couldn't shake the feeling that she had learned something significant last evening. But she didn't know what it was! She would just have to let it simmer and rise to the surface when it was ready.

Well, she had lots of things to think about. She had procrastinated long enough and had to make reservations for Sam's exhibit next weekend, prepare a guest lecture in Ben's class on how gender and race issues were often played off against each other, leaving those at the top secure in their position of dominance, and she had to do her laundry.

Sam had decided not to visit for Spring Break. Maggie was disappointed, but understood that the upcoming exhibit was paramount in Sam's mind, who had been trying for more than a year for a New York gallery to grant an exclusive exhibit. Now that it was a done deal, it was understandable that Sam would be nervous, having second thoughts about the quality of the photos, their arrangement, and other details. But it still hurt. Sam hadn't visited Maggie and while they wrote and spoke to each other frequently, she couldn't help wondering if something was wrong. They had had a wonderful time at Christmas and she had left feeling that they were as close as ever; but recently she had noticed a reticence on Sam's part. She attributed it to the upcoming exhibit, but still a nagging doubt remained.

She and Sam had been together since they were both students at Columbia. What had started as two friends interested in what the big city had to offer turned first into a mutual affection and then a deep love that has lasted for more than nine years. Considering that Sam was a photographer and looked at things with an artist's eye, and that Maggie was a philosopher who approached things with an analytic mind, it was all the more remarkable that they got along so well. But they did, and Maggie hoped that her fears were unfounded.

She spent the morning on-line trying to find a cheap flight to New York for the upcoming weekend. She knew she shouldn't have waited so long to make the reservations. It was going to be expensive, but she had to be there for the opening of Sam's show. Perhaps when the pressure was off, Sam would be more receptive to visiting at Spring Break. That would save Maggie from making two trips to New York.

Having succeeded at getting a ticket that would cost less than half a month's salary, she proceeded to the next item on her agenda–laundry. The apartment she rented did not have any laundry facilities so she used the laundromat down the block. *Jiffy Wash* was geographically convenient, but personally inconvenient. It closed at 6:00 p.m. and was busy during the hours that were more convenient for her. She usually took a book to read as the pile of laundry accumulated took almost three hours to complete. She realized that if she didn't procrastinate it wouldn't take so long, but laundry never seemed to get to the top of her "to do" list.

Today she used the time at *Jiffy Wash* to prepare her lecture for Ben's class. It was a topic she had lectured on many times before, but she liked to tailor the talk each time to the audience. Ben had told her what the students were reading, and what they had already discussed, so all she had to do was organize her remarks and decide which examples would work best for the class. By the time her laundry was done she had completed her notes for the lecture.

Sorting the laundry at home reminded her that she hadn't cleaned the apartment in two weeks, so the next hour was spent vacuuming and dusting, and trying to condense the jumble of papers into some sort of organized piles. Having accomplished the cleaning, and partly accomplishing the organizing, she realized she had not eaten anything since her morning coffee. It was now after 3:00, and she had made plans with Naomi for dinner so a real lunch was out of the question. She looked in vain for some fruit, opened the refrigerator to find only some old cheese and juice and some stale crackers in the cupboard. Eating some of the stale crackers and old cheese, she resolved to get to the grocery tomorrow.

....

At 7:00, Maggie met Naomi at *Willows*. As usual, Naomi had some departmental crisis she had dealt with the day before. This time, it was a disagreement between two of the men in her department that had escalated into a fist fight. They were both well over six feet tall, and in good form. While Naomi was a tall woman, she was clearly no match for the men. Even so, she tried to get between them without realizing that, given the state that they were in, they were just as likely to hit her as each other. She hadn't wanted to get the campus police involved as that would result in disciplinary action against at least one, perhaps both, of the men. And she was reluctant to call Dean Sweeney as he would most likely call the police. So she did what seemed reasonable: she got on a chair and yelled at the top of her voice "God damn it, stop!" That got their attention. When they realized that the secretary was crying, and the student workers were looking aghast at them, they came to their senses. They looked at Naomi on the chair, and sheepishly raised their hands in acknowledgement that the fight was over. It took probably five minutes total from beginning to end, but the aftermath lasted the rest of the afternoon. The secretary was so traumatized Naomi had to send her home, not sure that she would return on Monday, and after the men left Naomi retreated to her office with instructions to the students that she was not to be disturbed.

By the time she met Maggie for dinner and related the episode to her, she was able to laugh at the absurdity of it.

Maggie listened with amazement on her face. She had been fortunate to have grown up in a home where there had never been any sign of physical violence. The worst thing she had experienced was when her father had pounded the table when he heard that Bush had been elected–or, as he said, "stolen the election." Of course, she had heard about violence in the years she spent on the board of the domestic violence shelter, but that was different than experiencing it herself. The idea that two professors would come to blows amazed her.

"What were they fighting about?" she asked.

"Oh, something so trivial it's not worth going into. No one knows who threw the first punch, but as far as I'm concerned they both behaved like children. I sometimes wonder about these really big guys. Do they feel more comfortable resorting to violence because they feel less vulnerable? I don't know. I just hope that they're embarrassed enough to behave themselves."

They ordered their dinners–a combination of appetizers that Naomi ate with great relish. Her pronouncements of "delicious" were accompanied by such moans of delight that it reminded Maggie of the famous scene in *When Harry Met Sally* where Meg Ryan shows Billy Crystal that it is possible for women to fake orgasms. Maggie hoped that Naomi was also just faking it.

The rest of the evening was spent discussing Jane Austen and the Masterpiece Theater production of *Pride and Prejudice* that had been on the previous weekend. Naomi was a Jane Austen fan, having read all of her books, and she was concerned about the portrayal of Darcy in the TV production. Maggie had seen the program, but had not read the book since high school, and so had no strong opinion about the portrayal of Darcy except that Colin Firth was good-looking–not the kind of literary criticism Naomi was looking for.

It was after ten when they left the restaurant and the air had a faint smell of burning wood. The days were mild, but the evenings were still chilly and many people were still using their fireplaces. Spring was taking its time in coming this year.

. . . .

Dear Sam,

Well, just one week and I'll be in New York, celebrating your coming out as the next great American photographer. I know you'll be too busy–and nervous–to want to do anything before the exhibit, but we should do something special afterwards. Perhaps share a Famous Ray's pizza–I haven't had a good New York pizza since I left. Here, they think it's kosher to put ham and pineapple on it. Well, maybe kosher's the wrong word!

Speaking of food, there was a funny incident the other day regarding food. Doug, the one who dates his students, had gone to a Woody Allen film festival in Chicago this past weekend. He was in the department lounge yesterday and asked me why people in the audience had laughed at the scene where Diane Keaton orders a pastrami sandwich with mayo on white bread. What could I say except that everyone knows that pastrami goes with mustard on rye bread! I shouldn't be so flip, though. People here thought that my request at the student picnic last month for sauerkraut on my hot dog was bizarre.

But enough about food. It's your day, so whatever you want to do–or not do–is fine with me. See you soon.

Love, Maggie

Chapter 27

When Maggie arrived in New York, the city was shedding its winter coat, as were the people. Little remained of signs of winter except the occasional pile of dirty snow in dark alleys protected from the sun. Trees that just a few weeks before had been bare, were now filled with buds ready to burst into bloom. Birds could be heard outside of Sam's third floor loft as Maggie and Sam were having their coffee. Sam had made a special trip to the bakery before Maggie awoke to surprise her with freshly baked asiago croissants, her favorites.

Maggie had arrived the previous night, anxious to see Sam. Email and phone calls were one thing, but she would be able to understand much more when she could look at Sam. Was it simply worry or were feelings changing? They knew each other so well that a look told more than words.

They were preparing to go to the gallery to supervise the hanging of Sam's photos. The gallery had a professional "hanger," but often the artists had special requests for arrangements that they thought showed their work at its best. After they finished there, they had the day free until the exhibit opened that evening. Maggie could tell that Sam was nervous. She was wise enough not to initiate a discussion about their relationship before the exhibit. She didn't have what was considered an artistic temperament, but she had enough experience with Sam and other artist friends to know that timing was important. You would never want to ask them what they wanted to do "later" when they were engaged in their creative activities. At best, you would receive a shrug, at worst, a glare. And sometimes, you wouldn't even be acknowledged. Maggie had learned not to be hurt when Sam was so caught up in work that her presence wasn't even noticed.

They spent the afternoon browsing in the various galleries in SOHO, Maggie enjoying the various displays, Sam comparing the arrangements to the ones for the exhibit. "Do you think I should have placed my photos spread out like that instead of in groups?" It was clear that Sam was feeling insecure; after all, it was the first exhibit that would determine if there would be others. So much depended on the reviews one got at the first showing.

"I think the way you set them up is perfect. It tells a story; spreading them out would lose the power of the story."

Sam looked at her and took her hand. "Thanks. I guess I'm being a pain. After tonight, I'll be better."

"I think you're fine right now."

....

Maggie had bought a new dress in Michigan, which she hoped looked appropriate in New York. She wanted to look sophisticated, slender, and sexy–she hoped she succeeded in at least one of those areas.

The exhibit at the *Julie Saul Gallery* was a success. Of course all of Sam's friends and fellow artists were there. The gallery director had publicized the event in the major newspapers, and the gallery was filled to capacity. The typical fare of wine and cheese was served and everyone appeared impressed by the display. But the most important part was the appearance of Flo Jannings, the eminent photographer, whose opinion was more important to Sam than that of all the others in the room. Jannings could make or break a person's career.

Sam tried to look nonchalant, to exude an air of confidence–and partly succeeded. Only Maggie and close friends could see beneath the cool exterior to the underlying tension.

Maggie tried to keep an eye on Sam, while also keeping her distance. She panicked at one point when Jannings stood looking at one of Sam's smaller photos–the one Maggie liked the best. It was of a small boy sitting on a swing, while a group of similar-aged children played tag. The longing on the face of the child, the sense of being an outsider, was beautifully captured in the photo. Jannings looked at the photo for what seemed an eternity and then took out a small book, wrote something in it, and moved on.

Jannings showed no emotion as he moved around the room, examining each photo. No smile, no nodding head, nothing. Maggie could see that Sam was worried, but she could do nothing to help. Sam would have to deal with whatever the verdict was. Maggie thought that

Sam had enough confidence to keep at it, but it would be so much harder if the verdict were negative.

When Jannings finished his tour of the room, he retrieved his coat and walked over to Sam. They engaged in conversation for no more than a minute, and then Jannings left. Maggie couldn't contain her curiosity; she had to know.

"What did he say?" asked Maggie.

Sam, trying to maintain that air of nonchalance, shrugged. "Oh, something about showing my work at the *SOHO Photo Gallery*. He gave me his card—he judges for them and is going to ask them to give me a show!"

At this point, Sam's nonchalance evaporated and Maggie ended up engulfed in a big hug. The rest of the evening went by in a haze, followed by a celebration at the local bar with friends. By the time Maggie and Sam returned home, they were too exhausted to engage in any serious conversation and so went to bed, but not to sleep.

....

They slept late the next morning and lolled around, talking about the success of the exhibit and Sam's plans for the *SOHO Gallery*. Which photos would work best? What kind of work did they prefer? Maggie's plane didn't leave until 8:00 p.m. so that gave them the afternoon to visit the gallery, assuming that it, like most others, was open on Sundays.

The gallery was advertising a "Krappy Kamera Show" for the next few months, focusing on photos produced with equipment from the lowest end of the technological scale. As it said in its brochure, "The concept underlying this show is that in the hands of an artist, any piece of equipment can be used to create engaging photographs."

Sam was excited. All sorts of ideas came to mind. Maggie could see that for the rest of the afternoon Sam would be visualizing different shots and ways of arranging them. She reconciled herself to the fact that talk would not be productive.

When she was settled into her seat on the 8:00 p.m. flight, after having spent the rest of the afternoon listening to Sam's ideas about new shots, she found herself strangely contented. Yes, they hadn't had a chance to discuss their relationship, but the status seemed unchanged. She closed her eyes and woke only when they announced their imminent arrival in Detroit.

Chapter 28

The week since her return from New York had gone without incident and Maggie had been able to catch up with her writing. Her classes went well and she was getting ready to have coffee with Toby to hear his defense of a view she found problematic when David appeared at her office.

"Hi, David. I didn't see you in class today. Are things okay?"

'Yeah, I'm sorry about that. I'll get the notes from Josh. But I've been like real busy with this investigation stuff. It's like unbelievable what I'm finding out."

Maggie didn't comment on David's grammar again; she was anxious to hear what he had to say without interruption.

"I've been speaking to some of the guys in the Athletics Department—you know, guys on the teams—and boy do they have tales to tell. Some of the guys on the baseball team were like telling me about the jokes that go on in the locker room about the women coaches—in particular, about Dr. Redden. And they say that their coach is like present when these jokes are told and just laughs along with them. And I also talked to some of the women on the swimming team—my girlfriend's roommate is on the team—and it gets even worse. First, I found out that the women like don't get the same amount of money for dinners as the men when they have 'away' games and that Dr. Redden had like requested more money for them, but was refused. Then I learned that some of the men in the department would like go down to the pool when the women were practicing and make comments about like how they looked. In particular, laughing at how like Dr. Redden looked in a bathing suit with her nose plugs and bathing cap. It seems like the nose plugs really got them going. My girlfriend's roommate said the women on the team all felt sorry for Dr. Redden, but like didn't know what to do about it.

"But the most important thing I learned was that they—some of the men in the department—like wanted to get rid of her so that they could like hire some guy who coaches swimming at Central State. I couldn't find out names, but I did find out that the chair, Jack Sommers, was behind all this. I got that from one of the students who like works in the department office. She's a journalism major and is in some of my classes and we like got to talking about the Athletics Department and Dr. Redden's death and she just like told me things."

It took all of Maggie's self control not to comment on David's use of 'like' in every sentence, but she managed to focus on the content of his report. Not wanting to show how excited she was, she praised David for his information, told him to continue his investigating, and admonished him for skipping class.

....

By the time she met Toby for coffee, she could barely concentrate on their conversation. Toby was explaining the theory of "verstehen" or empathy—the method of understanding a person or situation by imagining that you are that person or in that situation. It has its application primarily in the behavioral or social sciences, but Toby was arguing that it was a perfectly appropriate method to use in the natural sciences. He had given a guest lecture in one of Maggie's classes last week and had started by saying "Imagine that you are a rock in a river." Then he would pretend to be a rock, drawing himself up into as close to the shape of a rock as is possible for a human. "Now imagine the water and the wind and the sun beating down on you for years, maybe centuries. Imagine how you would feel." All of this was accompanied by various contortions of his body, trying to simulate a rock being beat upon by the water, wind, and sun. His point was that you could establish causal connections and make predictions about rocks on the basis of this experience.

Needless to say, the students had difficulty in imagining themselves as rocks and giggles were heard from the back of the room. Maggie had shot the gigglers a warning look, but she sympathized with their difficulty. She, too, had trouble imaging herself to be a rock. What would it be like to be a rock? In fact, what is it to *be* a rock? Do rocks experience anything? She could imagine *herself* being in the river, with the water, wind, and sun beating down on her. She could also imagine the effects of the water, wind, and sun on a rock. But she couldn't imagine *being* a rock!

After a respectable time listening to Toby defending his position and making appropriate responses, Maggie excused herself, citing a previous appointment for her hasty retreat. She was on the way to see Fitzgerald.

....

"I've been doing some research on shrimp." Maggie was seated in Fitzgerald's office and held a handful of papers she had removed from her briefcase. " Did you know that shrimp is a member of the crustacean family? So are lobster and crab, but not mussels."

"And your point is?"

"Well, that's just a bit of information I found on the Internet. But I've also found out that one could have an allergic reaction to shrimp from injecting as well as ingesting–eating–it."

"I know what ingesting means, Dr. Bell."

Maggie realized that she had offended Fitzgerald, and hastened to make amends.

"I'm sorry; I'm so used to explaining what words mean to students that I forgot whom I'm talking to. Anyway, it's clear to me that Doris didn't eat the shrimp, but what if it was injected? That could make it appear that she ate it, couldn't it? Did the ME look for puncture marks?"

"That's a standard part of any autopsy. No puncture marks."

"Well, there's one other possibility. I saw it on a TV show–CSI. I won't go into detail, but it showed how stuff could be transferred to the blood through a mucous lining. Doris used nose plugs when she swam. Everyone joked about that. What if, somehow, shrimp got put on the nose plugs? That would explain how it was in her system without her eating it."

Maggie looked at Fitzgerald for his reaction, fearing ridicule. He didn't laugh. He just looked at her, then looked down at his hands on the desk. It was clear to Maggie that he was trying to decide what, and how, to say something. Having trouble dealing with the suspense, Maggie interrupted his silence. "It's not as far-fetched as you think. It's possible…"

Fitzgerald put up his hand to stop her. "Please, don't say anything for a change." He was silent for another minute and then said, "Nose plugs, though. How would it have gotten on the nose plugs? I don't mean who, at least not yet, I mean how. Rub a piece of shrimp on them?"

"How about shrimp paste? You can get tubes of shrimp paste in fancy gourmet stores. I don't know if it has much of a smell–not like anchovy paste, I'm sure–but I bet a very little bit would be sufficient to cause a severe reaction in someone so allergic to shrimp."

"But the shrimp was found in her stomach. I don't see how rubbing paste on nose plugs–and that is rather far-fetched–would show up as part of her dinner. Go home and let us handle this."

"Have the ME do a RAST test." Here Maggie pulled out a slip of paper from her purse and read: "radioallergosorbent test–it's supposed to measure the amount of immunoglobulin E antibodies in the blood–and I guess that tells you if there was shrimp present that caused the antibodies."

"Hold up, you're getting ahead of yourself. Obviously, you've been reading up on this, but we already know that she tested positive for the presence of shrimp. I bet that RASP test…"

"RAST"

"Whatever. I'm sure that test was already done by the ME. But that's irrelevant. It was in her stomach; obviously she had eaten it."

Maggie reluctantly conceded the point, but was not ready to give up. "Well, okay, but how would she have eaten it? Look, she would have had to knowingly eat it, accidentally eat it, or unknowingly eat something given to her. There's no way she would have knowingly eaten it, and no way, given how careful she was, would she have accidentally eaten it. So, that leaves the only other possibility I can see: she was unknowingly given it to eat by someone else."

"Dr. Bell, as usual your logic is fine, but your facts are weak. We don't have any leads on that part. Do you? Look, if you know something, I need to know. If it's only suspicions we can't do anything. We need evidence, we need to know where to get evidence. So far, we've got nothing–certainly no reason to question anyone."

Maggie put her head in her hands and just sat there. She looked up at Fitzgerald, took a deep breath and started to talk. She told him about the harassment Doris had been receiving; she told him about the visit to the Provost by some of the men in the department who were trying to get her fired; she told him about the locker room being open to anyone in the department, about Doris's "date" that evening, about her practicing for the swimming competition, and about the rumor that she was being fired to make place for someone. She wasn't at her most articulate, going back and forth between details. She would have been embarrassed at the disorganization if it had been a class lecture, but Fitzgerald listened patiently, asking questions for clarification when necessary.

"Okay, tell me about the harassment. About the department."

....

Maggie left Fitzgerald's office with the sense that, finally, something would be done. At least a serious look into the Athletics Department. And yet at the same time she felt frustration. How could she help? It was clear that Fitzgerald didn't see her as a partner in this enterprise—a nuisance would be more accurate. The sensible part of her agreed that she had done what she could and the rest was up to the authorities; but that other part of her, the part that typically got her into trouble—but provided most of the satisfaction in her life!—reminded her that in the past an "unofficial" approach had often proved more productive than an official one. By the time she reached her office, she had decided to contact Marge and get a first-hand impression of what was going on in Athletics.

Her call to Marge had to be delayed. Sitting outside her door, with a worried look on his face, drumming a pencil against his knee, was David.

"David, what's wrong?" Maggie was taken aback at David's appearance. He seemed so much more vulnerable than he had that morning. His excitement at investigative reporting, his bravado, had disappeared. She saw before her a scared young man. Had she gotten David into trouble?

"Dr. Bell, I'm sorry to bother you, but I didn't know who else to talk to."

Maggie's nervousness showed in fussing with her keys, trying to open her office door. She finally succeeded and motioned for David to come inside. When they were both seated, she turned to him and asked, "What's happened?"

David took a deep breath, leaned forward in his chair and replied, "You remember I like told you of my talk with a friend who like works in the Athletics Department office? The one who like told me about wanting to get rid of Dr. Redden?"

"Yes, I remember."

"Well, she was just like fired. Sommers, the chair, said that she had like behaved unprofessionally in talking to the press—even though nothing has been printed; and my girlfriend's roommate was just like kicked off the team for the same thing. I feel terrible. But that's not all. Some of the guys on the baseball team that I talked to are like angry at me. It seems they like got a real talking-down from the coach about talking to the press. They didn't like get kicked off the team, though, not like the girl."

Maggie knew this was not the time to praise him for the one correct use of "like" nor to comment on his use of the term "girl." There was a time to be quiet, and this was one of them.

"Do you think their anger could get ugly? Do you think it could turn violent?"

"Nah, I don't think so. If they had been like kicked off the team, then yeah. But they're just staying away from me now. Maybe they'll like make some remarks if I run into them at the bar, but I can handle that."

"David, you've been a great help. The information you gave me has convinced the police to look further into Dr. Redden's death. You can back off now. Let the police handle it."

David looked at Maggie, took a deep breath and smiled. "Hell, no. There's clearly something going on there. My editor thinks so, too. We're like going to do what we can. This is bigger than we ever thought. It could be like a major event for the paper. Just think, if we had like the first report on how Dr. Redden's death wasn't an accident, but murder. And if we could like name the murderer, that would put us over the top!"

David's enthusiasm scared Maggie. She spent the next ten minutes, explaining how if it was a case of murder, investigating it would be dangerous for him. She tried to explain that he could still write an article about the results of the investigation, and the important part he played in it, without doing anything more. He just had to have patience.

David looked down while Maggie was talking. When he looked up, he smiled. "I know you're like trying to protect me. But I'll be okay; I promise I'll be careful."

After David left, Maggie just sat at her desk, doing nothing, just sitting. One couldn't even describe what she was doing as thinking. She was blank; just sitting there. She felt drained and yet overwhelmed; too exhausted to move and yet too wound up to stay still.

The last time she had felt this way was when her father was dying and the family had to make the decision whether or not to remove him from the feeding tubes keeping him alive. He had been in a coma for four days, kept alive by machines that performed the functions his body used to perform for itself. Maggie and her mother had made the decision to remove those machines and just leave in the feeding tube to see if he could manage on his own. He did. His heart continued, his breathing continued, but he still remained in a coma. Maggie and Vivian went back and forth: he could come out of it; but what if he were brain-damaged, or completely dependent on others? He wouldn't have wanted that; but what if he were perfectly fine and could live a normal, or near-normal, life? How could they make such an important decision without knowing what the results would be?

The doctors tried to be helpful, but they could only quote statistics. There was a 10% chance he could come out of the coma and be able to resume some sort of life—but they were sure it wouldn't be life as he had known it, as he had suffered significant brain deterioration.

He had been a strong, active man, with a great passion for life. Even though he had never gone to college, getting a job and a wife as soon as he finished high school, he encouraged Maggie through all of her education. He delighted in listening to her discuss what she was studying—even philosophy!—and actually enrolled in some night classes at Boston University to get some, what he called, "culture." Would a man like that want to live a greatly diminished life?

After the 6th day of the coma, Doctor Jones, an African American young man who looked younger than Maggie, reported that there was a decline in Paul's brain activity and that full recovery was near impossible. Would they approve removing the feeding tubes, which were keeping him alive?

Maggie couldn't help but bring up the distinction between passive and active euthanasia, asking if they were going to do that, wouldn't it be more humane to simply painlessly end his life with an injection of something. Dr. Jones assured her that there would be no pain; they would keep him comfortable, but he would die "naturally" within two days. He pointed out that research showed that removing the feeding tube didn't lead to a more painful death; it just allowed the patient to die a natural death.

Maggie's mother wasn't convinced. "It'll be like starving him to death; I can't do that," she cried. Dr. Jones, while young, had the compassion that usually comes with years of consoling bereaved families. He sat down with her and took the time to explain that it would not be like starving to death, which was painful. As he explained, as one approached death most people did not want food, that they quickly became dehydrated, and while they might take sips of water to satisfy their immediate thirst, they did not crave enough water to prevent dehydration. He made it clear that her husband would not be starving to death, would not feel any pain or serious discomfort, but would just ease into death.

Whether Vivian was convinced, Maggie would never know, but at 10:00 that night they finally agreed to have the tube removed. Paul died the next morning. They never spoke of their decision again.

....

Dear Sam,

I think I made a fool of myself with Fitzgerald today. I obviously got carried away with my theory about Doris's death, and he rightly pointed out my inconsistencies. But, the good news is that he actually asked for some background about the Athletics Department and the reasons for my suspicions. I was able to tell him what I had heard about Doris's last evening— her mysterious date, her plans to practice for the upcoming swimming competition, and some of the harassment she had been subjected to. So I guess my wounded dignity was a small price to pay if he actually investigates further. After I left, I ran into my student reporter, who gave me some more examples of what has been going on in that department. I'm quite concerned about his safety. Those guys seem to play hard ball. (Yes, I know I shouldn't use sports metaphors, but I think this one is accurate, no?)

Anyway, I'm hoping to meet with one of the women in her department who may have some more information. Do I sound like Nancy Drew? At least she solved her cases!

Love, Maggie

Chapter 29

The next morning, Maggie put aside her fears for David and called Marge. When she finally got through, they agreed to meet for coffee that evening. Maggie didn't know what could be accomplished by the meeting, but she felt she had to do something. She was pleased that Fitzgerald was starting to take her concerns seriously, but she also felt that he wouldn't get the whole picture from an official investigation.

It was 7:00 when Marge joined Maggie at *Isis*. Marge ordered a mocha nonfat latte, which surprised Maggie as she thought Marge seemed more the type for straight coffee. When they were both seated at one of the tables in the back of the café, Maggie brought Marge up to date on David's information. Marge was clearly disturbed when she heard how the students were treated.

"I wasn't convinced when we met the other evening, but now I'm beginning to wonder. You remember, I mentioned that Doris seemed to be meeting someone the evening she died. I know she was also planning to practice for that competition, but she might have had dinner with someone before then. I have no idea who it was, but I wonder if Danny, our track coach, knows who it was. He said something a while ago that got me thinking. He was being awfully short with Stu Wentworth, his assistant coach. I overheard Danny laying into Stu about the responsibilities of a married man and something about vulnerable women. It may have nothing to do with Doris, but I got to thinking about her comment to me about seeing someone the night she died, and I wondered if maybe she was seeing Stu. It may be nothing; I could just be adding two and two and getting five, but it might be worth pursuing."

Marge said all this with an embarrassed air as if she was starting a rumor that might turn out to be false and in the process hurt Stu's reputation. She told Maggie she had respect for Stu and was fond of his wife. She hoped she wasn't being hasty in her suspicions.

Maggie listened quietly and assured Marge that she would be discrete. She, too, didn't want to jump to conclusions, but this was the first bit of information that seemed to lead somewhere.

"Do you think Danny would talk to me? I mean, is he one of the "old boys?"

"Well, he is an old boy, but I know what you mean. No, Danny sort of keeps to himself, does his job, works out, and goes home. He's older than most of the others, and I think he's just biding his time until he can retire. He's a pretty good guy, seems aware of the way the women are treated. He was fond of Doris. I think he'd talk to you. If you want, I'll let him know I've spoken with you—sort of let him know it's okay to talk."

"Thanks. I really appreciate your help. I feel as if I'm going off half-cocked, with suspicions, but no evidence."

"Well, anything I can do to help, let me know. I was fond of Doris; I wish I could have done more for her. I knew she was unhappy, but, you know, you get busy with your own stuff and being an adjunct I didn't want to get involved. Yeah, I know—that's the problem. We don't get involved."

"Don't blame yourself. There's nothing you could have done And what you're doing now is a big help. Talk to Danny tomorrow, if possible, and let me know if he has any problems with my contacting him, okay?"

Marge nodded and got up to leave. "Thanks for doing this, Maggie. Whatever happened, she deserves the truth to be known."

....

Two days passed with no word from Marge. Maggie was trying to concentrate on her own work, hoping to hear something, but resisting the urge to call Marge. She certainly didn't want to call Danny without knowing whether he was willing to talk to her or not.

Tonight was the annual Women's Studies dinner, always an elaborate feast, held at Jessie's home. It was officially a "potluck" with everyone bringing a dish to pass, but Jessie, as was her style, insisted on providing enough food for everyone, in addition to the various beverages. So, there was an abundance of food. And since everyone prepared a "special" dish, taking more time to cook and bake than usual, the food was great. The table was filled with appetizers and main dishes. There were ham and asparagus quiches, jalapeño cornbread, crab cakes with lemon pepper sauce, a wild rice risotto, and various desserts, along with the usual macaroni and cheese, lasagna, and tabouli salad. And, of course, Naomi's guacamole dip–which she was convinced was the best in the area, although it often went uneaten. Naomi was an excellent cook when it came to desserts; and she was one of the best at presentation; but she rarely seasoned her offerings and, with a crowd of hot pepper eaters, her food was often considered bland. Her confidence, though, was so strong that she just attributed the uneaten food as an indication that she had prepared too much!

This was the yearly event when the spouses of the members were invited. In the beginning years, the men were reluctant to attend, fearing that they would be bored with the conversation; but in recent years, the attraction of the great food, and the realization that a group of women could have intelligent and fun conversations made the annual event something to look forward to.

In addition to Jessie and her husband Mark were Sarah (with Nick), Naomi (with her husband Steve), Gail, Nina, Brandy (with her husband Todd), Olympia, Julia (with Ben) and Maggie. Julia, while not a faculty member, was the librarian for the Women's Studies Department, and, even though she couldn't often attend Women's Studies meetings, was considered a member in good standing because of all she did for the program. The only members who weren't present were Bob and Glen. Bob's wife had just had a baby, and with two other children at home he wisely chose to forego the good food to help out at home; Glen never came to these events–there was always something more important to do!

The conversation ranged from sharing recipes to stories about children to the latest scandal in town. While Maggie still didn't know many people outside the university, she found the stories entertaining, reinforcing her newly acquired opinion that small towns had as much dirt as large cities; in fact, it seemed easier to spot in small towns.

Later that night Maggie reflected on the evening. It had been lovely: the food was delicious, the conversations entertaining, no arguments between Gail and Brandy, but most importantly, it had been comfortable. Maggie felt as if she belonged, that these were her friends.

This all led to the nostalgic mood she found herself in. Remembrances of past dinners with friends, relaxed evenings discussing important as well as trivial events, the warmth of friendships.

It was probably the food at the retreat that reminded her of Elaine, a lawyer in New York whom Maggie had met while attending a conference on Women and the Law. They found they had much in common and formed a friendship which still lasted, although they saw each other infrequently since Elaine moved to Arizona. Elaine was a wonderful cook, the kind that didn't require recipes but just seemed to know what combinations would taste good. Maggie had fond memories of sitting around the table with Elaine's family—husband, two children, sister, brothers, in-laws, and anyone else who happened to be in town—and enjoying eggplant parmesan, pasta with sausage and peppers, homemade ravioli, and anything else that Elaine was in the mood to prepare. It was a feast—and the conversations were always fun to observe. Maggie would just sit there and listen to the "arguments" that seemed to hold the family together. Whose memory was more correct? Did grandma make the lasagna this way? Which cousin was getting married and which one was getting divorced? What did people think of Uncle Joe's new wife? Sometimes the conversation turned to politics. There were Democrats, Republicans, Socialists, and those who didn't care at all about what was happening in Washington so long as the stock market was up. All of these issues were discussed at high volume, everyone expressing their views with conviction, not to be dissuaded by others.

Maggie always felt welcome at these dinners. At first she found it alarming that people would argue so much and so loudly, coming from a family where raising one's voice was considered ill-mannered; but when she realized that it was just the normal way for this family, she relaxed. And through the years she came to realize that this family would always be a family, knowing that their disagreements were insignificant when compared to the bond that held them together. Remembering these times, Maggie resolved to keep in better touch with Elaine.

The nostalgic mood helped get Maggie's mind off of her conversation with Marge.

She hadn't heard back, but was reluctant to contact Marge again. It was clear that Marge was fond of Doris and would do what she could to help. Maggie would just have to be patient; she felt assured that Marge would get back to her when she had something to relate.

....

Dear Sam,

You would have enjoyed this evening's party. Good food, good conversation, good people. I think you'll really like some of the people I've met here. It seems people spend more time getting together here—probably because there's nothing else to do. Anyway, it was a lovely time.

Have you heard anything from that SOHO place about a date for your show? Kristi wrote me that you've been too busy to even drop by. I hope you're not doing your hermit thing. Even artists need time to relax.

Love, Maggie

Chapter 30

A few days later, Maggie heard from Marge. It was a go; Danny was willing to talk to her. When Maggie was able to get through to Danny, they agreed to meet the next evening–off-campus. Maggie wondered if he was worried about being seen talking to her. This was getting more and more complicated.

Since this was a non-teaching day, she decided to work on the revisions to an article she had sent off before arriving at Claxton. It had finally been accepted for publication in *Hypatia: A Journal of Feminist Philosophy;* the requested revisions were minor and she wanted to get it done so she could finish the article she was working on and then, hopefully, move on to the next article she had in mind.

"Have you heard the latest about the saga of the missing manuscript?" Maggie was at her usual table at *Isis,* busy at work, when Naomi came in. Naomi sat down with her usual "half-caf-quad"–she was rarely seen without a cup of espresso in her hand.

"No, what happened?"

"It was found by a student worker in the English Department who was asked to shred last semester's pile of papers from Grimsky's class. In the middle of this pile, there it was–the missing manuscript! Obviously, he'd dumped the manuscript onto this pile without thinking, and then just kept adding exams and papers to the pile. It's a good thing the student was alert or it would've been shredded along with the rest of the papers."

"What did he say when he found out? He's been accusing Andrews– has he apologized? You'd have thought he'd have looked through that pile before accusing anyone of theft, wouldn't you?"

"He's claiming that he didn't put the manuscript in the pile, someone else did–and of course he claims it was Andrews."

"What a strange guy! But what about the vandalism and hate mail? Do they have any idea who did that?"

"No, I think everyone's forgotten about that! At least there haven't been any more of those incidents that I know of. You know I do feel sorry for Grimsky. He's the butt of so many jokes around here, and nobody takes him seriously. Yet he's a decent teacher; a lot of graduate students like his classes and his publications are well received in the profession. He just annoys and antagonizes people and they respond accordingly—childishly at times."

Maggie found all of this bizarre. What she didn't know was the background for the antagonism between Grimsky and Andrews. When she asked Naomi about this, she was told that it had been going on from before her time at Claxton. In contrast to Jonathan Grimsky, a small, quiet man, Peter Andrews, professor of 20th century American Literature, was a larger than life man, with a booming voice. There was never any doubt whether he was in his office or not—you could hear him throughout the whole building. He was not called "Peter the Loud" for no reason. But worse than his voice was his laugh. For such a large man, his laugh was a high-pitched squeal, best described as the squeak of a mouse—a very loud mouse. And Andrews found much to laugh about. He was exuberant about life and seemed to find humor in life's daily events. He drove Grimsky crazy!

Naomi pointed out that one of Andrews's favorite authors was Henry Miller, whose works *Tropic of Cancer*, and *Tropic of Capricorn,* describing in detailed accounts the sexual adventures of a young American in Paris, were considered pornographic by people like Grimsky, and probably half the population of America, but were considered by Andrews as the works of one of America's finest writers. In fact, he included Miller in his survey course of great American 20th century writers. This enraged Grimsky, who claimed that Andrews was using Miller as an excuse to read pornography—both in the books and on the Internet.

Naomi went on. "It's true that Andrews visits a lot of sites that we would probably agree are pornographic, but his defense is that he has to know what's 'out there' in order to put Miller's work in perspective." She explained that Andrews believed that Miller has had a major influence on contemporary American culture, starting with the "Beat" generation of writers, most notably Jack Kerouac, up to the pop songwriter, Jewel. He had once defended his position by pointing out that his works were mentioned in film—as when the De Niro character in *Cape Fear* is seen reading Miller's *Sexus*–and in TV, as in the Seinfeld episode where Jerry is hounded by the librarian for not returning *Tropic of Cancer,* and he would cite the famous writers who had praised Miller's work.

"He claims," Naomi went on, "that Miller made it possible for people like George Orwell, Lawrence Durrell, and Norman Mailer to discuss sexuality without legal or social restrictions. Of course," Naomi continued, "none of this matters to Grimsky. He claims he knows pornography when he sees it!"

Unfortunately, Andrews's love of life and lifestyle that included dating curvaceous blondes less than half his 50 years did lead others to question his literary justifications. But, as Naomi pointed out, when questioned by Maggie, there had been no evidence of inappropriate behavior with students or with soliciting minors on the Internet, or things of that sort, so people just raised their eyes when his name was mentioned and ran when they heard his voice.

It was just Grimsky who couldn't let it be. And so the conflict between the two officemates continued.

....

Danny had been at Claxton for more than thirty years and his track team was considered one of the assets of the Athletics program, finishing in first or second place in the Mid-American Conference for the last ten years. Even though he had been in this country for most of his adult life, he still had the soft lilt of his Irish boyhood.

Maggie met him at the *Dogtown Tavern,* just off the highway, three miles north of town. Danny had chosen the place; Maggie hadn't known of its existence before then. It was connected to a motel, which advertised rooms with TVs and beds with Magic Fingers –all for $49.95/night! The tavern itself was dark, with the smell of spilled beer and cleanser permeating the woodwork. It was clear that Danny wanted to avoid being seen talking to Maggie as the place wasn't likely to be visited by anyone from the university.

After the usual pleasantries, and the serving of their beers, Maggie asked him about the rumor of Doris's affair. At first Danny was reluctant to discuss it, saying he had no proof of anything, but when Maggie persisted he responded by saying that one of his "lads" reported seeing Doris and Stu, Danny's assistant track coach, having dinner at one of the local restaurants. He, Danny, was upset because Stu was a married man with two young children, but since he had no proof that anything was going on he had said nothing to Stu until he noticed that Doris and Stu seemed to spend more time together than one would have expected. It was at that point that he talked to Stu, who denied that anything was going on and was offended that Danny would think otherwise.

"I took him at his word, and didn't raise the issue again. You're not thinkin' that Stu had anything to do with Doris's death, are you? I couldn't believe that."

"I have no idea, but even if he's not involved, he may have some information that might be important."

"I know I'm considered an old geezer, but it bothers me when married men fool around, especially with vulnerable women. She was a real nice woman, good at her job, always pleasant to me. I think the boys had it in for her–such a time they gave her for the teeniest violation of the rules, when the lot of them are always goin' round the rules as if they were made of silly putty and could be contorted into any shape that satisfied them. But I've been here a long time and know how to survive. I'm just doing my job as best I can until I'm out of here–which'll be in another year or so."

"Were you on campus the night she died?"

"Aye. The Tuesday night before the Thanksgiving break. I had me lads do an extra run around the track–indoors, of course, being there was so much snow that week–and so it was later than usual that I was finishin' up. Well, you know the lounge is between the two locker rooms–men's and women's. We all use the lounge for snacks, and stuff–it has a refrigerator and one of those micro wave things–faculty put their lunches in there, stuff like that. Well, after me lads had left, I went in there to get meself a cup of tea before heading out into the cold. I was surprised to see Stu there, talking to one of our students. He was getting something from the fridge and looked surprised when he saw me. Anyway, we nodded, talked about the weather–it was snowing again–and I got me tea and said goodbye. That's all I can remember. I don't know if that helps at all."

"Yes, it's very helpful. It may turn out to be nothing but, as I said, he may have some information that could be helpful. Thanks so much for talking to me."

They finished their beers, making light talk about the weather finally turning to spring, and left, with Danny promising to call Maggie if he remembered anything else. Maggie returned home with a slight headache–beer didn't agree with her–and various scenarios running through her head. She felt she was getting closer to what had happened, but still didn't have any evidence to support her suspicions, certainly not enough to convince Fitzgerald of foul play. She had to get more information, but how?

....

Dear Sam,

Sorry I missed your call the other night; but reading your email was just what I needed. I'm afraid I've bitten off more than I know how to handle. All I have are suspicions about Doris's death and that obviously isn't enough for the police. Perhaps I've lost my perspective and need to stop reading mystery stories. I've learned that Doris might have been having an affair with the assistant track coach. I'm going to pass that on to Fitzgerald; he can investigate since I obviously can't approach this guy and ask him questions about his private life. I just hope this leads to something.

But enough about that. I was excited to hear about the offer for the Krappy Kamera exhibit. What will you show? Old photos or have you some new ones?

I'm sorry you won't be able to visit during my Spring Break, but I certainly understand why you need to be in New York during that week. Perhaps you could visit later, near the end of the semester. Don't worry; I won't interpret a visit as a commitment to move here permanently! Things here are quite lovely with all the spring flowers blooming and the trees starting to sprout their leaves. The weather has turned warm, so we could have some nice walks along the river, or even take an overnight trip to the lake. Let me know what you've decided. I really would like you to see where I live and meet some of the people here.

I forgot to tell you about the President's annual talk the other week. It's supposed to be like a State of the Nation thing, bringing everyone up to date on finances, accomplishments, plans for the future, etc. It's required–they take attendance–so the auditorium was filled. He's a most unimpressive man, both physically and in substance. That's partly unfair of me–he can't help his physical appearance, but he is boring and shallow. He thinks the university is a business, and he's its head. He wants to be paid as a CEO of a large corporation, and he judges the success of the university in terms of its profits. If a program doesn't make a profit–off with its head! He recently proposed getting rid of the Anthropology Department on the grounds that it doesn't have enough majors to justify its existence. When someone pointed out that that was also true of the Physics Department he reconsidered. Everyone thinks that he's working behind the scenes on some new program that requires physics. Some think it's a medical school–which sounds strange to me as the state already has four medical schools, and the local hospital is certainly not equipped for internships and residencies. But perhaps they do things differently here in the Midwest.

Anyway, the fun part of the talk was when he went off on efficiency and effectiveness. Some of my friends call him "Double E"; he wants us to be more efficient, more effective. What that seems to mean is to increase products (i.e., students) more cheaply. When someone in the audience asked a question about the quality of education in his calculations, he responded by going into a tirade about faculty being opposed to change, about how we had to adjust to the new demands on education. He then compared the faculty to turkeys, who are so dumb that they would drown in the rain rather than adjust! People just looked around to see if others heard what they heard. Some laughed, some got up and walked out, and others just sat there.

It wasn't so bad for me, as I've only been here for a short time; but for those who have been here for a long time it was a slap in the face. From what I've seen, most of the changes that have occurred here–at least those in the academic area–have been proposed and carried out by the faculty. Anyway, I walked out with the others.

Afterwards, I talked to some of my colleagues. I found out that there had been an attempt to organize and join a union, but that the effort had failed. The reason given was that many of the faculty didn't see themselves as workers but as professionals. I also think that many people think they don't need a union to protect them; they think they're so good that the administration will, on its own, recognize their accomplishments and reward them accordingly. I've never worked at a unionized place, but I can certainly see some of the benefits a union would provide here.

Okay, enough about the fun times at this place. Let me know how plans for the exhibit are going.

Love, Maggie

Chapter 31

Maggie had already taught her two sessions of introductory philosophy and was looking forward to having an hour to herself before her last class of the day. All of her classes were going well, but her favorite was the social philosophy one, which she would be teaching in an hour. She considered herself a good teacher, and students seemed to appreciate the various techniques she employed to help them grasp the concepts and engage in significant discussion on the issues. But she didn't think she was exceptional, nor that she had some "special" techniques to share.

Charles had set up a session for later in the day when she would explain to her colleagues what she does in class. He seemed to think she had some secret for effective teaching! She was preparing herself for a disaster. Would they think she was full of herself? Imagine, giving advice to colleagues who had been doing this longer than she had—some of whom were acknowledged to be excellent teachers. She had heard good things about Ben's and Doug's teaching—although with Doug one was never sure what the raves were about! Well, she would make sure they understood that she was just sharing, not recommending. What worked for her might not work for others.

She closed her door, turned off the overhead lights, and folding herself between two chairs she had pulled together, closed her eyes and immediately fell asleep. She considered sleeping to be one of her talents. She had never been bothered with insomnia, falling asleep as soon as she put her head on her pillow, and could sleep most any place. She had perfected the technique when riding the New York subways. She could catch a few winks holding onto the overhead straps, awakening at her stop as if she had an internal alarm clock. She found that talent very handy now as she could refresh herself with a 20 minute nap between classes. So far she had never overslept.

When she awoke she found that she had ten minutes before her next class. Since she had already prepared the lecture and discussion for the day, she leisurely walked down to the classroom to set up the media she would use that day. Maggie preferred the old-fashioned chalkboard, but had adjusted to student demands to use the new technology. Students felt cheated if you didn't use it. She didn't like Power Point, felt it hindered spontaneity of discussion, so she compromised by putting up outlines of the general topics of the day on the visualizer, a modern form of overhead projection. That was her concession to technology–and the students didn't protest. Perhaps if one gives the impression one is using new technology that's sufficient to satisfy them.

The topic for the day was Mill's essay "On Liberty," with the focus on the question: Under what conditions is the state justified in interfering in the lives of its citizens? In order to ensure that at least some of the students had done the reading before class, she had assigned them a list of situations to consider and then compare their views with what they thought Mill would say about them. Situations such as: regulating the foods we eat; restrictions on smoking; requiring motorcyclists to wear helmets; removing children from homes where parents aren't taking "proper" care of them; sexual relations between, and among, consenting adults, etc. These, and other, topics usually elicited good discussions in class, as students tended to hold different opinions and felt sufficiently motivated to engage in discussion. Of course, for Maggie, their particular opinions were not the focus, although she had her own views; to her, the reasons they gave to support their opinions was what she was looking for–in addition to their understanding of the reading. She was quite aware that most of them would never have to refer to Mill again, but that the habit of offering reasons to support their positions would be a skill that would serve them well in whatever they ended up doing with their lives.

She was pleased to see that David was in class. He was always ready to voice his opinion, which helped to generate other student responses. He started with a general opposition to state interference in any part of a person's private life, which immediately led to hands raised throughout the room. Obviously, others disagreed–some with the scope of his claim, others with the substance. After about twenty minutes of rather heated argumentation, Maggie went to work. What would Mill say about it? What general principles is he using? Are you using any general principles in your arguments? What are they? Are you willing to apply these principles to other situations, or just to the one you're discussing? What's the difference? And so on.

The hour flew by with Maggie trying hard to keep the discussion focused, and not always succeeding. Not as much material was covered as she had planned for the day, but that didn't bother her. It was more important that what was covered was understood and if that took more time than planned, so be it. She couldn't understand colleagues who kept to such a rigid schedule that even if a topic wasn't adequately finished, they moved on to the next scheduled topic.

After class David asked if he could speak with her. Following her to the office, he continued to defend the position he had taken in class, only stopping when they reached Maggie's office. She was pleased to see that he appeared less troubled than the last time she had seen him. "So, what's up?" she asked.

"Well, I thought you should know that we're still like working on that story about Dr. Redden, you know? We're considering like writing an article raising the question about her. What do you think?"

Maggie, once again, controlled her impulse to correct his grammar and focused on his question. "Well, what would you say? You can't make any accusations without evidence, and the police haven't declared it anything but an accident. You have to be careful with what you print."

"Yeah, we know that. But we were thinking of like using it as a springboard to raising the issue of like how women are treated in some departments. We're going to like interview women in different departments, investigating whether they think they're like treated the same as the men—things like that. What do you think?"

"I think that would be great. But be careful what you say about Dr. Redden. The case is still under investigation and you don't want to do anything to mess that up. But be aware that many people might not want to tell you how their situation is for fear of retaliation by their colleagues. You might have to guarantee anonymity for those who talk to you. In fact, you should talk to Dr. Sloan in Sociology. She's an expert on survey research; she'd be able to give you some guidance on what types of questions to ask— legality, you know, things like that."

"Yeah, that's a good idea. Thanks. Well, I've got to get to my next class. I'll keep you posted on what we're doing."

Maggie was pleased with the discussion. At least David was safe and engaged in what might turn out to be an important expose´ of sexism in departments. Anyway, it would focus his attention on something other than Doris's death for a while—at least until there was more information available.

By the time David left her office, it was time for Maggie to present her teaching "secrets" to her colleagues.

....

The next day Maggie sought out Jessie. She hadn't spoken to her since the last Women's Studies meeting and wanted to bring her up to date on the information from Danny. She found her in the English Department office, negotiating next fall's schedule with the secretary. Her position as Director of Women's Studies was a part-time one requiring her to teach one class each semester. She had been assigned an early morning slot for her advanced Shakespeare class and was trying to explain why that would not work. Many of the students who took that course were English teachers in the public school system who didn't get off work until late afternoon. That was why the class was typically offered in the evening. The department had a new chair, who obviously hadn't been brought up to speed about the scheduling requirements for various courses. Of course, the secretary had been there for twenty years and should have known, but Jessie was too aware of the importance of staying on the good side of secretaries to point this out.

When she saw Maggie, she smiled and motioned for her to wait up. After a few minutes Jessie left the office, thanking the secretary for her help, and joined Maggie. They walked down the hall to Jessie's office, where coffee and oatmeal raisin cookies awaited. One of Jessie's cookies was enough for a meal for an average person, and since Maggie had already had her oatmeal for breakfast, she valiantly declined the offer and settled for coffee.

Jessie was surprised at the information Maggie had been able to get, although she cautioned her that there was still no "smoking gun" and that the police wouldn't act without more evidence.

To this, Maggie replied: "But isn't it their job, not ours, to get the evidence? I'd have thought that raising suspicions, pointing out inconsistencies, connections, possible motivations, things like that, would be enough to get them to investigate. And I think we have enough info for that."

"But what would Stu's motivation be? Why would he want to harm her? I don't get that part."

"Neither do I; but remember, he's a married man. Maybe she wanted more than he was willing to give; maybe he was afraid she was going to talk to his wife. Who knows what could have gone on between them?"

"But, Maggie, we don't really know that there even was anything between them. All you have is a report that they had dinner together and that they *maybe* were in the lounge at *maybe* the same time. That's scanty evidence of an affair. Good lord, we don't want to encourage people to assume that every time a man and a woman are seen together in public they're having an affair!"

"I know, I know. But I'm going to give the info to Fitzgerald anyway and he can investigate it. What have I got to lose? I don't have much credibility with him anyway."

Jessie shook her head, apparently not at all satisfied with Maggie's decision. She pointed out that going to the police with only the suggestion of Stu's involvement could turn out to be extremely embarrassing, if not harmful, to Stu–if he was innocent.

Maggie agreed, but said, "Yes, but I don't see any alternative."

Realizing that Jessie was not going to be convinced, Maggie changed the topic. "On another issue though, I have good news. Sam is coming here at the end of the semester. I'm so anxious for the two of you to meet; you 'artsy' people will have a lot in common."

"I'm so glad to hear that–not about being artsy, but about the visit. I'd be pleased to host a party. You choose the people and I'll worry about the food. Just let me know what works for you."

"Oh, I hate to put you to all that trouble. There are so many people I want Sam to meet. I'm on a mission to make this place look interesting enough so that there won't be any problem explaining why I've decided to stay on another year. Yeah, the department has sent up my reappointment papers, and they tell me there shouldn't be any problem with getting the Dean's approval."

"Wonderful, congratulations. I never had any doubts about your reappointment. But, getting back to the party, it's no trouble. I have a big house, and a husband who loves to clean. In fact, if it makes you feel better we can ask some of the people to help out with the food–but let's not make it a potluck; that gets too iffy. You weren't here at the time, but once we had a Women's Studies potluck where everyone brought chocolate–chocolate cake, chocolate mousse, chocolate cookies; even the one dish that wasn't a dessert was chicken molé!"

Maggie laughed. "Okay, we'll organize the food. I appreciate this. I'm really nervous about Sam's visit. Transplanted New Yorkers are the worst. Sam comes from Kansas, of all places, but thinks that there's nowhere worthy of even a visit outside of New York. I, on the other hand, spent my early childhood in New York and while I like it there, I'm not fanatical about it. Maybe it has something to do with growing up in Kansas. Now that's a typical New York attitude!"

The two women chatted a bit more, chuckling over the Grimsky manuscript recovery, agreeing that professors, especially the men, were truly a strange lot. Maggie took her leave, promising to let Jessie know about plans for Sam's visit.

....

Dear Sam,

It was great talking to you last night. I understand your not visiting at Spring Break, but I'm so glad that you've agreed to leave the splendor of New York and condescended to visit the dreary, prosaic Midwest later in the semester. When will you arrive? How long can you stay? I'll arrange to have more free time than usual so that we can take a few days to travel in the area.

Spring has come early this year. It's quite pretty here now. The crab apple and cherry trees are budding, and the tulips are still blooming, along with the new irises and early lilies. In all, it's quite a pretty sight. I know you hate photos of puppies and flowers, but perhaps you could expand your sights to do some "interesting" flower photos.

Well, nothing new on my murder investigation, but I do have an appointment to talk to Officer Fitzgerald about the info I told you I got from Danny, the track coach. Maybe that will give the police something to question people about.

The latest buzz around here has been about an invitation to bring to campus an alumna who has made a fortune in the sex toy business. The campus paper had a two-page story on how she has revolutionized the business by marketing merchandise toward women. They showed pictures of gadgets that boggled my mind. They come in different colors, some made of colorful plastic, others of "sparkly" silicon, and still others of glass. For the life of me I can't imagine how some of these things would be used. I guess my age— and sheltered life—have limited my imagination. The controversy isn't about what she does and how she made her money, but the impression that is given by using her as a model of a successful alum. It seems that a few years ago, Claxton was listed in *Playboy* as one of the top "party schools" in the nation. The university has been trying to overcome that image, especially since it wants to be known as a serious research institution, and this seems to drag it back to the old days. But I'm just an interested bystander enjoying yet another episode of life in the "dull" Midwest.

Well, it's time for bed. I have a busy day tomorrow trying to explain to students why citing from anonymous blogs isn't an acceptable source for their term papers, and meeting with Ben and Olympia to finalize plans for diversity week next fall.

Wish you were here. I need some of that snuggling you're so good at. I wish I were better at expressing my feelings in writing, but you'll have to be content with declarations of my love and wait until we're together for more!

Love, Maggie

Chapter 32

"No, just because something is on the Internet does not make it a credible source."

Maggie was instructing the students in her introductory classes on how she handled cases of plagiarism on term papers and that had led into a discussion on how to cite one's sources. Students seemed to think that if it was posted on the Internet it was fair game for citing. Many of them used "blogs" as if that person's opinion was clearly as authoritative as a respected scholar's. It was difficult to get the point across without seeming to be biased toward printed material. Many of them couldn't see the difference between citing *Wikipedia* and citing the *Encyclopedia of Philosophy*, a peer-reviewed publication. Pointing out that acceptable sources were reviewed by people in the field seemed to the students as another sign of snobbery. She ended up, as many parents do, resorting to "because I say so"—not the most sophisticated response, but an effective one.

After classes she met Ben and Olympia to discuss plans for next year's diversity programs. They had worked on the proposal for a required course on diversity for students and that was now going through the torturous curriculum process. The course had to be approved by the various departments and colleges which would be involved; then it had to be approved by the necessary curriculum committees; then it went to the Academic Senate, a body of faculty and academic administrators. If it was approved all the way, then it would be added to the curriculum. But that wasn't the end. Then it had to be considered as a required course, which meant it had to be sent to the Committee on Standards, which made recommendations on requirements for the various degrees to the Academic Senate, which would once again be asked to approve the new requirement. All of this would take at least a year, but it was out of their hands now, which meant that they could focus their attention on programs for next year.

Olympia came in with some suggestions for workshops and the data from a campus survey on student attitudes on diversity. The workshops were the typical ones used at universities and corporations to help people working together to be more sensitive to racial diversity. In Maggie's view, most of these workshops were unproductive. A three-hour session on diversity didn't overcome whatever attitudes people had; in fact, some of the studies she had read suggested that, if handled poorly, these workshops increased racist attitudes. But what were the alternatives? Clearly change was needed, but how to accomplish it on campus?

Maggie raised this point as gently as she could as she didn't want to imply that Olympia's workshops were unproductive; perhaps they were instrumental in the improvement shown by the data that had been collected on the campus survey.

The discussion turned to some of the recent racist events on campus. The interesting thing was that the survey Olympia shared with Ben and Maggie showed that the vast majority of students—black and white—approved of more diversity on campus. Of course, the question regarding whether one had been the recipient of racial attacks was answered differently by blacks and whites, but that was not surprising. After looking at the data, Maggie thought that most of the racial attacks could be accounted for by a small, well-organized group out to do as much harm as they could.

The latest incident involved the hanging of four nooses in a classroom. Now, for someone like Maggie, nooses were equated with lynchings, and that was equated with the lynchings of blacks in the South. But to many students lynchings were equated with cattle rustling in the old West! Clearly, there was a problem here. The black students were up in arms at what they saw as a racist symbol aimed at them; many white students didn't understand that and thought the black students were overreacting, making something into a racial attack that was never intended as such.

The university was looking into the incident, but the real problem was how to sensitize the campus to the racist implications in such actions. Maggie recalled a conversation she once had with a colleague who tried to convince her that the swastika was not necessarily an anti-Semitic symbol as it was used by many ancient cultures as a symbol of prosperity and good fortune, way before the Nazis appropriated it as a symbol of hatred. Maggie was unconvinced, but then she remembered when she had thought that the confederate flag was just a remnant of Southern attitudes toward the North, not seeing anything racist in it. Clearly, developing sensitivity was a lifelong process. Their job was to at least start the process with the students now.

Ben made a few suggestions about how to create an atmosphere where students would feel comfortable sharing their experiences, citing a very successful forum a few years ago where this was accomplished. The problem was that each year there were new students on campus, and so there was always a need for such programs.

By the end of the session, they had outlined a year of programs, including workshops, forums, and speakers. Olympia's office would take charge of setting up these programs as some would require funding from her office. They agreed to meet again at the beginning of the fall semester to see where things stood. All in all, everyone agreed it was a productive meeting. On the way out, Ben reminded Maggie of the department party that evening.

"Oh, thanks, I almost forgot about that. I'm not used to official functions during the week."

"Well, Mrs. Richards–you know we never call her by her first name, in fact, I can't even remember her first name!–thinks things will end earlier if people have to work the next day. Obviously, this is something she doesn't really want to do, but does because Charles is chair. Now if it were a meeting of 'important people' she'd be thrilled."

Maggie laughed and waved good bye. She had completely forgotten about the party; now she would have to go home and change her clothes.

....

It was a tradition for the chair of the department to host a party before the end of the semester. Department members were invited, along with their spouses or guests, and invitations were given to "special" guests, such as Sarah and Nick who were longtime neighbors of Charles.

This year, everyone in the department attended–even Barbara. Doug brought along a new girlfriend–an attractive young student who worked in the department office–and everyone was torn between being polite to her and indicating their disapproval to Doug. Fortunately the young woman was so excited at being included in the party that she was oblivious to the coolness that greeted Doug.

Leo and his wife, Susan, were there. She was the antithesis of the stereotype of a school teacher: smartly dressed, perfect make-up, and a mod hairstyle. In addition, she was a fascinating conversationalist, giving the impression of having read every book on the *New York Times* best seller list!

Ben and Julia arrived late, having had difficulty in getting a baby-sitter for the children. The oldest boy was twelve but they were reluctant to leave him in charge, given his propensity for teasing his sisters. Julia was a strikingly attractive woman with short dark hair, big brown eyes, and a figure that most younger women would die for. She worked out, and it showed. If she was a typical example of what librarians looked like these days, more men would be spending their time in libraries.

Louise was in the kitchen with Mrs. Richards, arranging the *hors d'oeuvres* on platters. Her husband, Joe, was in the living room talking sports with Charles and Ben. Charles, as host, was supposed to be serving drinks, but got dragged into the conversation by Joe who, as a fan of the Pistons, was chiding Ben's criticisms of the losing team. It didn't take long for Mrs. Richards to find Charles and remind him of his duties. This she did with the sigh of a frustrated, but patient, parent chastising a forgetful child.

Henry and Toby were off on the side discussing the latest book by Robert Curtis on "What is Art?" Toby was defending Curtis's thesis, and Henry was arguing about the style of the citations.

Felipe was trying to convince Doug to come on board and support the cognitive science program, which had been tabled once again at the last meeting. With each new drink Doug was getting more and more convinced.

Barbara was sitting at the feet of her husband, Ken. She was dressed in black, wearing a low-cut camisole which not only showed cleavage but also left nothing to the imagination about what she was wearing underneath. She had served him a platter of food, explaining that he had a bad back and found it difficult to get up out of the chair. He responded by patting her on the head and calling her his "little servant girl," at which she had the grace to look embarrassed. He was expounding on the importance of professors using the latest technology in their classes. According to him, the most important thing a student could learn in college was the use of technology. "Every class should use the latest technology—and it should be an integral part of the class. That's the most important thing a student can learn at a college—how to use technology," he proclaimed.

Nick, who was seated next to Ken on one of the many sofas in the room, looked at him with such a scowl that Sarah quietly elbowed him, trying to avoid what she knew was coming. She failed. Nick leaned forward and poking his face right up to Ken's said, "What are you—a moron? Or just out to maximize your profits? That's the trouble with you fucking capitalists. All you can think of is what will feather your own nests. What students need is not spending their time learning the new technology—my God, they do that on their own. What they need is a good awareness of how this society works, who pulls the strings, whose interests are served by the policies put in place by you and your cronies. Go peddle your goods elsewhere, leave the universities alone to do what they're supposed to be doing: educating young people to understand the society they live in so that they can change it for the better. That's something people like you don't seem to understand—that change is needed. We can't continue to see the rich getting richer at the expense of the masses...."

Nick would have continued, but at this point Ken stood up and motioned to Barbara that they were leaving.

This exchange was witnessed by everyone in the room—Nick had not used his "indoor" voice. Some of the people looked worried, as if it might escalate to a fist fight; others were amused; and still others were nodding in agreement with Nick.

Mrs. Richards had come out of the kitchen at hearing the commotion. She was clearly disturbed that there should be such an occurrence at her party. She looked to her husband to see what he was doing to stop the disturbance, but what she saw was a smiling Charles. When she pointedly confronted him on his lack of leadership, he laughed and pointed out that Nick had simply said what others thought but were too polite to say.

Maggie thoroughly enjoyed the party. Nick's lashing out at Ken seemed to loosen everyone up and the party moved to a new level. Jokes were told, banter about winning and losing teams was tossed around, gossip about disliked administrators was gleefully shared. All in all, it was a fun evening. Some, when leaving, thanked Mrs. Richards for such a lovely evening–the best party ever. She was not pleased.

....

Dear Sam

I had a marvelous time at the department party tonight. Nick, Sarah's husband, lit into Ken, Barbara's husband, for his views on education, causing Barbara and Ken to leave, amusing everyone at the party except Charles's wife, who was quite distressed. I'm sure she thought Nick was out of line, but Ken deserved everything he got. That man is so pompous, claiming knowledge about things he's really ignorant of, that it was good to see him shot down. Of course, he'll just go on believing that we're all foolish academics who don't understand the modern world. Anyway, it was fun, and everyone seemed to have a good time–especially after Nick's tirade.

I was glad to hear that you spent some time with Kristi and Wayne. How are their kids? Has the little one settled down any? I hate to see people use Ritalin on kids just because they're active, but I don't think I've ever known such a hyperactive child. Maybe Ritalin might be better than what they're doing now–drinking! But I'm no expert on child raising; they're probably doing the best they can.

I'm off to bed now. I'll call this weekend.

Love, Maggie

Chapter 33

Maggie slept late. The party had been such a success after Nick's outburst that people didn't leave until well after midnight, everyone joking that it was way past their bedtimes. After a shower and a leisurely breakfast of yogurt and fruit she dressed in jeans and a bright orange shirt, topped off with a light jacket as the mornings were still cool. She had called Fitzgerald and was told he would be available to see her at 11:00 so she gathered up what she would need to work on later in the day and left the apartment.

She was shown to Fitzgerald's office by the receptionist, this time a young woman with pink spiky hair and a nose ring. Maggie was impressed that the police department would hire someone like that. It showed more tolerance than she had come to expect.

Fitzgerald stood up to greet her and gestured for her to sit down. When Maggie was settled, he said, "Well, what's up?"

Maggie found herself tongue-tied, not at all sure any longer of what she had to say. Taking a deep breath, she finally spilled out her suspicions of Stu's involvement with Doris. Fitzgerald listened, taking notes as she talked, and then asked, "Do you have any reason to suspect that he harmed her? I admit, though, if they were having an affair–and we don't know that–it opens up possibilities. We'll look into that. But you stay out of it! This is a matter for the police, not for someone who's read too many detective novels. Do you understand?"

"Yes, I understand, but I resent your characterization of me. If it weren't for me, you wouldn't even be investigating her death!" Clearly, Fitzgerald had struck a nerve and Maggie was angry. He did nothing to soothe her hurt feelings, but simply repeated, "Stay out of it."

Maggie, doing what she could to maintain her dignity, rose, nodded to him, and left the office, heading for *Isis,* where she was hoping to work on her lectures for the next day.

Still smarting from what she perceived as an unfair scolding, she had difficulty focusing on her work. Getting up from her table to get a refill, she spotted Rachel Browne working at one of the tables and joined her for a brief chat and catching up.

Rachel, an assistant professor in the History Department, also used *Isis* as an office away from the office. She was coming up for tenure next year, and was hard at work on her book on military schools during the Civil War era. After seeing Rachel at work for a few weeks, Maggie had approached her and introduced herself. They found that they had enough interests in common and enjoyed each other's company. They would occasionally take a break and chat while Maggie drank her coffee and Rachel drank her Thirsty Turtle concoction, a drink made of Ghirardelli chocolate syrup, caramel, praline, and espresso. Maggie marveled that she could drink two of those while at *Isis*–each one probably containing at least 500 calories–and still remain so slim. Clearly genetics didn't play fairly.

Rachel was in a department of twenty, with only two other women. One of the women had long ago realized that her input wasn't welcome and, like others in similar situations, had simply withdrawn from involvement in departmental matters. The other, a relatively new hire, probably learning from the experiences of other women in her field, had become one of the boys. Figuring out who were the "important" men in the department, she had set her focus on joining that faction in departmental decisions, and so guaranteed for herself support for reappointment and other personnel matters.

Rachel didn't play the game, whether out of ignorance or principle, didn't matter. The result was the same. She was fairly isolated in the department. She wasn't one of the boys, and the other faction–those that disagreed with the direction the department was taking–was so disorganized that there was no effective opposition to the decisions of the important guys.

But her book was coming along, and her teaching was certainly acceptable, so she wasn't worried about her tenure decision. However, it hurt not to fit in, not to be treated as a colleague.

One day, while Rachel and Maggie were taking a break and catching up on plans for their weekends, a group from the History Department entered. They sat down at a table right behind Rachel and ignored her. When Maggie asked her what was going on, Rachel replied,

"They're interviewing a candidate for women's history." Asked why she wasn't being consulted, Rachel said, "They never include me in these interviews. I guess they think my opinion isn't worth very much."

Maggie found this incredible, pointing out that simple manners required they at least acknowledge her presence and introduce her to the candidate. At first, Rachel just shrugged, saying this was typical. But after urging by Maggie she approached the table and introduced herself to the candidate, a young woman who warmly greeted her and obviously had some questions to ask. The men were appropriately embarrassed and went out of their way to invite Rachel to join them, which she did for a short time.

This was not a one time event, though. Another time, with another candidate being interviewed, the same thing happened. Again, it was a woman applying for the same position. When the men again ignored Rachel, Maggie, who was leaving, walked by their table to say hello and mention that Rachel was at a table in the back. The woman looked surprised and seemed only moderately impressed by their belated invitation for Rachel to join them.

Perhaps it was coincidence, but neither of these women–the department's first and second choices–accepted the position. Maggie liked to think that it was the sexist treatment of Rachel that had convinced the women that this was not a good "fit" for them!

Maggie and Rachel chatted for a while and then each turned to her own work. Maggie found it difficult to concentrate, her mind filled with replaying the conversation with Fitzgerald, anger mixed with feelings she could only label as guilt. Had she accused Stu prematurely? Jessie might be right; perhaps there was another explanation. But surely, that was up to the police to determine. She had no authority to ask questions of Stu.

She stayed at *Isis* for a short while but, finding her efforts at working unproductive, decided to head to the office. There she ran into Louise trying to explain to Henry why it was too late to change his schedule for next fall: the master class schedule was being printed as they spoke; extra rooms were impossible to secure at this point; and any change in his schedule would require a change in someone else's. To Maggie's amazement, Henry persisted.

"I can't have a class at 2:00. I have to rest after lunch–doctor's orders, you know–and I have lunch at 1:00."

"Why didn't you say something when the schedule was being set up? You knew you were scheduled for 2:00 and you didn't say anything."

"I don't remember seeing the schedule; perhaps I missed that meeting."

Louise took a deep breath, deciding not to remind Henry that the draft of the fall schedule had been distributed via email to everyone in the department and that that was the time to make adjustments. Instead she pulled out a folder and looked up the schedule.

"Why, Henry, you have the noon hour free. Why can't you have lunch at 12 and rest from 1 to 2?"

"No, that won't work. Noon is too early for my lunch. I have breakfast at 9:00 and can't eat again until 1:00. Besides, I have to dash home at noon to make sure Minette is okay, and that wouldn't give me enough time to eat before 1:00 anyway," Henry replied.

Louise looked in desperation at Maggie. Maggie just looked back in amazement. This was a grown man, an educated man, behaving worse than a child.

Louise then did what she was good at. "Henry, I'd love to accommodate your request, but I don't know how to do it without making major changes in other people's schedules. I'll take it up with Charles and see what he can do."

Henry seemed to find this acceptable. When Henry left, Maggie approached Louise, a big grin on her face. "Brilliantly done. How do you put up with that man?"

Louise groaned. "I know that Charles has even less sympathy for Henry than I do. But Henry will accept a decision from him more readily than from me. You know, it's all I can do to be civil to him. And if I hear any more about Minette and her needs I'll scream. Can you imagine what he must be like in class?"

Laughing, Maggie rolled her eyes and waved goodbye.

....

Dear Sam,

Well, I did it. I told Fitzgerald about my suspicions of the assistant track coach and I think he'll follow up on that, but he made it clear that my help wasn't wanted. I hope I'm not causing problems for an innocent man, but I really don't think anything will happen otherwise. Am I too involved? Am I overly obsessed with Doris's death? What if it was simply a stupid accident? I'm so confused it's actually affecting my work. I don't know what time is good to call you tomorrow so give me a call at home—I'll be here all evening. I need to talk to you. It's at times like this that I especially miss your input.

    Love, Maggie

Chapter 34

Maggie was in her office reading the latest edition of the *Chronicle*, checking out the ads for positions back East she might apply for. She wasn't unhappy at Claxton, but she missed Sam. If a position opened up in her area, anywhere on the East Coast, she would at least be closer to New York, and therefore closer to Sam.

She was so absorbed she didn't notice the man standing in her doorway, looking at her. When she glanced up she smiled and said, "Hi, can I help you?"

"Are you Margaret Bell?" he asked. When Maggie nodded, he stood there, stony-faced, and introduced himself as Stuart Wentworth. "Do you know me?" he asked.

"No, we've never met," replied Maggie.

"Then why are you spreading lies about me? Why have you gone to the police with those lies?" Stu was clearly struggling to maintain his composure, to control his rage. Although he was a big man, Maggie was surprised to find she wasn't afraid of him. His demeanor spoke of genuine puzzlement as well as anger, but he didn't appear violent.

"Whoa, we need to talk. Please sit down." He stood in the doorway, glaring at Maggie. After what seemed like an eternity, he entered and took the other chair in her office, straddling it as if riding a horse. He raised his eyebrows, spread his arms, and said, "Okay, let's talk. You first."

Stu was tall, with a long lean body and curly brown hair which fell over his brow giving the impression of a younger man. His skin was brown, whether from a mixed racial background or from many hours in the sun Maggie couldn't tell. What she could tell was that he was handsome. Under different circumstances she might have noticed a twinkle in his eyes when he flashed his bright smile, but today that was not apparent.

Taking a deep breath, Maggie began. "Mr. Wentworth," she said, "let me start by saying that I was fond of Doris. That I don't believe her death was an accident. I believe she was murdered. I have tried to convince the police to investigate her death as a murder, but I've not been successful. I had no evidence, no likely suspects. When I heard that she and you have been seen together I thought that the police should know about that. After all, if I had come to you asking questions about your relationship with Doris, you would have told me to go to hell. Well, you can't say that to the police."

"No, I certainly found that out," said Stu. "Look, I was also fond of Doris—not in the way you think. And if her death wasn't an accident I also want to know who's responsible. I just want you, and whoever else you talk to, to know that I was not having an affair with Doris. She was a friend, a good friend. She was the only one around here who went out of her way to talk to my wife at social events. It wasn't easy coming to a place like this from Chicago where my wife has family. She gave up a good job to follow me here, and she's had a hard time finding friends. She's busy raising our two girls—one just started kindergarten this year—and she doesn't get out much. Doris would come by with donuts and have coffee with her, or push me to take care of the kids so Talia—my wife—could go to the movies with her—things like that. Why, she taught my kids to swim when they were just babies. Doris understood what it was like to be alone in this town. I think she derived as much pleasure as Talia did from their friendship. And any time I was with Doris alone it was all aboveboard. We were friends—nothing more."

"I assume you told the police all this and that you're no longer a suspect?" Maybe it was Stu's look of sincerity, but Maggie believed him when he nodded. She asked, "Do you have any idea about what could've happened? Did she say anything to you? Was she afraid of anyone? You know she filed a grievance against the department, against the chair, in particular. She'd been getting harassing, even threatening, calls at night. I didn't know her very well, but I could tell she was frightened those last couple of weeks. Did she talk to you about any of this?"

Stu turned away from Maggie, his eyes focused on the floor. When he looked up he said, "Yeah, she told me about the phone calls—and she showed me some of the pictures she'd gotten. God, I feel I let her down. I didn't take it all that seriously. I just told her to ignore it and enjoy her new social life–I think she was seeing someone, although she wouldn't say who. She certainly deserved a little happiness."

"Well, I think a lot of people didn't take it seriously. Look, I'm sorry if I caused you any embarrassment, but I'm really floundering here. If you have any information about who could have done this, please tell the police. They gave me the impression that if we could give them specific leads they would follow them up–as you painfully know!"

Stu rose to leave and nodded to Maggie. "If I hear anything I'll let you know. Doris didn't deserve any of this. She was a good person."

....

Maggie had an hour before her social philosophy class and took the opportunity to check in with Louise. She hadn't had a chance to talk with her for more than a week and liked to keep in touch. Louise, like most executive secretaries, was the backbone of the department– but, more importantly, she was the source of most of the gossip going around. The informal network of secretaries was alive and well, each individual contacting her counterparts around campus informing them of the latest happenings of faculty and administrators. Maggie liked to hear some of the antics of other departments; it made hers look normal.

The latest minor scandal was about the professor in Foreign Languages, an elderly, overweight man who dressed in shiny navy suits, displaying lots of dandruff on the collar. He was being accused of sexual harassment–more specifically, sexual solicitation–by one of his female students. His defense was that she had asked him what she had to do to improve her grade in his introductory French course. He took that as an invitation for sex! He told her to close the door and they could "do it" right there. She panicked and ran out of the room. Obviously she told her friends, and eventually her parents, who complained to the President, who called the Dean, who called the chair, and the rest is history. The professor still doesn't see what he did wrong; after all, he said, female students have been propositioning him for years. He admitted, though, that none had taken him up on his offer, and that this was the first time anyone had complained. The money was on his being offered early retirement–the university's way of getting rid of odd balls near retirement age and preventing any bad publicity. The younger odd balls were more difficult to deal with.

....

Maggie's class went as well as she had expected. This was the session where students gave their group presentations. Each group had been given a contemporary issue and some readings on proposed solutions to, and analyses of, the issue. The students were asked to work together and come up with a presentation giving the pros and cons of the various proposals, and their group's response, if possible. It's not that the students did a poor job; the presentations were usually accurate, it was clear that they had learned something, and it was also clear that most of the students had formed an opinion on the issue. It was just that it was so boring to listen to! Most of the students mumbled through their individual reports, requiring Maggie to ask them to speak up, and when they did express an opinion it was usually in the form of, "I agree with what the author said."

The only bright spot was David's report. He found problems with all of the readings assigned! He had a different spin on what the problem was and found that none of the authors addressed the real problem. While Maggie thought he had misunderstood the point of one of the articles, she appreciated his attempt to get at the root of the problem and, as usual, his intellectual creativity. At least, she didn't have to fight sleep listening to his report.

After class, David and Maggie walked down the hall to her office. They didn't speak until the door was closed and both were seated, and then both started to speak at once. Maggie laughed, "You go first."

"It's fantastic! People like actually responded to our survey. You were right. People didn't want to speak to us, but Dr. Sloan helped us like design an on-line survey that guaranteed anonymity and, boy, did people respond. She said our response rate was like above the average for surveys like that."

"Great! What did you find out? Have you analyzed the results?"

"We've like hired one of the grad students in statistics to help with that. We should have the official results soon; but what we can tell from like just looking at the responses is that a lot of the women faculty feel they're treated like shit in their departments."

"David, we're planning to have a forum where the results from your study would be the focus. If you could get the results to me as soon as they're available I could work on the program. But that would have to come after the paper prints its story. We want people to be aware of the problems so they'll be motivated to come. We obviously don't want to point fingers at any individuals or departments, just make the point that there's a major problem and something has to be done. Pointing fingers will come later!"

"No problem. The guy says he'll like have the numbers for us right after Spring Break. Any news on Dr. Redden's case?"

"No, it's still ruled an accident. If you hear anything, let me know. And remember, there's an exam next week."

"You're really like going to give the exam the week before Break?"

"Why not? Spring Break doesn't start until Friday, the exam is on Wednesday. It's a one-week break, not one and a half, or two weeks. I'll see you in class, right?"

David shrugged, then smiled. "Right."

Maggie shook her head when David left the office. She had barely noticed the "likes" in his speech. Soon she'd be talking the way students did! She already had to resort to the dictionary to check the spelling of "existence." Having seen it spelled "existance" so often she was no longer sure which was correct.

....

Dear Sam,

Well, just one more week before Spring Break. I wish I could be with you, but I'm consoling myself by planning to get so much work done that the rest of the semester will just fly by. The results of the survey that the student newspaper conducted should be available next week and we're planning on using that info to kick off some activities on campus. But I feel out of sorts. I'm just frustrated at not being able to do anything about Doris's death. I have nothing but vague suspicions which gets me nowhere with the police. Maybe I should just leave it up to them and stop playing detective? (Nah!)

I was sorry to hear that Gwen and Tim's divorce isn't going well. I guess it was naïve to think that they could split up after all that time and not have hard feelings—especially when Gwen feels so betrayed by Tim's affair. I'm not sure I understand why a brief straying outside the marriage can turn love to hate so quickly, but it seems to make a difference to most people so I guess I'm the one who's out of the main stream.

Speaking of couples, what have you heard about Janet and Lily? Are they back in town yet? I assume they're still together—if not, don't tell me! If you see them, give them my love and tell them I'll see them this summer.

Well, it's off to bed for me. I need my strength to face a week full of meetings and students worrying about exams.

Love, Maggie

Chapter 35

The next week was spent with department meetings, and students coming in with questions for the exam scheduled that week. One of the frequent questions was: "Can I take the exam after Spring Break? I made plans to go to Florida with friends and they're leaving tomorrow!"

Maggie reminded them of the make-up policy she had announced, and had made sure was on the syllabus handed out at the beginning of the semester: all make-ups would take place during final exam week, when there was a day set aside for just such situations. It didn't please the students, who rightfully were concerned that they would forget the material for this exam by the time final exam week arrived; but Maggie had found that allowing make-up exams turned out to be unfair to those students who took the exam as scheduled. Not only did it give the late-takers more time to study, it was difficult to construct an alternative exam that was truly equivalent to the regular one. And to give the same exam to the late-takers raised the possibility of cheating.

She had once used the policy of allowing make-up exams if students had a good reason. But she was such a softie that almost any reason a student gave she considered a good reason. She realized this when a young man explained that he had missed the exam because he had a hangover. Maggie thought that was quite a good reason! After that, she initiated her new policy, which didn't require any judgment on her part.

Almost all the students showed up for the exam. The only one missing was Adam, whom she had not seen for many weeks. She had assumed he would officially withdraw from the class, but just before the deadline for withdrawal he had appeared in her office, explaining why he had missed so many classes. It was truly a sad story involving the death of a grandparent, the illness of a brother, and the depression of a parent. Maggie had learned not to question these stories, as quite frequently they were true. But she did point out that he had missed so much of the semester that she didn't think he could pass the course. Well, Adam believed he could catch up and promised to attend all the remaining classes. Maggie told him what he had to do and he promised he would come in during her office hours with any questions he had. Maggie never saw him again!

Since Maggie had given an exam to one of her classes, and a "thought paper" to the other two, she had plenty of work to do during Spring Break. She usually spread out her class assignments so that she wouldn't have that much grading to do at one time; but since she was not going to New York she actually looked forward to having a lot of work to do. Of course, she could have used the time to do her own writing–the article on the views of men and women on friendship was still in the research stage–but she knew she wouldn't be able to concentrate on that, with all that had been happening these past few weeks.

But before she could get to the grading, there was a Women's Studies meeting to attend.

....

Gail tromped into the Women's Studies meeting, banged her briefcase on the table, grabbed a cookie and sat down. Everyone present looked at her, startled to see how flushed she was, wondering what had happened. Jessie's look of concern prompted Gail to explain her behavior.

"I just came from a meeting with the head of the maintenance division and the VP for facilities. You all know that the bathrooms on the third floor of this building are not working, right? Well, I assumed that maintenance would like to know about the situation, so I sent them an email requesting someone to come over and take care of the problem. Well, I never received a response, so I wrote to the VP for facilities, asking to meet in order to explain the situation.

"I just got out of that meeting and I'm furious. I was told that the water pressure in the building is no longer sufficient to handle so many flushes at one time, and since the 15 minutes between classes is the most popular time for people to use the bathrooms, they decided to send out a notice *not* to use the bathrooms on the third floor during the break between classes. There's going to be a sign put up to that effect later today."

Gail stopped her recital to grab another cookie and continued. "All of my arguments about the insanity of that proposal fell on deaf ears. The fact that students, and faculty, were more likely to use the bathrooms *between* classes rather than *during* classes didn't seem to impress them. They were like robots–smiling, saying how they appreciated my concerns, and yes, it would be an inconvenience, but there was nothing else they could do. When I mentioned fixing the plumbing, or getting new plumbing, their response was well, that would cost too much money–it wasn't in the budget! When I pointed out that I had three classes in a row on the third floor, and that their solution would require that I wait until my last class was over to use the bathroom, they nodded. Well, I lost it at that point. I suggested they use some of the money they have squirreled away for the athletic program, or the money they are going to spend on refurnishing the Welcome Center building, but they said that that money comes from another budget. 'We can't use those monies for maintenance.' I was so angry I just got up and left."

"That's a pile of shit!" Sarah charged, always quick to point out the problems with the bureaucratic decisions made by the administration..

"Well, technically, they're correct," interrupted Naomi, who, being a chair, was more familiar with the budgetary aspects of the university. "They make up a budget, allocating the available funds to different areas–some to the academic division, some to maintenance, some to Athletics, etc. But what they're leaving out is that they decide what the allocations should be."

"That's what I said: it's a pile of shit," repeated Sarah. It's clear that they have their priorities, athletics being the number one priority for the Board. Convenience for students and faculty–not to mention the whole academic enterprise–is not at the top of their list. But what can you expect when the place is run like a corporation where the main goal is profit–and appeasement of the members of the Board of Trustees. Remember, the Prez is a fucking accountant who probably couldn't have gotten a job in the private sector, at least not one that would've given him the salary and perks that he gets here. And the Board's made up of the governor's friends–payback for contributions to his campaign."

Brandy, as usual, thought that Sarah had gone too far. "Well you have to admit that the inconvenience is rather small; people can always use the bathrooms on the other floors. And remember, athletics does bring in a lot of money to the university."

"A small inconvenience?" bellowed Gail. "Why should I have to walk down to the second floor in the 15 minutes I have between classes in order to use the bathroom? All your classes are on the second floor, so it's no inconvenience to you!"

Sarah also wasn't going to let Brandy's comment go unchallenged. "You've been listening to the university's propaganda again! The university gives more than $14 million each year to support the athletic programs. They're not self-funding. Even football, with its gate receipts, doesn't support itself."

After more grumbling about the warped priorities of the administration, Jessie finally managed to get control of the meeting and turned to the agenda, the main item being a discussion on women faculty and their experiences on campus.

Jessie was urging the group to sponsor a forum where women could report how they were treated in their respective departments. Clearly, some of what Doris had gone through seemed to be present in other departments.

Brandy was the first to respond. In her charming Southern drawl she said, "I just don't think many people will be comfortable discussin' their situations in a public forum. I know I wouldn't be." Brandy's Southern accent grew stronger as she became more agitated.

"What about that forum you were setting up for the fall?" asked Naomi, who had a good memory for detail. "Remember, you and Gail were going to set something up so that women who were having trouble in their classes could get some advice."

"We just haven't done anythin' yet," replied Brandy. Looking at Gail, she asked, "Do you think this kind of a forum would really work or should we just stick with the classroom problems?"

Gail, ever reluctant to agree with her, hesitated. "Well, I guess I have to agree with Brandy. I think we should keep the two functions separate."

Sarah then asked, "Isn't there some way we can hold a kind of private meeting where women would be comfortable expressing their concerns?"

At this point, Jessie intervened. "I don't know how we could do that and invite women all over the campus. We're bound to have people there who will worry that what they say will get back to their departments."

"Well, here's an idea," suggested Maggie. "A student of mine works on the campus paper and they've conducted a survey on the treatment of women in departments–Naomi worked with them on that. Maybe that will give us a focus. If we find out that similar problems exist for women in different departments, we could focus on those problems without citing specific individuals. I haven't spoken to my student recently, but I'll see him in class this afternoon and check on how far they've gotten with the analysis of the data."

Everyone agreed that using the survey information would serve the function of bringing out classroom problems as well as the treatment in departments, and therefore one forum would work. Names were tossed around and by the time the meeting was ended, there were enough people for Jessie to contact to form the panel. It would be easy to get the experts; what would be more difficult would be to find a few women who were willing to talk about their own experiences.

When some members started to leave for their next class, Jessie adjourned the meeting, staying behind to work with Gail and Brandy on setting up plans for the forum.

....

As planned, Maggie spent most of the Break grading papers and exams. What had seemed like a good idea at the time, was turning into a nightmare. She had started by sorting the exams and papers into piles and grading ten at a time, at the end of which she would take a break. Within two hours she found she couldn't sit through ten exams, so the piles were reduced to five. Unfortunately, the breaks she took typically ended up at the refrigerator or cupboard. It didn't take her long to realize that, at this rate, by the time she finished her grading she would have gained twenty pounds!

She packed up her exams and papers and headed for *Isis*, which stayed open during vacation times for just such people as Maggie. At least here her breaks would be accompanied with coffee, not food.

By the middle of the week she had finished all the grading and was ready to reward herself. But how? Most of her friends had left town to visit family or just to get away. Sarah and Nick were up north at their cottage; they had invited Maggie, but she had declined, expecting to need the whole week to finish her grading. Naomi was in Chicago visiting her husband; Nina was busy with preparations for the play she was directing; and Jessie and Mark had taken off to visit their newest grandchild. Maggie was preparing to just get in the car and drive when Gail called. Gail, too, had stayed in town to finish some work and was ready for some fun.

They decided to have dinner at the fancy restaurant at the Casino as Gail, a regular visitor, had "earned" enough points for two free dinners. "Earned" was a euphemism for having lost a certain amount on the slot machines. After spending an hour on the machines—Gail on the slot machines, Maggie on the poker machines—they decided to cut their losses and go in for dinner.

The restaurant was beautifully decorated with a Native American motif. The murals and rugs were authentic native themes, designed by a member of the local tribe. The table settings were modest: the gold-colored charger plates were beautifully decorated with subtle green herbal borders which stood out against the cream-colored plates. The small vase holding spring flowers put the finishing touch to the display.

The food was also beautifully presented. However, both Maggie and Gail were more interested in the taste of the food than in its presentation. While the restaurant specialized in buffalo, elk, and venison, Maggie chose the whitefish while Gail ordered the filet. Both were pleased with their meals and decided to celebrate the end of their grading by indulging in dessert—chocolate mousse for Gail, peach cobbler for Maggie.

At the end of the evening, they agreed to meet the next day to take in one of the new films in town. It had gotten good reviews which meant that it probably would not be around for long!

The next day brought a soft rain, which seemed to turn everything green. All of a sudden the trees had blossoms on them, the scent of lilacs was in the air, and the dandelions had sprouted on all the lawns. Maggie liked the look of dandelions, at least until they turned to fluff and spread their seeds all over. But while they were in bloom, they made a lovely landscape.

Maggie met Gail at the theater that evening. They had their choice of seats, as there were only two other couples in the theater. With most of the students and faculty out of town, most places were quite empty.

After the movie, Maggie and Gail stopped off for drinks. Maggie had a glass of cabernet and Gail, who didn't drink alcohol, had a diet coke. After discussing the movie, which they both liked, they turned to the upcoming forum.

Gail, who, along with Brandy and Jessie, had organized the event, explained their plans. "We've got a panel organized. It was difficult finding women to talk about harassment in their departments, but we did find three who were willing to share their experiences."

It became clear, as she continued to talk, that Gail was upset with Brandy. "She's worried that their being on the panel might lead to unpleasant consequences for them. She's being so over-protective it's frustrating. I keep telling her that it should be up to the women to make that decision. And, besides, the whole point of the forum would be lost if they're not on the panel."

Fortunately, Jessie had agreed with Gail, having being convinced that the women were willing to be on the panel and were aware of the possible ramifications of their participation. After all, she had argued, wasn't it another case of discriminatory treatment to assume that women couldn't make these decisions for themselves?

Gail continued to point out Brandy's faults, until it became clear to Maggie that they needed to change the topic. Maggie agreed that Brandy was naïve and easily co-opted, but she found her pleasant and well-meaning. While Brandy was interested in many of the same intellectual issues as Maggie, she approached them with such a different mind-set that they really had nothing to talk about. Maggie, for good or ill, needed evidence to support factual claims, whereas it seemed that Brandy could accept these claims if they sounded good and fit in with her general perspective.

Perhaps what Maggie liked most about Brandy was her commitment to social issues, and her willingness to do more than talk. She was in charge of a long-running program on campus where current issues were discussed, using faculty and student participants. These programs were very well attended and required a great deal of preparation—all of which was done by Brandy. So Maggie cut her considerable slack—unlike Brandy, most people were more talk than action.

The rest of the week was spent with Maggie cleaning her apartment, doing laundry, and stocking up on groceries. She bought some flowers, which she placed in a vase on the kitchen counter, and even considered doing something to make the apartment more cozy. But the thought of decorating so tired her, she flopped on the couch and took a nap.

....

Dear Sam,

Well, Spring Break is just about over and I've been very good—finished grading, cleaned the apartment, and actually cooked myself a regular meal last night. I never realized how much I appreciated your cooking until I came here and now have to do it for myself. Somehow it doesn't taste the same!

Are you all set for your show? I think the idea of windows is brilliant, especially in black and white. Which camera did you use? I assume it was the old one, to fit in with the theme of art not requiring fancy equipment. You've been rather quiet about the show. Are you all right with it? You know the fact that you were asked to submit your work, and then chosen to exhibit it, should be enough validation that you're good.

I'm sorry I can't be there, but please tell me all about it—send me pictures and describe the reactions of the viewers. I'm counting the days until you're here.

Love, Maggie

Chapter 36

Classes had resumed and Maggie found herself pleased to see the students back in town. Usually, she regretted the end of Spring Break, but at Claxton it came so late in the semester that she greeted it as just one week closer to when she would join Sam in New York for the summer.

She was sitting at her usual table at *Isis,* working on her manuscript, when Marge came in, looking flustered. She joined Maggie and started in right away. "I've been talking with people and I just have to let you know what I've heard. I don't know if it means anything. I certainly don't want to get anyone in trouble; I don't want to have Stu's situation again, but you've got me so concerned I don't know what else to do."

Maggie listened, quietly encouraging Marge to continue.

"Well, you know Stu realized that it was Danny who told you about him and Doris, and so they had it out. But after Stu met with you, he seemed to be okay with Danny and they're on good terms again. But that got Danny thinking about the night Doris died. Stu reminded him that a student was in the lounge that night, too. He didn't know who the student was, but Danny did. It's an older student who's one of the stars on the baseball team. When Danny talked to me about it, I thought it was certainly possible that he, the student, was the one Doris was meeting that night. Why would a student be eating in the lounge on that night? It certainly is possible that he was waiting for Doris, who might have been practicing in the pool. I know this is pure speculation, but it's at least a possibility. If the police took seriously the suspicion that Stu was involved, certainly they should look into this student, don't you think?"

"I don't know how much credibility I have left with the police but, yeah, they should look into it. Do you know the student's name?"

"Wally something. I can check it out on the team roster and let you know. I just wanted to see if you thought it was worth pursuing."

"Definitely worth pursuing. Get me the name and I'll try to get Officer Fitzgerald to listen to me once again—if he'll let me in the door! Thanks. Maybe we're finally on to something here."

Marge left, promising to get her the name before that evening. Maggie stayed at *Isis* for another hour, but, finding it impossible to concentrate on her work, headed home for an early dinner.

The days were warm and the evenings pleasantly cool. Maggie had walked to campus and used the twenty minutes to calm down and think about what she would prepare for dinner. She needed something to occupy her mind so she wouldn't focus on the information Marge had delivered. Tomorrow would be soon enough for that.

When she arrived home, there were two messages waiting, one from Marge with the name of the student, and the other from Naomi asking her to join Sarah and her for drinks at the *Penguin*. Since Maggie knew that drinks always led to food, she put back the eggs she was going to scramble and headed out the door. Naomi would surely have some absurd incident to report on; that would be sufficient to get Maggie's mind off of Doris's case.

The *Penguin* was unusually crowded and it took Maggie a few minutes to find where Naomi and Sarah were seated. She could tell from the half-empty wine glasses on the table that they had been there for a while. She could also tell from Naomi's arm gestures that she was in fine form relating some incident. They beckoned to her and she asked a waiter walking by for a scotch—neat—as she sat down.

Naomi brought her up to date on the latest administrative snafu. It seems that when a student went in for a conference with one of her colleagues, who has an office in the basement, the student became violently ill. The paramedics were called and took the young man to the emergency room. The doctors there diagnosed the problem as respiratory distress brought on by a sensitivity to mold. When this was reported to university officials, they sent in a team of investigators who found "black mold"—lots of it, hidden in out-of-the way places along the outside walls. All the offices in the basement were then evacuated, using empty classrooms as temporary offices for the faculty and staff.

That wasn't the problem, though. As Naomi explained it: "I understand it's not their fault that the basement walls get damp and that mold grows—although you'd have thought the builders would have anticipated that. The problem is that within two days they sent people back to their offices—and you know they haven't solved the mold problem in that short a time. One of my new department members who has an office down there has been down with respiratory problems at least ten times this year. We all just assumed she wasn't used to Michigan's environment and was having allergy problems. Now she's wondering if she's contacted some mold disease. I told her to get to her doctor right away. But what about the people who haven't had any symptoms? They might be infected. I don't even know how dangerous black mold is, do you?"

Naomi turned to Sarah and Maggie for an answer. They just looked at each other and shrugged. Maggie had never heard of black mold—except in science fiction movies.

The conversation then turned to the movies in town and which ones were worth seeing. That wasn't a problem for Naomi as she only went to PG movies, claiming that reality was disturbing enough. Sarah, on the other hand, only wanted to see reality films, preferably documentaries. Maggie, a true film buff, was clearly on her own here. She liked most genres of films, and was known to even enjoy a sappy "boy meets girl" film occasionally. She wasn't into the lives of the actors and didn't really care about the directing, as most film buffs would; she was primarily interested in the plots and the characters. She justified her interest as necessary to keeping up with popular culture for her classes, but that was only what she told people: she just loved the movies! Even Sam teased her about her taste—or lack of it. But that never deterred her from spending a few hours in a theater watching a two-star film. She and Sam had subscribed to Netflix, but Maggie liked the experience of sitting in a theater, preferably one with few other people in it, where she could be completely focused on the screen, knowing that, short of a fire, there would be no interruptions.

They spent the rest of the evening talking about Doris's case and what the police were doing about it. Maggie reported her last conversation with Fitzgerald: "Stay out of it!"—and the egg on her face from her premature suspicions of Stu. She didn't mention the possibility of the student's involvement as she had even less reason to suspect him than she had Stu.

The evening didn't end in dinner, but they did indulge in snacks—

all fried!–along with their drinks so that when Maggie reached home dinner was no longer on her mind. She put on a recording of Dianne Reeves, curled up on the couch with a book, and promptly fell asleep, only to be awakened an hour later by Sam's phone call. After an incoherent five minutes, Sam told Maggie to go back to sleep–they would talk tomorrow.

Chapter 37

Maggie and Danny were once again at the *Dogtown Tavern*. She had called Danny, anxious to follow up on Stu's recollection of the night of Doris's death.

After the usual pleasantries were exchanged, Maggie asked, "Do you remember a student in the lounge that night–the night that you saw Stu there?"

"Aye, there was a young lad there. I didn't think much of it at the time; I was busy jokin' with Stu about bein' on campus so late on the night before vacation. Teasin' him about avoiding goin' home to the wife and kiddies. But, aye, there was a student there–Wally, I think his name is Wally. Nice young lad; older than most of the students, though. I think he'd been in the army a few years before comin' to Claxton. Why are you interested in him? You're not thinkin' he had somethin' to do with Doris's death, are you?"

"Well, I don't know. But it looks as if she was seeing someone that night–like a date. I'm just wondering if maybe she was seeing this Wally kid. Why would he be in the lounge, anyway? Is he on one of the teams, your team maybe?"

"No, not mine; he's the pitcher on the baseball team. Got a good future, from what I hear."

"But why would he be there at that time, on that night?" Maggie persisted. "Do you remember anything else? Like what he was doing there? Was he just sitting around, looking for something, waiting for someone?"

Maggie realized that Danny's silence was not from a reluctance to talk, but from an attempt to remember. When he finally spoke it was somewhat hesitant, as though he was retrieving memories as he spoke.

"Well, I seem to remember that he was sittin' at the table when I came in. I didn't think much on it at the time as I was surprised to see Stu there and we just got to talkin'–but it is a bit strange, now that I think on it. The lad just sat there while Stu and I joked. But I think–now mind you, I can't swear to it–I seem to remember seeing Wally go to the refrigerator. I assumed he was going to eat something, though why he would eat there I can't say. That's about all I can recollect. Sorry. Does that help at all?"

"Yes, it's very helpful. Do you remember what Wally took from the refrigerator–was it a drink, or maybe a sandwich?"

"No, I don't remember. I seem to remember he had both hands full, though, as he closed the fridge with his butt, but I really didn't pay him no mind."

"Do you remember what time you left?"

"It must've been close to 8:00. Me lads had finished their run about 7:30 and by the time I got to the lounge and talked with Stu it would've been comin' near 8:00."

"This Wally, was he there when you left?"

"Aye, he looked like he was getting' ready to have his supper–at least, he was diggin' around in the drawer for some forks and stuff. I assumed he was goin' to eat right there."

"And did you see Doris at all that evening?"

"No, she wasn't in the lounge, and I wouldn't know if she was in the women's locker or the pool. Sorry."

"No, that's fine. You've been a big help. Oh, I never asked. Who is the baseball coach?"

"Why that's young Kevin, Kevin Marshall. A nice young lad."

Maggie drove home with her head full of scenarios, but the one that stuck had   Doris dating Wally and meeting him for dinner after she practiced for her competition. Now if she could only get Fitzgerald to take her seriously–again.

She hadn't eaten anything since breakfast and the beer she had just finished had the effect of reminding her that she was hungry. Knowing that the only things at home were eggs and some frozen dinners, she stopped at the grocery on the way.

Arriving home with an already roasted chicken, cole slaw, and fresh bread, she made herself a hefty sandwich. She flicked on the TV as she sat down on the couch, sandwich in hand. There was nothing she wanted to watch, but she needed to get her mind off what she had learned from Danny. There was no sense in spending time preparing what she would say to Fitzgerald tomorrow when she called him; she knew what to say.

....

The next afternoon, Maggie ran into Jessie–literally–causing papers to go flying through the air. After helping Jessie gather her belongings, she followed her to her office.

Maggie needed to share her latest information with someone. She had spoken to Fitzgerald that morning and he was going to follow up on her suspicions; but she was worried that perhaps they were too far-fetched to be taken seriously.

Jessie brought out the muffins she had baked that morning and poured two cups of coffee. Looking at Maggie she said, "What's up? You look terrible."

Maggie grimaced. "Is it that obvious? I feel like I'm really out of my depths here and it's worrying me." Maggie then proceeded to relate the information about Wally that she had already told Fitzgerald and waited for Jessie's reaction.

Jessie took another bite of muffin, a sip of coffee, and wiped her mouth on a napkin. She didn't say anything at first. Finally, when it became clear that Maggie was waiting for a response, she said, "Go through it again. Why do you think this kid would want to kill Doris?"

Maggie, clearly agitated, answered: "Look, people in her department were trying to get rid of her; if she were to leave, that would open up a position for this guy they wanted to hire; she was preparing for a competition and practicing that evening; she was, probably, seeing Wally, the baseball student; he was in the lounge that evening, when there was no other reason for him to be there than to see Doris; Danny saw him remove at least two things from the refrigerator; as far as we know, no one else was in the area after Danny and Stu left, but for Wally and Doris. Now if we could just think of how shrimp could have been put into her food without her knowing, we certainly have a plausible scenario. Don't you see, there must be a connection between Wally and Kevin. After all, Kevin is Wally's coach–maybe that's the connection."

"That's stretching quite a bit, isn't it? Wally dates Doris so he can kill her so that what? He can impress his coach? I don't know, that sounds quite far-fetched, probably too far-fetched for the police to take seriously."

That wasn't the response Maggie wanted, but she had to admit that Jessie's reaction was reasonable. After all, there were lots of possible holes in her account. But, damn, it was the only scenario that fit the facts, limited though they were.

She finished her coffee, and muffin, hugged Jessie and left.

....

The next few days seem to drag on. No news from Fitzgerald. Perhaps she had jumped to conclusions again and caused a young man the same embarrassment she had caused Stuart Wentworth. Why did she think she could solve a case that the police couldn't? But Doris's death clearly wasn't an accident, she was sure of that. She may have the wrong person, the wrong scenario, but she knew she was right.

She was planning on spending a quiet evening at home watching a video and munching on popcorn. The papers that students had just handed in would have to wait. Grading was not on her mind tonight.

She had just settled down when the phone rang. Thinking it might be Sam with a rare call, she picked up the receiver only to hear a strange voice say, "Stop your snooping or you'll be sorry."

"Who is this?" she demanded, but, instead of an answer heard a click on the other end. Trying not to overreact, she returned to the couch to watch the video. After twenty minutes she realized she had no idea what she was watching–not the fault of the video, just her inability to concentrate. Her immediate response was to call Sam, but she quickly put that thought aside. The call was probably a prank and she was overreacting. No need to upset Sam and cause unnecessary worry. She turned off the TV and started pacing. Her apartment was so small, however, that pacing was not much better than standing still. She needed to do something. Grabbing her jacket, she left for a long walk. Fresh air would calm her down and then maybe she'd stop off for a hot tea at *Isis* where she could think and be among other people.

Isis was crowded. She had forgotten that it was open mic night. A young man with long brown hair, and big brown soulful eyes was reading his poetry. She sat in the back, .drinking her tea, trying to listen to him. The crowd, mostly students, seemed engrossed, but Maggie couldn't concentrate.

She was spooked, she had to admit that. So this is what Doris must have felt, she thought. But, she told herself, even if it was a prank call, it meant that she had stepped on someone's toes. Which, in her eyes, proved that she was on the right track!

By the time she returned home, she was feeling less vulnerable. She was determined to be more insistent when she called Fitzgerald in the morning. Surely he had to take her seriously now.

....

Fitzgerald was out when Maggie called the police station. Leaving a message for him to call her, she headed to campus for her classes. Not wanting to miss his call, she kept her cell phone turned on while in class, but no call came through.

The day went by without any contact from Fitzgerald. Maggie had calmed down since the threatening phone call, so she agreed to go *Willows* for dinner with Sarah and Olympia. The food was good, the conversation better; all in all, a lovely relaxing evening with friends She had not intended to stay long at the restaurant and had left her car on campus, planning to walk back since the evening was warm and she enjoyed the walk. However, they had stayed later than anticipated, enjoying the relaxing atmosphere and conversation.

By the time they left the restaurant it was after 10:00 and the streets were quiet. Refusing a ride with Sarah, saying she preferred to walk, Maggie set off for campus. Finding her car was easy as it was the only car remaining in the faculty parking lot. She unlocked the door, climbed in and started the engine, only to find a piece of paper attached to the windshield wiper on the passenger side of the car. Thinking it was a parking ticket–although she couldn't think why she would have gotten a ticket, or why it would be placed on the passenger side–she got out of the car and retrieved the mysterious paper.

WE'RE WATCHING YOU, it said.

She looked around, her heart racing. There was no one in sight. She quickly got into her car, locked the doors, and took off. Her heart rate didn't slow down until she was parked in front of her building.

Checking to see that there was no one hidden in the shadows, she got out of the car, and hurried to her apartment. Locking the door behind her, she stayed in the dark, not wanting to turn a light on lest someone was out there looking to see which apartment was hers. She sat there for what seemed like an hour, but was only 10 minutes, before putting on a light.

First thing in the morning, she was going down to the police station. She would sit there until Fitzgerald, or some other officer, would listen to her. This was more than a prank.

....

Maggie left her apartment at 8:00 and drove to the police station. Again, she was told that Fitzgerald was not in. Pulling herself up to her full height, she said, "I'll wait," and proceeded to sit down on the bench, pull out papers to grade, and make herself comfortable.

The young woman at the desk—the one with the pink spiky hair—looked over at Maggie. "He probably won't be in until noon," she said. "I can have him call you when he gets in."

"No, that's okay. I'll wait."

The young woman shrugged and went back to her work. Maggie started reading the student papers. They each worked at their respective chores, the young woman occasionally looking up to see what Maggie was doing, shrugging, and then going back to her work.

At 10:45 Fitzgerald walked in. The young woman caught his eye and nodded her head toward the bench where Maggie was sitting. Fitzgerald acknowledged her warning and, taking a deep breath, walked over to Maggie.

"Good morning, Dr. Bell. What can I do for you this morning?"

"I've gotten some threatening messages. One was a phone call, and the other was this piece of paper that was left on my windshield last night."

Handing the paper to Fitzgerald, Maggie kept silent while he read the brief message. He looked down at her and motioned for her to follow him to his office.

"Okay, tell me about the phone call," he said after closing the door.

Maggie proceeded to fill him in on the phone call and her theory on how Doris had died.

"Have you spoken to that Wally kid?" she asked.

"Contrary to what you obviously think, we do know how to conduct an investigation. No, we haven't spoken to Wally, yet. But we have spoken to some of his team mates."

"And?"

"They don't know of any connection between him and Dr. Redden, but some thought that he was secretly seeing someone. I guess he was usually quite talkative about the women in his life, so being secretive about whom he was seeing seemed strange to them."

"So what are you going to do?"

"I'm going to do my job–that's what I'm going to do. Now you go home and let me do it. And be careful. Lock your doors and don't go walking around by yourself. Use the 'buddy system' like you did when you were a kid."

Maggie put her head down and took some deep breaths. She looked up at him and said, "You will look into this, right?"

Fitzgerald got up and walked to where she sat. "Dr. Bell, I do take this seriously and I am looking into it. I'll be talking to Wally this afternoon. You know I can't accuse him of anything, but I will get to the bottom of this. Now, go home. Leave this to me–and be careful. If you get any more threats, let me know immediately. We don't have a large staff here, but we can get someone to watch you if you think it's needed."

"No, I'll be all right. Just let me know what you find out, okay?"

"Okay."

....

Dear Sam,

I'm sorry I worried you last night; I'm really okay and the good thing is that I've finally got Fitzgerald's attention. He's interviewing the kid today, so we'll have to see where that leads.

I had a nice time with Sarah and Olympia last night–before I found the message on my car! I haven't told anyone about that, except for Fitzgerald. It's probably nothing and I don't want to get people to be all solicitous about me. What a nuisance it is when people start feeling sorry for you.

Other than that, everything here is pretty much the same. Classes are going well and I'm looking forward to your visit. So, don't worry about me, and get going on your plane reservations.
Love, Maggie

Chapter 38

The next few days were uneventful; no threatening notes or phone calls, and no message from Fitzgerald. Maggie knew not to contact him again, but found herself more and more anxious as the days went by.

There had been some of those "hang-up" phone calls, but nothing was said so she couldn't report them as harassing. She just wished she knew what was happening, what Fitzgerald had found out about Wally. The fact that he hadn't called made her wonder if she had once again targeted the wrong person.

Well, she wouldn't worry about that this evening. She was meeting Nina at the theater to see a student production of *Born Yesterday*. She was not expecting it to compare to the film version with Judy Holliday, but, given the shows she had attended at Claxton, she expected it to be a solid student production.

Nina was already at the theater, talking to some of her students. Maggie enjoyed seeing the interaction between Nina and the students. Theater people were so different that it was like looking through a peephole at another world. Hugs and kisses, sprinkled with shrieks of delight, accompanied by effusive hand gestures and facial expressions, all seemed over the top to Maggie, who viewed the scene with amusement.

Nina was dressed in black: black slacks, black shirt, black coat, and black hat. The only touch of color was the red flower in the hat, which on someone else would have looked odd but on Nina seemed at home. Taken together, the outfit emphasized her slenderness while imparting a dramatic aura around her. Clearly, this tall, slender figure in black would be noticed.

After greeting each other with hugs, they took their seats as the lights dimmed, signaling the start of the play. As usual, Nina took out her notebook for another review of a colleague's production.

At the intermission, Maggie turned to Nina and, with a twinkle in her eye, asked, "Am I enjoying this?"

Nina laughed. "Yes, it's a good production. You see how they're using the full stage? And they're not always facing the audience, but talking to each other. That's good. And the students are projecting well. Yes, it's a good production."

"Good. I thought I was enjoying it!"

After the play, they walked to the parking lot, talking about the strong performances of some of the students. Maggie found herself agreeing with Nina's assessment of the play, realizing that she had learned quite a lot from Nina and, as a result, her appreciation of theater had significantly increased. Now she focused on more than the story line; she was becoming better at evaluating the actual performances and the skill of the director–something she had never considered before.

When they arrived at their respective cars, Maggie was distressed to find that one of her tires was flat. She had not had a flat tire in many years and at first didn't know what to do. It slowly came back to her that one has to change the tire! She knew how to do that, but was not dressed for manual labor.

"Why don't I drive you home. You can have the car towed tomorrow," Nina suggested.

Maggie hadn't thought of that. But when Nina pointed out that her insurance probably had towing included, Maggie agreed. She went around to the side of the car to get her briefcase when she noticed a note on the windshield–again, on the passenger side. This one said:

YOU WERE WARNED!

She didn't want to explain the note to Nina, so, tucking it into her purse, she got into Nina's car. Fortunately, the ride home was short as she had trouble following the conversation. She had all she could do to mumble a few words of agreement as Nina continued her analysis of the play. Her heart was racing, she was short of breath, and she was scared. Thanking Nina for the ride, she got out of the car and quickly ran to her building. Her apartment was dark. She had left a light on, not wanting to come home to a dark room. Did the bulb burn out? Was the electricity off? Knowing in her gut that neither was the case, she made extra sure that the door was locked and then, using all her strength, succeeded in moving the desk against the door.

She slept with the lights on that night.

....

The next morning she appeared at the police station at 8:00. Fitzgerald was in. She showed him the note and reported the invasion into her apartment. To his credit, he didn't ask if she, perhaps, had left the door unlocked, nor whether she was mistaken about having left the light on. He left the room and returned with a young officer.

"Dr. Bell, this is Officer Palinski. He's going to be your personal body guard for the next few days, until we get this sorted out."

"You think it'll be settled in a few days?" asked Maggie.

"Yes."

"Could you say more?"

"No."

"Okay."

Maggie left Fitzgerald's office with Officer Palinski trailing behind her. She turned to him and said, "We may as well walk together. It's not like we're trying to hide the fact that you're with me."

"Yes, ma'am," he replied. "I'll follow you to your apartment; you can leave your car there."

"I walked. My car is still at the theater parking lot. My tire was flat and I haven't had a chance to call the tow truck to get it fixed."

"Well, then, let's do that right now." He placed the necessary calls and together they drove to campus in his car, with the words "Police Department" clearly visible. Maggie wondered what her colleagues would think with her driving up in a police car with a police escort! She was partly embarrassed, but immensely relieved to have Officer Palinski nearby.

The day passed with much time devoted to explanations about her police escort. Louise was concerned about Maggie's safety; Toby was confused about why she needed a police escort, not being able to think that a student could be responsible for the harassment; Ben and Leo were incensed that the police had waited so long to offer her protection; and Doug was interested in just how much togetherness she and Officer Palinski would be sharing! Charles, to his credit, made sure that campus police were brought into the picture so that there would be no confusion about jurisdiction. And, of course, Maggie's friends were concerned, offering to stay with her at night. Jessie suggested she move in with her until the police found the culprit. Maggie, pointing to Palinski, assured them that she was well protected.

By the time she got to class, the rumors had started and students were talking in hushed tones about the death threats their teacher had received. Maggie spent the first few minutes of each class explaining that she was fine, that the police protection was just a precaution, and that now class would begin!

Even though the day was uneventful, Maggie was exhausted when she returned home. Palinski had arranged for her car to be delivered to her apartment, where it was waiting for her, repaired tire and all. There had been a tear in the tire, leading Palinski to conclude that the tire had been slashed.

Contrary to Doug's salacious expectations, Palinski planted himself outside Maggie's apartment, after making sure that the door was securely locked, the desk having been returned to its proper place.

....

Dear Sam,

You'll be happy to hear that I now have my own personal bodyguard, compliments of the police department. It's simply a precaution—nothing to get excited about. But it is fun to watch people's reactions, especially the students', when they see me with a police officer. I think some of them think I'm being arrested!

Doug, with his usual fixation on sex, asked, with a wink, if the officer would be staying overnight. I wonder if he would have asked that if the officer were a woman. He's really clueless.

But not to worry. Officer Palinski quite appropriately stayed outside my door all night, guaranteeing that my good reputation would not be tarnished! I think being seen on campus with a police escort has scared off the caller. He probably thinks the police have secret ways of knowing who's calling.

Well, I'm sure I'll sleep well tonight.

Love you, Maggie

Chapter 39

Maggie was seated in Fitzgerald's office, waiting for him to finish his discussion with Palinski. He entered the room, holding a stack of papers and started to speak to Maggie.

"What did you find out? Did you talk to that kid?"

Fitzgerald looked at her.

"I'm sorry, I interrupted you. You were going to tell me something important, I hope?"

Maggie leaned forward in her chair, anxious to hear the reason she had been called down to the police station.

"As much as I hate to admit it, you were right. It wasn't a simple accident. I ordinarily wouldn't be sharing this information with a civilian, but this situation is unusual. We wouldn't have looked into anything if it hadn't been for you, so I feel I owe you this.

We brought in the Walters kid—do you know his name is Walter Walters? That's as bad as Gerald Fitzgerald! Anyway, the kid was denying everything at first, but he was nervous as hell. It didn't take long for him to admit dating Dr. Redden and not much longer to admit that he had seen her that evening. With a little prodding, everything came out. It was as if he was relieved to tell his story. Sometimes basically decent people really can't live with the guilt.

"Anyway, it started as a prank; he had been asked to 'spike' her dinner with some shrimp so that she would fall ill, wouldn't be able to practice, and then wouldn't do well in the competition. I guess some of her colleagues were out to get her and thought that her not doing well in the competition would be held against her.

"Unfortunately, she didn't have her medication with her and Wally panicked when she couldn't catch her breath. Instead of getting her medication, which was in her office, down the hall—or calling 911—he called his coach, Kevin Marshall. By the time Marshall arrived, she was dead. Then they both panicked and called Sommers, the chair. These clowns then decided to make it look like an accident, and dumped her in the pool. And the rest you know."

"How did Wally get her to eat shrimp? She was so careful about that."

"He claims that he slipped some mushed up shrimp into her chicken salad. Obviously, she trusted him and didn't examine the salad–although it's not clear she could have seen the shrimp, it was so well blended into the rest of the stuff."

"Was he the one leaving me those notes and the phone calls?"

"He hasn't admitted any involvement in that, though it's most likely that he, or one of his friends, is responsible. We're still looking into that, but it's going to be difficult to prove unless one of them turns on the other."

"Well, I'm not so concerned about that, so long as it stops. What happens now?"

"Well, clearly Marshall and Sommers are involved in at least a cover-up. But according to Walters, Marshall was the one who told him to spike her dinner. So, we're looking at a murder charge against Marshall and Walters. We've turned over the case to the DA, who'll decide on the specific charges. They might let the kid off in exchange for his testimony."

He looked at Maggie. "You've got some serious problems on campus, Dr. Bell. This seems to have been simply a case of trying to get rid of someone they didn't like. Even if she was an annoying bitch, as they are claiming, that doesn't justify their treatment of her, and it certainly doesn't justify murder. What the hell's going on up there? Doesn't the university monitor these things?"

"That's the question I started with. We filed a harassment charge against the department, only to be stone-walled and then dismissed when she died. I'm hoping to be able to use your findings to get some action on campus. You know Doris's case was extreme, but there's still a lot of that 'old boy' stuff going on, especially in departments where there are few women. We keep hearing about these things, but so many of the women are either afraid to come forward, or just go along and try to keep out of the limelight. I'm hoping this case will make a difference."

"Well, all I can say is good luck. And, contrary to what you're probably thinking, it was actually a pleasure to work with you—although I hope I don't have the pleasure again." Having said that, Fitzgerald rose and extended his hand to Maggie, who took his hand in both of hers and thanked him for listening to her.

Now that the legal case was in good hands, she could focus on matters closer to home: harassment on campus and Sam's visit.

When Maggie arrived home, she called Helen. Even if the police had notified her, she felt that Helen deserved a personal call. Helen had not yet been notified by the police, and cried when she heard the findings. She was comforted by the closure, but was left with a feeling of emptiness. Why hadn't she taken Doris's complaints more seriously? Wasn't there something she could have done? Why hadn't she called her more often? She would never find an answer to these questions, her guilt would gradually fade, leaving her to simply mourn the loss of a loved one.

....

Dear Sam,

Well, finally the truth is out. The police have arrested three guys for Doris's death. It seems it was a prank gone wrong. In any case, Helen, Doris's sister, is in shock. I guess we never expect someone we love to be murdered. She's wondering what she could have done to prevent Doris's death, and nothing I can say makes her feel any better.

I, too, feel kind of strange; relieved that it's over, but still feeling I should be doing something—although Fitzgerald has made it clear that I'm to stay out of it now.

I wish you were here. You can always keep me focused. Well, hearing your voice this weekend will have to do. Until then,

Love, Maggie

Chapter 40

"Can I ask what's happening with Dr. Redden's case?"

David was sitting in Maggie's office, discussing the results of the survey the newspaper had taken. It was going to be published in the paper that week and he wanted to give her a heads-up.

"What do you like know about Dr. Redden's investigation? You, know, about her death?"

"Well, all I can tell you is what's in the paper. Her death wasn't an accident. You might want to contact Officer Fitzgerald for the specifics—it should be public information. There have been some arrests and the case will go to the DA. There's not much more for us to do there; it's in the hands of the police and DA. That's why we're trying to focus on the campus environment which seems to have been responsible for what happened. By the way, without the information you gave me, I don't think this case would have been solved. So your first investigative reporting case was clearly a success. I'm only sorry that you got harassed about it."

"Ah, it wasn't too bad. I think I like overreacted."

"Well, I'm glad you're okay. Now go write your story. We're going to use the results you print in the paper as the basis for our forum next week. You might want to have someone cover that, too."

"You bet, I'll be there for sure; and we might even like get some of the other papers in the area there, too."

....

Maggie headed for another Women's Studies meeting, the last one before the forum was to take place. Everyone was talking about the news article concerning Doris's death. When Jessie could get order, she turned the meeting over to Maggie, who gave a general report, without going into specific details, about Doris's case.

Gail, clearly upset, demanded that they do something soon. "If we let this murder go without comment, what kind of feminists would we be?"

"At the least we need to write a letter to the editor, condemning the department's involvement," suggested Sarah.

Maggie was pleased at the support for doing something, but worried that the focus would be on Doris's murder and not on the treatment of women faculty. Most people would easily condemn murdering a woman, but would they see that their treatment of female colleagues needed changing? She raised this point, and was pleased to see Sarah agreeing with her. It was decided to use Doris's case as an extreme example of what sexual harassment can lead to, and tie it in with the results of the survey.

Jessie volunteered to write the letter and pass it around for approval before sending it off to the newspaper. Arrangements for the forum were confirmed: the posters announcing the forum would be distributed around campus in plenty of time; the radio and TV station had been notified; there would be microphones for the audience as well as for the panelists; and there would be flyers with a summary of the results of the newspaper survey. The panelists were on board and Maggie was all set to introduce and moderate the program.

The meeting was adjourned with a sense that something important was about to happen.

....

The day of the forum had arrived and the small auditorium was filled to capacity. They had not reserved a larger room, assuming that a small room filled looks better than a large one half-empty. Maggie started the forum by thanking those who attended.

"I'm delighted to see so many people here today; I'm especially glad that you agree with us that the issue of sexual harassment on campus is important enough to take valuable time from your busy schedules. Some of you may have read the full report of the results of the survey conducted by the student paper regarding the experiences of women on campus, but in case you haven't had a chance to see it, we're passing around the summary sheet.

"What we want to accomplish today is two-fold: one, we want to further the discussion of the chilling climate that women seem to be experiencing on campus, and two, we want to change that climate.

"Let me give you some background. The student paper got interested in the issue of sexual harassment as a result of Dr. Redden's death. We now know that Dr. Redden's death was not an accident and that people have been charged and will stand trial for murder. That's now in the hands of the DA. But the university also bears a responsibility for her death.

"When many people think of sexual harassment they think of things like *quid pro quo*–you sleep with me and I'll support your promotion; or they think of double entendre jokes or flirting on the job. To many people these are relatively harmless things, and that only overly sensitive feminists with no sense of humor are offended by them.

"I want to explain why we think that sexual harassment was a major factor in Dr. Redden's murder. In other words, why a climate that ignored, maybe even condoned, sexual harassment led to her death.

"She worked in an environment where some of her colleagues were allowed to make fun of her and to encourage their students to make fun of her. Male students, and some of the faculty, would stand in the balcony overlooking the pool and laugh at her when she was teaching a swimming class. Admittedly, it was a strange sight to see a swimming coach with an old-fashioned bathing suit, bathing cap, and nose plugs. Did that deserve organized public ridicule? I think not. She was subjected to lesbian-baiting, finding pictures of women in erotic positions posted on her door; she was accused of sexual assault on students because she touched them when she was teaching them to swim. Note that no student ever complained of being touched inappropriately, but two of her male colleagues complained about it to the Provost. She was assigned a differential teaching schedule, teaching more courses and more students than any of the other regular faculty in her department–all men; and she was subjected to sexual jokes at department meetings.

"When she finally had enough and brought a grievance against her department, she started receiving anonymous deep-breathing messages on her phone late at night, and one time she actually received a threat.

"All of this was reported to her chair, Jack Sommers, who told her to—and I quote—'Lighten up, can't you take a joke?' All this was reported to her dean, Dean Morris, who sat on the grievance for two months, finally deciding that since Dr. Redden had died there was no longer any need to investigate her allegations of sexual harassment.

"Who knows what would have happened if the university had taken seriously any of the allegations Dr. Redden had made against members of her department? Perhaps it wouldn't have made a difference; those who were out to get her might have simply continued their behavior. But perhaps it might have made those who thought it was simply fun to tease a woman who didn't fit in with the 'old boys' think twice about the trouble they could get into by their actions.

"I don't know if those responsible for her death intended to kill her. Perhaps it was—as some are already saying—just a prank gone wrong. But why was such a prank ever considered appropriate? What do we say of an institution that allows such childish behavior to go unchecked? What kind of message are we sending to our students if our university ignores allegations of such behavior? We're past the time of accepting the excuse that 'boys will be boys' and looking the other way when women are treated as lesser human beings.

"The survey reported many examples of women feeling that they are not treated respectfully by their colleagues, or by their students. And we have on the panel this evening some courageous women who are willing to share their stories with you. I know that there are those in the audience with your own stories but who, for very good reasons, are reluctant to talk about them in public. I just ask that you listen, and, if you are comfortable doing so, share your stories. It helps to realize that you're not alone and that if we work together we can make a change here. We can't change the world, but we can change our university."

With that, Maggie introduced the panel, starting with the legal expert and then the sociologist putting sexual harassment into a context of sexism in society. Next came the emotional part of the session: two women who had themselves experienced sexual harassment on the job, and one woman whose best friend had left Claxton for a less desirable position because of the sexually charged environment in which she had been working. These women all talked about how they felt like outsiders in their own departments; about how they were subjected to, at best, condescending reactions to their comments at meetings, or, at worst, simply ignored; about how they had to put up with double entendre jokes and comments about their appearances.

Some of the experiences they described were not technically sexual harassment, but sexual discrimination: for example cases where there was no sexually charged environment, but simply a case of not being treated the same as the men in their departments, of not fitting in. But all of the situations spoke to the fact that many women were not accorded the same respect as their male colleagues.

After the panelists concluded, Maggie turned the session over to the audience. She was pleased that her fears about lack of audience response were unfounded. There were around one hundred women–and some men–in the audience and, after a slow, hesitant start, many women rose to share their experiences. Some had good things to say about their departments and its male members; some, while admitting that they had not had any problems, recounted tales of other women's problems.

Some of the women in the audience were quick to point out that they were not feminists, but simply women who wanted to be treated the same as the men in their professions. Many of the women in the audience seemed shocked at hearing about the treatment of other women, perhaps a testament to the fact that their departments treated them fairly.

The forum lasted beyond the scheduled two hours, at the end of which Maggie and Jessie stayed behind to meet with other Women's Studies members to plan the next step. The newspaper article had attracted the attention of the administration and Naomi pointed out that some members of the administrative staff had been present at the forum and were undoubtedly on their way to make their report to the Provost. Brandy noted that some reporters of the local newspaper, as well as the student paper, had been there. Perhaps there would be stories in the papers tomorrow.

Everyone agreed that it was important to keep the pressure on; it was all too easy for things to go back to "business as usual" after such a catharsis. But how to do so was the question.

They decided that they needed to brainstorm and the best way to do that was to go out for drinks and snacks.

It was a quiet night at the *Penguin* and they were able to get seated at the large table in the back. After ordering drinks, and some snacks, Jessie tried to get the group to focus on planning the next step. Not having any success, she just let them talk. Obviously they were not yet ready to focus!

Sarah was the first to speak. "I can't believe how many women claimed not to be feminists, when it's clear that what they want are the very things that feminists are fighting for."

Brandy, in typical fashion, responded, "Yes, but wasn't it good to see how many of them reported that their male colleagues treated them well?" Sarah cast a disapproving look at Brandy. "So you're saying that there really isn't a problem of sexual harassment on campus?"

"I'm not sayin' that," Brandy replied. "It's just that we shouldn't jump to the conclusion that all men are at fault here."

Gail, ignoring Brandy, indicated surprise that no one had mentioned the discrepancy in salary between men and women, while Maggie was impressed that so many women were willing to share their experiences in a public forum.

When everyone had a chance to vent, Jessie turned to the reason for their meeting: what was the next step? Suggestions were made: picket the administration; name the departments that were involved in sexual harassment; circulate a petition demanding that new policies be developed and implemented; follow up with interviews with the media throughout the state; contact state legislators; file law suits charging discrimination; and so on. Gail even suggested that they picket Jack Sommers's home because of his treatment of Doris.

Jessie noted all of the suggestions and agreed that, before they did anything, they should get legal advice.

Sarah, having dealt with the university on legal issues before, said, "Remember that the university's legal counsel's responsibility is to keep the university out of trouble, so don't go there for advice."

Gail supplied the name of a lawyer friend in Lansing whose main focus was women's rights and volunteered to contact her. At the end, everyone left with a feeling of empowerment: something would get done.

....

Dear Sam,

Tonight's forum went beautifully. I was a bit nervous—what if no one came, or no one said anything. But I needn't have worried. It seems that

Doris's murder has gotten to everyone and people shared and shared and shared. Afterwards, some of us went out and, over drinks, brainstormed about what to do next. There were some good suggestions—some wild ones, too—and we're hoping that the press covers the event and the results of the survey, which the student newspaper has made public.

Now, tell me about your show. I know you'll probably be reading this tomorrow morning as you're out celebrating your success right now. (I already tried calling and you weren't in!)

Call me tomorrow with a full report—all the details: who was there, what were their responses—although I already know you were a hit!

Love, Maggie

Chapter 41

The feeling of empowerment of the previous evening was reinforced by the news that the administration was looking into the Athletics Department. The university's legal counsel had finally decided that there might be some problems in that department and that the university could be legally liable if it didn't do something about it.

Jack Sommers and Kevin Marshall were under indictment for involvement in Doris's murder, and the university had suspended them, pending the results of the trial.

Wally Walters was suspended from the baseball team and was working with the prosecution in exchange for immunity in his own case. He claimed that he had really cared for Doris and that he thought it was just a joke to "spike" her food with shrimp. Those who knew him doubted the accuracy of this claim. After all, she was in her forties, a not particularly attractive woman, and he was the star of the baseball team, the object of adoration by many of the coeds on campus. He had never struck any of his friends as a particularly sensitive, mature guy. The word was that he had been trying to please Kevin in order to get his support for being recruited by major league teams.

But the DA's office wasn't really concerned about Wally's motives, only about his actions and those of Sommers and Marshall. If it took immunity for Wally in order to prosecute Jack and Kevin, so be it.

Jessie had done a good job of following up the original letter regarding Doris's death by a subsequent letter denouncing the prevalence of sexual harassment on campus and calling for the administration to clean house. After the newspaper accounts of the forum, and the follow-up interviews with some of the local TV stations, it was getting impossible for the university to claim ignorance.

Jessie had received letters and calls from Women's Studies programs at other universities around the state, indicating their support and admitting they had the same problem on their campuses. She even received calls from people around the country, as the report of the murder, and the forum, had been picked up by the *Chronicle,* a national publication for higher education. Now the job was to keep the pressure on the administration so that real change would occur. It was all too easy to expend great energy at first and then, when the eyes of the public had turned away, to go back to business as usual.

The next few weeks flew by in a flurry of activity. Maggie was emotionally exhausted by all the publicity and calls for interviews. But she was also exhilarated by the reaction of her students. Students she had considered total airheads, unaware of and unconcerned about anything but the next kegger and what the latest fashion was, came up to thank her and to share their experiences of harassment in some of their classes. Some of it was subtle: a professor expressing surprise that a woman was taking advanced calculus–and doing well!; a professor discouraging a woman from majoring in engineering; and, most disturbing, a member of Maggie's own department telling students in class that there were no women philosophers worthy of study, because women weren't capable of abstract reasoning! Maggie resolved to bring this issue up at the next department meeting.

....

Dear Sam,

I can hardly wait for next week. I'm trying not to plan too much, so that we can just do what we feel like doing. I've arranged to take some time off–no committee meetings and my classes have out-of-class projects to work on, so I'll have more free time to spend with you. I know you'll be bringing along some work, so I've included some free time for you as well.

Well, I guess my age is showing. The warm weather had brought out what seems to me to be inappropriate clothing. Students are appearing in what are clearly pajamas! When I questioned one of the guys why he was wearing his pajamas to class he told me it was quicker: this way he didn't have to spend time getting dressed in the morning. And the young women and their cleavage! I didn't think such petite young women could have such large boobs. One of the guys in the Accounting Department showed up in class the other day with a Victoria's Secret *catalog and told the students "If you can find it in here" –pointing to the catalog–"it's not appropriate* to wear in here"–pointing to the classroom. He said the men laughed, but not the women.

There seems to be an incident of academic dishonesty afoot. One of the men in the history department had written a book on the history of the American Boy Scout Movement. It was well reviewed in the professional journals and had been cited in other works. He just received a copy of a dissertation being written in the Education Department here on the Girl Scout Movement in America–in fact, it's already written, and the person is coming up for her defense. The history guy was sent a copy by the woman's mentor as a courtesy, as he knew of his interest and thought it was a well-done study. Well, it turns out it's completely plagiarized! Where the original talked about boys, this one talks about girls. The history guy–I don't know his name–thought it all seemed so familiar that he went and checked his book to see if she used the same sources. He wrote the book five years ago and hadn't looked at it since, so he didn't recognize his own words at first. I don't think she'll receive her degree!

See, I told you this place was fun. What have you been shooting lately? I was pleased to hear how well your Krappy Kamera show went, not only in terms of approval, but in terms of money! What's next?

Love, Maggie

Chapter 42

It was the last monthly meeting of the department before the end of the semester and Maggie was hoping that it wouldn't last too long as Sam's plane was scheduled to arrive at 6:00. It was an hour to the airport and while department meetings started at 2:00 p.m. and usually ended by 4:00, you could never tell what issue would keep the group going until after 5:00.

Charles started the meeting with the usual announcements, and then turned the meeting over to Barbara to report on the programs scheduled for the following year. There had been complaints about the speakers she had invited to campus during the current year, and people wanted to have more input in the decisions. In her lovely, soft voice she outlined the plans she had tentatively made for the following year. Most of the suggested speakers were non-academics who came from the private business sector; many of them would come for a small honorarium as a favor to Barbara's husband. That was a major selling point for her: she could bring in more speakers because of their connection to Ken than if she had to pay the outrageous fees of these famous people.

Ben's response was that these "famous" people were not academics, who typically didn't charge much, but were business executives.

"We don't need so many business executives speaking to our students; we need more variety. What about some philosophers whose works relate to themes discussed in our courses? What about some activists who could talk about current issues and their philosophical implications? We could attract an audience from other departments with similar interests and at least show that philosophers have something to say about these things."

The upshot was a decision that people would give Barbara suggestions for next year's speakers and she would bring back to the department a list of who was available, at which time the department would make the decision on whom to invite to campus.

She was not happy with this and threatened to resign from the program committee. At that point, Toby intervened. "No, please don't. You've done a brilliant job, splendid programs. Just add a little variety, that's all."

She relented, citing her commitment to bringing quality speakers to campus, but Maggie wondered if her main reason for relenting was a reluctance to give up such a great opportunity to hobnob with "famous" people.

That being settled, it was now time for Felipe to raise the issue of the cognitive science program.

"This has been tabled since the beginning of the year. It's time to take a stand—up or down. You've had enough time to get all the information you need in order to make a decision. I move approval of the program."

Charles recognized Felipe's motion and called for a second. Doug seconded it, and discussion followed. When Henry tried to table the motion again, Ben stepped in and, agreeing with Felipe, suggested that they "fish or cut bait"—in other words, make a decision. Since no one seconded Henry's motion, a vote was taken and— it passed! It seemed the conversation Felipe had with Doug over drinks at the department party had convinced Doug, who then convinced Toby. So, after two years of discussion, Felipe's cognitive science program would now be sent up the line to Dean Sweeney who, while not in support of it, might consider it more favorably now that it had departmental approval—or so Felipe hoped.

The meeting had so far only taken an hour and since there was not much more on the agenda, Maggie raised the issue of sexism in their classes. She reported her student's comment about the philosophy professor who claimed there were no women philosophers worthy of study because they lacked the ability for abstract thinking. She didn't name the professor, whom she knew was Henry. Maggie had learned that sometimes students exaggerated, or even misunderstood, a professor's comments, and she didn't want to charge Henry with anything without some evidence. As it turned out, she didn't have to worry. Henry admitted that he had made that comment in class and that he stood behind it! His defense was that there were no famous women philosophers in history; that if there had been quality thinkers among them, we would have heard of them.

Maggie was stunned. The temptation was to lecture him on the many reasons why we didn't know of women philosophers of the past, and to point out the work done by contemporary women philosophers–much of it in the philosophical mainstream. But before she could gather her wits to respond, Charles, Ben, Toby, and Leo exploded.

"That just shows your ignorance," shouted Ben. "Do you want me to cite the exemplary work done by contemporary women philosophers or don't you care about the evidence?"

Leo picked up the attack. "Perhaps you're also ignorant of the work done by women in the past," and then went on to name some. Unfortunately, most of those around the table were as ignorant of these women as Henry!

Toby, who had sat quietly through these attacks, piped in: "But what about our own students? What must they think if that's what you're saying in class, Henry? Think of the young women who have to listen to your comments about their lack of philosophical ability. I'm surprised there hasn't been a bloody uprising in your classes."

Charles, clearly disturbed by Henry's attitude, spoke up: "I want to see the grades you've given for the last three years. If I find that there is a disparity between the grades given to women and to men in your classes, I'll take this up with the Dean."

Henry, turning first an ashen white, and then a frightening red, sputtered incoherently at first, and then in his thin reedy voice proclaimed his innocence.

"I resent the implication that I would ever grade on the basis of anything other than the quality of a student's work. That would go against the rules. There have been women in my classes who have done quite well; not showing outstanding originality, but certainly adequate mastery of the material. I don't have many women in my upper-level classes–I think that shows that they're not really interested in philosophy; most of the women in my classes have been in the introductory courses, which they take to fill general distribution requirements. I don't require originality in those classes, so they can do quite well. But, I stand behind my claim that women don't do as well as men when it comes to genuine philosophical ability."

It was Ben who spoke up next. "Why do you think there are so few, if any, women who take your upper-level classes? Almost half of our majors are women, and they all take the required departmental upper level classes. And some of the most outstanding papers have been written by these women. Last year, for example, Kristen Jacobs received the Dean's prize for the best essay written in the college, and the previous year it was received by Laura Kowalski. And the placement rate in graduate schools for our majors shows no discrepancy between the men and the women. Perhaps women don't take your classes because they know how you feel about their abilities."

Maggie finally spoke up. "I've heard Henry's arguments before. It's something women of my generation had to deal with. I had hoped that it had been laid to rest by now, that the work of women philosophers during the last thirty years had proved their right to be called philosophers. I won't bother to list the outstanding work done by some of these women—names even Henry will have heard of. It's clear to me that nothing we say is going to change Henry's opinion of women's intellectual abilities; but I think it's important that we let our women students know that he is a voice from the past, a voice that has no support from the rest of the department. I don't know how to accomplish this, though…"

Charles interrupted at this point. "We typically have a meeting of our majors, and potential majors, in the fall. I'd like to suggest that one of the themes of that meeting would be the issue of women philosophers. Perhaps we could have a short presentation of the contributions women have made to philosophy—in the past and in the present. Maggie, is that something you could prepare?"

"Definitely, I already cover that in some of my classes. All I'd have to do is shorten my lecture."

"Great. Henry, I do want to see the grades for your classes, though. You have the right to your views, even though they're based on gross ignorance. But I need to be assured that your views haven't been influencing your grading. The chilling atmosphere for women in your classes is another matter. We'll need to talk about that, too."

The meeting ended with plenty of time for Maggie to get to the airport before Sam arrived. On the drive she found herself alternating between anticipation of seeing Sam, and kicking herself for her less than impressive response to Henry. There were a lot of clever "I should've said" responses she could now think of, but at the time she had been taken aback by Henry's comments. However, the remarks by the men in the department more than made up for her lapse. She was developing a strong fondness for them. It was true that neither Doug nor Felipe had spoken up, but their facial expressions had shown their disdain with Henry's views. Even Barbara, who had been silent throughout the discussion, clearly disagreed with Henry. Maggie had the feeling that Barbara, without Ken, would be a much better colleague, maybe even someone Maggie could work with.

....

The small airport was crowded and parking spaces were hard to find. After looking for a space close to the terminal, Maggie ended up parking at the very end of the lot. Worried that she would be late for Sam's arrival, she dashed through the parking lot, only to find that the flight was just landing. She had barely caught her breath when the passengers started coming through the doorway. A tall, curly-haired blond woman waved at Maggie, who marveled that, after all this time, she still felt like a giddy schoolgirl when she saw Sam.

Sam patiently stayed in line behind a young couple who were struggling with a toddler and all the paraphernalia that accompanies traveling with children these days. Finally, the stroller, and the diaper bag, and the carry-all bag, as well as the tired, cranky toddler, were all under control. She walked over to Maggie. They looked at each other and embraced, both women oblivious to the stares of the people walking by.

Since Sam had only carry-on luggage, they left and walked to the car. Sam teased Maggie about how far the car was from the terminal, surprised that at such a small airport there were that many people using it. Being used to La Guardia, an airport with only two gates wasn't really an airport to her. Maggie laughed, admitting that after a year in the Midwest, it was nice to be reminded of New York snobbery.

By the time they arrived at Maggie's apartment, they had only touched upon all the news from New York: Gwen and Tim's divorce;

how Wayne and Kristi were adjusting to marriage after living together for seven years; and how Janet and Lily were doing. Sam briefly talked about the Krappy Kamera show, but wanted to wait to show Maggie the photos before going into any detail.

After looking at the contents of the refrigerator, they decided to eat out. Sam, who did most of the cooking when they were in New York, was appalled at the lack of food in Maggie's apartment. "What the hell do you eat? All you have here is junk food."

While Maggie agreed that the cupboards were bare, she found herself becoming defensive. "I've been busy these last few weeks and haven't been able to get to the store. It's not usually this bad."

Sam smiled. "Bullshit! I know you too well. But it doesn't matter; I'm here and I'll cook. But tonight, let's go out for drinks and a meal. My treat, okay?"

....

It was after 8:00 when they arrived at *Willows* and the restaurant was quiet with only a few tables occupied. Maggie found herself apprehensive. Would Sam find the restaurant mediocre? Would it just reinforce the view that it was too far a step down from New York to consider living here?

Sam perused the menu, ordering the house cabernet, while Maggie stayed with scotch—more for moral support than desire. It was an odd feeling for Maggie, but she felt protective of the town. She could certainly see its limitations; in fact, she commented quite frequently on them. But she wanted Sam to see some of the things she had come to appreciate and to understand why she would stay another year.

They ate their meals, continuing the saga of their friends back home. At the end of the dinner, Sam looked at Maggie. "That was a really good spanokopita! Good flavor, good texture. Really nice." Maggie smiled, and found herself relaxing. Maybe it would turn out okay, after all.

When they arrived back at the apartment, Maggie filled Sam in on the plans—tentative plans, though—for the week. There was the dinner at Jessie's, a dinner with some of the people in her department, and then there were the various places they could visit. She wanted to show Sam around the area, hoping that she would find things to photograph while

Maggie was in class. Not only did she want Sam to have something to do while she was busy, she realized that they both needed time alone. Living together had taught her that. What had made them compatible all those years was the fact that they both needed private time away from each other: Maggie with books, and Sam with cameras.

Sam looked at Maggie with feigned horror, pretending to be overwhelmed by her plans for the week. After an attempt by Maggie to promise that it wouldn't be too hectic and that, except for the dinners, plans could be changed, Sam smiled and suggested they go to bed and discuss plans in the morning. Right now there were other things to do and they could be done most comfortably in bed.

Chapter 43

Saturday was spent shopping. Groceries came first, but then Sam declared that Maggie's apartment was dull; it needed sprucing up. So off they went to the local *Bed, Bath, and Beyond*. They found some colorful pillows for the daybed and small pots of tuberous begonias, which would do well on the balcony; they hung some photos from Sam's recent exhibits; and they rearranged the furniture, allowing more space for seating and a more comfortable work area for Maggie.

Sam was all set to start cooking, but Maggie insisted that they have lunch first and then drive around the area looking at local "treasures." Since they were expected at Jessie's for dinner that evening, Sam could cook tomorrow.

The first place they visited was the Casino. That wasn't on Maggie's list of things to do, but Sam had seen signs at the airport advertising "the largest Casino in the Midwest" and was curious. The first thing she noticed when they entered the Casino was the smoke. While smoking was banned in most places by this time, the Casino, being on Native American land, was not subject to state regulations. As such, people smoked. After a while, unless one was extremely allergic to smoke, one could ignore the general haze and concentrate on losing one's money.

They played the poker machines for about 30 minutes, just long enough to lose the $20 each had put into the machines, and then wandered through the hotel and restaurant areas. Maggie had raved about the rugs and murals, leaving Sam surprised that she had even noticed such things, no less been impressed by them. Maggie was known for not noticing her surroundings. There had been the time when Sam had repainted their small loft and rearranged the photos on the walls; Maggie hadn't noticed until friends over for a visit commented on the changes. Many people wondered that Sam, a true artist, put up with such a lack of observation in her, but she responded by saying that one artist in a relationship was enough; two was a disaster.

But Sam had to agree with Maggie's judgment this time. The rugs were beautiful– woven by a wool factory in Ireland, in original patterns designed by a member of the local tribe. The colors were muted, mauves and slate blues, and yet vibrant because of the design and the placement of the colors. The murals were of similar colors and shapes, contributing to the overall harmony of the various areas, while at the same time evoking a feeling of tranquility in such a public place.

Sam was impressed and sought out the manager to make arrangements to return for a photo shoot. When she explained her interest in exhibiting some of the photos in a future show in New York, the manager was more than willing to give his approval. They made arrangements for Sam to return the next morning when the hotel and restaurant areas would not be so busy.

After a quick lunch back at the apartment, Maggie took Sam for a drive through the rural areas surrounding the town. While the cherry and crab apple trees were heavy with blossoms, it was still too early for the crops to be flourishing. Fields of what would soon be soy beans, barley, corn, and wheat were just acres of dirt with little green patches. Sam, having been raised in Kansas, understood this, but commented on how small the farms were compared to those back home. Maggie, never having been on a farm in her life, was surprised that these were considered small farms; what would a large farm look like?

Sam, finding interest in the old barns, many of them deserted and falling down, decided to revisit them under better lighting conditions. Maggie was pleased that Sam had already found things of interest to photograph; at least, she would have something to do while Maggie was busy in classes.

They returned to the apartment and settled down to watching the last few innings of the Tigers game, during which Maggie fell asleep, not being able to maintain interest in the game. They showered and dressed for dinner, remembering, as they were leaving, the bottle of wine they had bought to take to Jessie.

....

When they arrived, Maggie introduced Sam to Jessie and Mark. Sam extended her hand and said, "Hi, I'm Samantha, but everyone calls me Sam."

Jessie responded by saying, "We know an awful lot about you, Sam. Maggie talks about you all the time. I feel I already know you. Come, let me introduce you to the others."

Jessie had invited some of Maggie's friends, limiting the number to what her table would accommodate and what would allow easy conversation. In addition to Maggie and Sam, she had invited Sarah and Nick, Naomi and Steve, Nina, and Gail–and, of course, her husband, Mark.

Jessie had organized the dinner so that desserts and salads were brought by the guests, but the appetizers and main dishes were provided by her. What was to be a dinner had been turned into a feast, with a table full of marvelous dishes accompanied by an unending supply of drinks. As a result, the conversation flowed as freely as the wine.

Nick was the first to raise the issue of Maggie's involvement in the solving of Doris's murder. Waxing eloquently about her courage and stubbornness, he said, "Without her involvement, those guys would have gotten away with murder."

Maggie tried to change the topic, but Nick ignored her interruptions and went on to give his rant about the "sexist bastards" in the Athletics Department.

"I know it's hard to believe," he said, patting his stomach, "but I was an athlete in my youth. So I'm somewhat familiar with the mentality of athletes. It's drummed into you that you're the important people on campus; women will flock to you and you can have your way with them; and so long as you are loyal to your teammates, you'll be protected." But, as he pointed out, most of the athletes he had known did not go about killing women!

Sarah then brought up the statistics about sexual abuse being connected to alcohol use, and how fraternities were just as guilty of date rape as athletes were. Everyone then had something to say about young people today and the rise of violence against women–and gays.

Sam quietly listened to the conversation, joining in after a while to compare the situation in New York. "The violence against women in New York is not primarily date rape, which seems largely restricted to young people on college campuses. It's against women in general. Domestic violence is a major problem–especially when the economy takes a dip; and random violence against women in public places, especially minority women, is on the rise. But," she agreed, "most of those cases are connected with alcohol or drugs."

At this point, Nick pointed out that alcohol should be banned and marijuana legalized. "Nobody ever raped while on pot!" he declared.

Jessie brought out some more drinks, which allowed the conversation to change direction. Nina, interested in Sam's photos, asked how themes were chosen. "Are they chosen with particular exhibits in mind? Does something just catch your eye? Do you think in terms of themes, or does that come later?"

"Yes, to all of that," Sam replied. "Sometimes a scene just calls out to be shot. It may not relate to anything else you're working on, but it just needs to be shot. Maybe you'll use it as part of a show; maybe it'll just be a single photo. At other times, there's something I want to say, something I want to show in the only way I can. I've heard photography called 'visual poetry' and that works for me. Words are not my forte–I leave that to Maggie. I work in images and if I want to make a statement, for example, about the increasing poverty in the city, I'll take pictures of the homeless sleeping in doorways and subways. Sometimes one picture alone can carry the message; other times a series works best. But to be honest, since this is how I make my living, sometimes I have a particular show in mind, so I'll gear my shots toward that, hoping that they'll include them in their exhibit."

"Have you thought of using videos for some of your work?"

"Yes, and no. I've thought about it. In fact, I tried one a few years ago. But I don't have a feel for that–at least not yet. Perhaps because it involves more than images–dialog and action–and I'm not comfortable with that. But, who knows? I'm always looking for new themes, and new techniques. And I do believe we can all learn new things, so maybe you'll see my name on a documentary one of these days. But don't hold your breath!"

Steve then asked, "Have you found anything of interest here?"

"I was really impressed by the hotel area of the Casino. I've got an appointment to go back tomorrow to take some shots. And it's been so long since I've seen barns, that I might do a series of deserted, dilapidated barns–reminiscent of my childhood in Kansas. I come from a farm family that was basically bought out by the big agribusiness companies. It's been a long time since I've been home; most of my family has moved to the West coast, so it was kind of nostalgic to see these old barns. It looks as if farmers here aren't doing so well either, though."

"That's true, but there's a movement now to support local farmers rather than buying produce from China and other places," said Sarah. "We've bought a share of one of the farms here—you get a certain amount of produce each month. Of course, it depends on what's growing that month. One month we had more corn and zucchini than we could handle! How many zucchini breads can you make? But the obvious limitation is that you get only what is in season—no strawberries in January."

Gail responded to Sarah at this point by saying that she wasn't ready to give up her strawberries in January yet. Besides, the farmer's market, which opens in June, is another way to support local farmers—though she wondered how many of them were truly organic as advertised.

Sarah started to embark on a lecture as to why it was important to do more to support local farmers, but Nick interrupted, holding up a strawberry from the fruit tray Jessie had supplied, and proceeded to compose a limerick about strawberries and fairies. It made no sense, but it did create a diversion—and, as usual, it was funny!

The rest of the evening was spent in discussing the recent decision of the Board of Trustees agreeing to allow one of the local big-time landlords to put up a hotel on university property for the cost of $1/year—thus avoiding state taxes since it was on public property! The defense offered was that the hotel would provide internships for the students majoring in hospitality services—or at least three of them!

The evening ended when Nina noted that Naomi had fallen asleep on the couch; everyone then agreed that perhaps it was time to leave. On the drive home, Maggie was apprehensive about Sam's view of the evening. It was important to her that Sam had a good time, otherwise the possibility of moving here would be nil. Sam, sensing Maggie's concern, smiled, saying, "That's a nice group of people. I can see why you like it here."

Chapter 44

The next morning Sam arrived at the Casino at 8:00 a.m., anxious to get started. There were a few people mulling around, but not enough to cause a problem. She took some photos of the general area, including the people sitting in the chairs by the fireplace, waiting for their luggage to be taken to their cars.

She was using the murals and rugs to form impressionistic, not realistic, photos. There was no need to use a different lens; a slight change of focus would create the desired effect, maintaining the integrity of the objects while blurring the boundaries, creating a canvas of colors and shapes leaving the interpretation to the imagination of the viewer. This was a departure from her usual approach; it wouldn't tell a story or make a statement. It was an attempt to create a canvas with a camera.

It was noon by the time Sam returned to the apartment. Maggie was busy working on her laptop, papers and books strewn around the couch where she was sitting among the new pillows they had purchased the other day. She looked up as Sam came in and smiled. Her impression that it had been a productive session was supported by the enthusiasm with which Sam described the morning. It took Maggie to feign hunger pangs in order for Sam to agree to sit down for lunch at 2:00. Sam's enthusiastic description continued, stopping only to take a bite of the chicken wraps that Maggie had prepared for lunch.

Finally, Maggie suggested that they spend the rest of the afternoon cooking up some of the food they had bought yesterday, as she knew cooking was a second love for Sam. Having complained about the lack of food in Maggie's refrigerator, she was only too willing to agree. They spent the next few hours preparing some of Maggie's favorite meals. They cooked up a pot of split pea soup, a vegetarian lasagna, and a batch of potato gnocchi, all of which could be frozen and eaten later when Sam had left. Her famous paella came next, along with gazpacho and a chicken marsala, which they could eat in the next few days. Maggie insisted that there be some desserts, so Sam baked cookies and prepared the makings for peach cobblers. By the time the cooking was done and the kitchen cleaned, it was time for a relaxing drink before eating the gazpacho and paella.

The rest of the evening was spent watching Masterpiece Theater, with its production of Jane Austen's *Persuasion*. Halfway through the program, Maggie fell asleep, awakened at the end by Sam who teased Maggie about not finding the trials and tribulations of the heroine sufficient to keep her awake. Maggie replied "For heaven's sake, why don't they just say to each other what they're thinking? It's so tedious to watch them misunderstand each other."

"Oh, you're such a pragmatist."

"No, that's the wrong use of the term. I'm just an impatient realist. You're such a romantic!" responded Maggie.

Laughing, they both turned to convert the couch to its bed form and called it a night.

....

The next morning Maggie left for school while Sam was still in bed. They made plans to meet later that morning for lunch at *Isis*–Sam was anxious to see where Maggie spent so much of her time.

Jessie was the first one Maggie saw as she entered the building. She again thanked her for the wonderful dinner and told her how much Sam had enjoyed the evening. "Well, does it look good for a permanent stay for Sam?" asked Jessie.

"It's too early to tell. So far, it's been great. A lot of excitement about the pictures of the Casino, a lot of ideas floating around, and we've been having a really great time. But we haven't discussed any plans yet; I guess I'm afraid to raise the issue."

"Well, it's best not to push things. You have options even if she doesn't move here. Charles tells me that your schedule for the fall gives you longer weekends. You could use that to visit New York or she could come here when you'll have more time to be together.

"On another issue, I wanted to tell you about the effect of our forum and the publicity it's had. The President has formed a task force on the campus climate for women and has asked me to suggest some members. Obviously, I'm going to suggest you–unless you have some problems with that."

"No, that's a committee I wouldn't mind being on. At least to see that it doesn't lose its focus. Thanks."

"And the latest news is that Jack Sommers has pled guilty to a cover-up and received a two-year sentence. Obviously, he's been dismissed from the university. Let's see if he can get another job with that on his record. Kevin Marshall has been charged with something like second-degree manslaughter and faces a prison sentence of 15-20 years. He's pleading not guilty, but the case is so strong with Wally and Jack testifying against him that I'm betting he gets convicted."

"What about Wally?"

"All I know is that he received a six month sentence, with two years probation, in exchange for his help in the case against Jack and Kevin. But I do know he was kicked off the team and lost his scholarship. I don't know if he's coming back in the fall or whether he's switching to another school. I do feel sorry for him; he was a jerk for letting himself be used that way. But I don't forgive him for his treatment of Doris. She was so vulnerable for someone like Wally to come along and pay her some attention. He's old enough to have known better."

Maggie hugged Jessie and took off for her intro class. Today was the day they were discussing determinism versus free will and she had assigned them to read Clarence Darrow's defense of Leopold and Loeb in the murder of Bobby Franks in 1924. Darrow's defense was a masterful defense of determinism, arguing that the two men should not be held responsible for their actions as their actions were the result of prior causes over which they had no control. She was anxious to see what the students thought of that argument. Most of them would be believers in free will and would probably disagree with Darrow. She was interested in how they would defend their position. Usually, they responded by simply disagreeing; but occasionally a student would come up with a well thought-out response to Darrow and it was those occasions that made teaching a delight for Maggie.

After class, Maggie met Sam at *Isis*. Maggie had her usual coffee, but Sam amused her by ordering a Nutty Irishman latte, along with a tuna wrap, called "The Neptune." Maggie shared the information she had received from Jessie and they talked about what the Task Force might be able to accomplish.

Before leaving for her afternoon class, Maggie reminded Sam that they had been invited to Ben and Julia's for dinner that evening. Sam was planning on spending the afternoon playing around with some of the photos she had taken the other day. With digital photography, the creative aspect could be done on the computer, which allowed her to work without a darkroom.

....

Leo, and his wife, Susan, were at the dinner, as was Toby. Julia was not only a charming hostess, but a wonderful conversationalist. She and Ben were so much in agreement that he often just sat back and beamed at her as she eloquently expressed their shared views. The children had eaten earlier, and were content to politely greet the guests and then go about their business, which was TV for the younger children and video games for the older one.

Toby was wearing his lovely jacket with the tear in the back. Sam started to point this out to him, but Maggie gave a small shake of her head and any embarrassment was avoided. It was clear that either Toby didn't care that his jacket was torn or that he liked to be considered above worrying about such small details. In either case, avoiding any mention of the tear seemed the wiser way to go.

Dinner was lovely, with Ben attending the grill. He and Julia were great barbeque fans; whenever Maggie had eaten with them they had always prepared an interesting meal of ribs or chicken with delicious sauces. Tonight, however, the weather had turned cool and was threatening rain, so Ben was alone outside with the grill. People joked about keeping him company, but no one moved!

Susan was helping Julia in the kitchen, who refused any other help. So that left Leo and Toby to visit with Sam and Maggie. Sam, knowing from discussions with Maggie about Leo's interest in Hume, asked what Leo was working on now. That led to a short, but adequately detailed, description of Leo's controversial view about Hume's view of causality. Sam, not being a philosopher, had no comments to make about the substance of Leo's view, but shared with him the importance of following your own lead. "It's the same in art. When you do something that doesn't fit the accepted models, there are all sorts of criticisms–until others join you. And sometimes no one joins you! But you never know what future people will say, so you simply go ahead and do what you have to do."

Just then Ben came in with a platter of ribs and announced that dinner was ready. Julia and Susan appeared with bowls of tossed salad and Julia's special sweet potato casserole. Maggie had eaten that before and thought it was the closet thing to a healthy dessert–a sweet but healthy vegetable dish that one could eat without guilt!

The conversation then turned to their various impressions of the Midwest. Leo had been born and raised in Toronto and was interested in seeing if others had the same reaction to a small Midwest town as he had when he first arrived. Toby, coming from California, surprisingly had adjusted easily to the small town environment. But it was Julia who admitted that she had not yet found the charm of the Midwest.

"It's only recently that I can find the greens that I like at the local supermarkets. And forget about haircuts! I know some of my girlfriends go to one of the salons here, but I had to go to Saginaw when I first came here–no one could do 'colored' hair!–and I still go there."

"But you have to admit that things have gotten better," said Ben, looking at Julia with a soft smile.

"Well, yeah, after ten years. It's a good thing that soul food has become fashionable for white folks; otherwise I still wouldn't be able to get my greens!"

Julia turned to Maggie. "What's your reaction to this town? You come from a big city–how do you find this place?"

"I admit I had trouble getting used to the pace here. It's so slow! And I missed the things that big cities have– you know, theaters, museums, restaurants, things like that. But I also have to admit that I've found plenty to do here. Maybe if I weren't working I'd find it boring, but with teaching and writing, I really haven't been bored. But then I've been lucky in finding a great group of people here–both in the department and outside–and that makes a big difference."

"And you've been busy playing detective–that certainly added a special flavor to your first year here," broke in Ben, with a smile.

"Sam, you're the outsider here. What's your impression of the town?" said Leo.

"Well, I'm no stranger to small towns. I spent the first twenty years of my life in Dodge City, Kansas, a million miles from anywhere. When I left there I swore I'd never again live in a town with a population of less than a million. New York was my salvation. I had good folks, though; they understood that I didn't fit into Dodge City life. They sent me to the University of Kansas in Lawrence, even though none of the other kids in town ever went to college. After that I left for New York. My folks moved to California a few years later and so I haven't been back to Kansas since I left. Now this place isn't like Dodge City, but it is small."

"Do you think you could do your work here?" asked Julia.

Maggie, growing concerned that Sam would think she had asked people to press the issue, jumped in. "Oh, she could work anywhere. It's a matter of access to places to show the work, though. And that's not so easy to do outside of the big markets. Anyway, I haven't finished showing her the town, so it's too early for an opinion."

Sam smiled at her, saying, "I'm keeping my options open."

Chapter 45

The week flew by. By the time Sam was scheduled to leave, Maggie was convinced that everything between them was fine, but that Sam would not be moving to Michigan. It was clear that a small town, no matter how charming, just did not hold the interest for her that New York did. Maggie couldn't disagree with that; after, all, if she didn't have a job that demanded her full involvement, she, too, would be bored. And Sam needed stimulation from outside in order to be creative. Whereas Maggie could work in any environment–reading, writing, and thinking could be done anywhere–Sam required more, and that wasn't available here.

But it was also clear that she had had a good time visiting and would be returning. They had discussed schedules and had actually set up times during the next year when they would be able to get together–in New York and in Michigan.

While Maggie was disappointed that they wouldn't be living together as they had in the past, she was content to know that the separation this year had not affected their feelings for each other. In fact, with email, phone calls, and visits they seemed able to share as much of their respective lives as they had when they were together. And their times together, perhaps because of their rarity, were extremely satisfying! Anyway, she would be spending the summer in New York and that was only a few weeks away.

After dropping Sam off at the airport, Maggie returned to campus to pick up her department mail. Louise beckoned to her with a conspiratorial look. When Maggie approached her, Louise whispered, "Jessie was looking for you. Have you seen the recent report on promotions? Of the 24 people who applied five were turned down–all women! Jessie was furious. She's in her office now; go see her."

Jessie was indeed furious. When Maggie entered her office, she found Jessie on the phone, expressing more anger than she had seen before.

"I don't care what the Provost says: there has to be further study. This has been happening for years now, but never so blatantly. Daniella has made a national name for herself in her field—with her publications and her programs—and they turn her down for promotion! She's more qualified than the rest of the clowns in her department, but then, they're all men. And so was the Provost's advisory committee—all men! Clearly, reporting on sports is more important than reporting on injustices to women! Yes, I know—I'm sorry—I shouldn't be yelling at you. I'm just so tired of fighting these battles. Okay, we can raise the issue at the meeting this afternoon. See you then."

Maggie sat in the chair in front of the desk. Not knowing who Daniella was, she just raised her eyebrows at Jessie. "What's up?"

"I just found out that all five of those denied promotion this year were women. I don't know about the other four—I'll have to look into that—but Dani Jackson is a first class journalist and teacher. She had worked for the *Washington Post* when she was in DC, but her husband got a job at the Henry Ford Hospital in Detroit and she wanted the family to be together, so she took a job in the Journalism Department here. She still freelances and has had her work accepted by the *Post* and the *New York Times*, not to mention featured articles in *Atlantic Monthly* and others. The trouble is she writes about social and political topics, mostly those dealing with women—in particular, African American women. Her department rejects these publications as not 'neutral' journalism, even though her work is well-researched and respected by others in her field. In fact, I've used some of her work in my classes, especially the article she wrote for the *Times* exposing the differential treatment African American women receive from their physicians. Did you know that a disproportionate number of African American women using drugs while pregnant are reported to the authorities than are pregnant white women using drugs?

"Well, enough of that. I'm going to raise the issue at today's meeting of the chairs, but I don't expect anything to result. I think we're going to have to tackle this issue ourselves. Are you up for another round?"

Maggie hesitated before responding. "What about that new task force you mentioned? Wouldn't that be a place to deal with this?"

"Yes, it would. But you'll be one of the few people on the committee with an enlightened perspective. People are really reluctant to interfere in department decisions. You'll have your work cut out for you. And we'll have to get more information–especially about the other four women. I know it's asking a lot of you–after all you've been through with Doris's case–but you're really the ideal person to handle the grievance for Dani."

"Let me think about it, okay? I'll certainly do what I can on the committee. But I just don't know how much time I can spend on anything else. I'm leaving for New York right after final exams. I'm going to spend the summer with Sam, maybe finish that article on gender perspectives on friendship I've been trying to work on. And Doris's death really hit me hard. I know we're not talking about another murder, thank God, but I don't know if I have the energy to take on another case. I'll let you know before I leave for New York, okay?"

"Of course. After all you've done this year, no one'll fault you for wanting some relief. Take your time and whatever you decide will be fine."

They spent a few more minutes discussing plans for the summer, agreeing to get together for a relaxing evening before Maggie left for New York.

Later that night Maggie received a call from Sam, who had arrived home safely and on time. When Maggie told her that she had been asked to work on another grievance, but that she didn't want to get involved, Sam laughed. "That'll be the day when you refuse to get involved."

They talked about their respective schedules for the next two weeks, developing the Casino pictures for Sam, and preparing final exams for Maggie. They were both looking forward to Maggie's joining Sam in New York for the summer.

....

Dear Sam,

I am so missing you. Spending last week with you just reminded me how much so. But knowing that we will have three months together this summer makes it tolerable. All my friends were impressed by you–by you as well as by your work. They're anxious for you to return. So, you see, I'm not the only one here who wants to see more of you.

I've made my reservations and arrive a week from Wednesday. I'm counting the days.

Love, Maggie

Chapter 46

A few days before Maggie was set to leave for New York, she was sitting with a cup of coffee at her favorite table at *Isis*. A short, plump, middle-aged African American woman, wearing a chartreuse cap with purple running shorts, carrying a large cup of black coffee, approached her, smiling. "Hi, I'm Daniella. I'm so glad you agreed to help me on my grievance in the fall."

Dani joined Maggie, where they planned the strategy they would use in the fall for appealing the negative decision on her promotion. At least, Maggie thought, she takes her coffee straight!

THE END